His kiss deepened—demanded more—and suddenly she was nervous.

"Caleb…stop, please."

He squeezed his eyes shut and then, breathing hard, pulled back. "You do realize this changes things?"

At her silence, he looked up from his task.

"It can't change, Caleb. I can't—"

Thunderclouds gathered on his brow. "I must be the biggest fool west of the continental divide. Even now you are thinking of going through with marrying Rowlings?"

"Don't you understand? I can't think about just me!"

He stood and buckled on his gun belt, shoving his gun into its holster. "Don't explain it. I don't want to hear it again. Look. I don't fault you for being loyal to your family, but you need to figure out if that is more important than being loyal to yourself."

AUTHOR NOTE

I've had several readers write and ask what happened to Hannah, the little girl from my first book THE ANGEL AND THE OUTLAW. She's all grown up now, and it is a pleasure to bring you her story here.

I enjoy the colourful history of my hometown, San Diego. Many of the unique facts I learn show up in my stories. 1888, the setting for THE GUNSLINGER AND THE HEIRESS, was a time when Wyatt Earp owned three businesses in town, when the famous Hotel Del Coronado had its grand opening, and when a young boy stumbled into town saying he had been living with pirates off the coast. No one believed him until he produced a few items from the stolen pirate booty.

I love to hear from my readers. You can find me online at www.kathrynalbright.com, on Facebook, and at Goodreads. Stop by and say hi.

THE GUNSLINGER
AND THE HEIRESS

Kathryn Albright

Published in Great Britain 2015
by Mills & Boon, an imprint of Harlequin (UK) Limited,
Eton House, 18-24 Paradise Road, Richmond, Surrey, TW9 1SR

© 2015 Kathryn Albright

ISBN: 978-0-263-24758-9

Printed and bound in Spain
by CPI, Barcelona

An obstetrics nurse, sonographer and medical writer, **Kathryn Albright** was delighted to add 'published novelist' to her bio when her first completed manuscript made the finals in the Romance Writers of America Golden Heart Contest and was picked up by Harlequin® Mills & Boon. She writes American-set historical romance, and her award-winning books are inspired by the real people and events of the past. She lives in the Midwest and loves to hear from her readers at www.kathrynalbright.com

Previous novels by Kathryn Albright:

THE ANGEL AND THE OUTLAW
THE REBEL AND THE LADY
TEXAS WEDDING FOR THEIR BABY'S SAKE
DANCE WITH A COWBOY
  (part of *Wild West Christmas* anthology)

For my sons—Beau, Zachary and Cole.
You are my inspiration for every hero…

Prologue

San Francisco Bay, 1883

"Look lively, Scrapper. We be dockin' soon. Need you on deck."

Caleb opened his eyes, letting in a sliver of light.

In response, Squid squared a hard boot to his side, rocking the rope hammock in a violent arc.

"Back off!" Awake now, Caleb stretched his back against the stiffness that had taken over his body, and then swung his feet to the plank flooring. He rubbed the remaining sleep from his face, wincing when he discovered his bruised and cut bottom lip.

"Gor. Look at you."

"Trask and Corcoran deserved everything they got," he muttered. He'd only protected what was his.

"Good thing you're getting off. Corcoran is fair anxious to have you gone."

"That makes two of us. I didn't sign on to dance with him." All he'd been lookin' for when he'd boarded the clipper in Windham Bay was to work his way south. It had been the captain who had offered a bonus if he'd stay on. The permanent crew, namely Trask and Corcoran, had taken offense. Last night their petty jealousy had turned on a new tack, bypassed annoying and headed straight to ugly when they'd learned he'd had some luck in the gold fields. It wasn't information he bandied about, so how they'd come across it was a mystery. Whatever the case, they'd come out of the scuffle in worse shape than he had. Gingerly, he touched his lip again. Scabbed over. He'd heal. He always did.

Squid gave him the once-over, apparently decided he was up and moving and left.

Caleb walked to the porthole and surveyed the shoreline. The ship maneuvered through the deepest channel of the harbor toward the docks. Shipyards and warehouses lined the waterfront in a familiar pattern like every other port he'd ever entered. But this was San Francisco, which made all the difference. It wasn't home. Not once in his twenty-four years did he remember having a true home, even though his sister, Rachel, had tried her best. He let out a long breath. No, Frisco wasn't home, but when her letter had finally tracked him down, he'd known he had to come back. He'd read it in the spaces between her words. With her first baby on the way, she was scared—scared things might be the same for her as it had been for their mother the night he was born. Heck, he was worried, too. Rachel had always been there for him. It was time he returned the favor.

A thick border of red and blue flowers bobbed in the summer breeze, issuing a light scent along the stone path to the front door. Rachel would know their name. She'd planted them on his last visit, talking on and on about how they'd look when he came back in a year.

That had been four years ago.

And that was why he stood before the cottage on Sand Pebble Road with his canvas duffel bag slung over his shoulder, bracing himself for the meeting ahead. A tongue-lashing was to be expected—and not the enjoyable kind with a willing woman. The scolding wouldn't change a thing, but it would make Rachel feel better, make her feel as if she had done her duty as his stand-in mother.

Either way, a place like this—a place he could hang his hat—just hadn't been in the cards for him. *Too much gunpowder inside,* one black-eyed Sitka woman had said. That had been true once, but now…now he might try staying put—for a while or possibly longer. Rachel would be plumb tickled at that prospect.

He pounded on the door, stepped back and listened for sounds from inside. Silence.

Briefly, he considered heading back to the bar he'd passed on the waterfront. He could come back later—when Rachel or Stuart was home. Trouble was, Trask and Corcoran were probably there by now. Better to sit that one out. He tried the door latch, sure it'd be locked tight, only to feel it give under his hand.

Striding inside, he dropped his duffel on the parlor floor. Sunlight through the window turned the sitting room and entryway into a yellow and rust-red kaleidoscope of color, but the house was eerily quiet. He'd expected Rachel to be home. After all, it was near time for the baby to come. Wasn't she supposed to be sitting in a rocking chair knitting socks or blankets or something? Course, he hadn't sent word ahead that he was coming. There hadn't been time.

A scrap of paper, blown from the tea table by the breeze he'd created on entering, floated down to the dark plank flooring. He crouched and picked up the note, his gaze falling on a familiar name. He rose to his feet, smoothing out the crease as he read. Hannah's birthday. He'd missed the date by a few days, but apparently a party was happening even as he stood waitin' for company. No doubt he'd find Rachel there.

Hannah. If Rachel had had to take over being his mother, it was Hannah he thought of as his kid sister. She'd been a skinny mite the last time he'd seen her. Rachel had mentioned Hannah didn't come by anymore, didn't have much to do with Stuart either, no matter that the man had been a stand-in father and raised her those years at the lighthouse. When her grandfather finally found them, he'd insisted she live in the mansion as her birthright.

Guess he might as well head there and see what she looked like after all these years. It was as good a time as any to give her that trinket he'd been carrying around. Taking a small leather pouch from his duffel bag, he stuffed it into his vest pocket and set off for the Lansing estate.

The property encompassed the entire crown of a prominent hill. He stopped before entering the wrought iron gate and checked the view of the harbor below. A long, low whistle escaped. Several sailing vessels with their tall masts lined the wharves beside smaller fishing boats. Beyond them, a swath of deep blue water glistened under the setting sun. Hannah must have felt like a queen to see this every day.

He turned and strode up the long cobbled drive. Around a tree-lined bend, the mansion emerged—elegant white stucco surrounded by an expanse of green grass. The place hadn't changed much since the last time he'd seen it. Five black carriages were parked in front of the estate, and more conveyances had pulled off under the trees. Gas lanterns spilled light along each side of the marble staircase leading to the front entrance. At the base of the stairs, a large fountain sprayed sparkling water into a shallow pool.

He swallowed, feeling wholly out of his element. At the door, the butler pursed his lips, but reluctantly allowed him in. He stood in the entryway under thick cherrywood beams that crisscrossed the white domed ceiling. Down the wide hallway came the sound of deep voices interspersed with high twittering and the smell of something sweet baking—cookies or maybe a cake. The flash of a dinner jacket at a doorway had him looking down at his leather coat and canvas pants. Guess he was a bit underdressed for the occasion. He wore his Stetson—the only new thing he owned.

When someone finally emerged to meet him, it wasn't Hannah or even Rachel. It was Dorian Lansing. Leaning slightly on the cane that had always been a statement of his power, he strode down the hall decked out in a stiff new suit. The ruffles at his collar seemed out of place on such a man. His appraisal was quick, but Caleb felt as if he'd been turned inside out and inspected thoroughly for bugs.

Dorian nodded briefly. "Mr. Houston. It's been a while."

"I've just arrived in town. Thought I'd let my

sister know I was here and say hello to Hannah. Don't mean to interrupt anything."

Dorian peered at him with those piercing blue eyes. The years might have watered them down some but hadn't blunted their sharpness. "You'll understand if I don't invite you in. This is an exclusive gathering. I will inform my granddaughter you stopped by." Without waiting for a response, he turned back toward the party.

Caleb hadn't expected to be treated like royalty, but then he also hadn't expected to be treated like dirt. He took two steps following Dorian. The butler blocked him from going farther, so he called over the man's shoulder, "I'll see Rachel. Just to let her know I've arrived safely."

Dorian paused halfway down the hall. He didn't look back. "Very well. I'll send Mrs. Taylor out."

Caleb tried to corral his retaliatory thoughts. He'd better not be waiting until Christmas.

Sudden movement from a nearby doorway caught his eye. A young woman stood there, frozen like a deer in the woods before it breaks and runs. Recognition hit him like the wallop of finding gold at the bottom of the Indian River. Hannah. Last time he'd seen her, she'd been in braids and wore a pinafore to her shins. Now her fancy white dress hugged curves of a waist he'd never seen before—and her shoulders were bare. Bare! Where had he been while all this came about? She wasn't quite a woman yet—but she was close, mighty close.

He tipped the brim of his hat and then signed her name. *Hannah?*

A smile transformed her face, dimples forming on both cheeks. She ran toward him, her arms stretching wide to hug him the way she always had.

"Miss Lansing," the butler said, and coughed discreetly.

Immediately Hannah slowed, and the smile disappeared into tightly pressed lips as she lowered her arms. The transformation cautioned him. Guess she was a young lady more than a girl now.

She stopped a full three feet from him. *Hello, Caleb,* she signed. *How lovely to see you.* She was suddenly so stiff and formal that he half expected her to curtsy. Before he could answer, she wrinkled her small nose. *You smell like fish.*

He raised a brow. So the imp was still inside her. Reading her sign language came back to him naturally, as if he'd never had a four-year hiatus—a surprise after all he'd lived through in the north country. He looked closer at her, noting the changes. Still the same heart-shaped face, the same big gray eyes, but the young waif was turning into a butterfly. She carried herself as if she was royalty coming to call. A comb sparkled in the upsweep of her pale blond hair. Diamonds? Most likely…

"Miss," the butler cleared his throat again.

Her hands flew in beautiful rhythmic patterns. *I'm fine, Edward. Really. You may go.*

Caleb hadn't expected the way she spoke with her hands to be so elegant, so...so graceful. It was like a dance—mesmerizing.

Edward frowned but did as he was instructed and disappeared into a side room.

"Well, aren't you all grown up, *Miss* Hannah?" Caleb emphasized the *miss* to tease her. He'd never called her anything but Hannah or peanut. She might not be able to speak, but her hearing was just fine. "And looking mighty pretty for your birthday celebration."

Her cheeks colored. That was new. She'd never blushed before when he teased, and he always teased her. Mostly she'd tease right back or stomp off in a huff.

Laughter filtered in from down the hall, drawing her attention. She turned back to him. *Won't you come join us?*

He'd rather drink a gallon of seawater. "I don't fancy meetin' a bunch of strangers just now. I'm fresh off the boat and could use a shave and a haircut." He ran his palm over the four days' growth of bristles on his face in emphasis. "Just let Rachel know I'll be at the house."

But you just got here! I want to hear all about what you've been doing.

The warmth of her greeting relieved him. He

hadn't known how she would be—growing up in this huge mansion and after all these years. He'd halfway wondered if she'd forget about him.

She glanced down the hall, pressed her finger to her lips and then grabbed his hand and pulled him the other way—outside. She led him down the front steps and onto a path through a flowering trellis that led to a large rose garden. Their floral scent filled the warm evening air along with something he hadn't smelled in years—night-blooming jasmine. In the center of the garden, a bronze sundial stood next to a wrought iron swing. She sat down, a conspiratorial smile on her face, and patted the bench seat beside her.

He took care not to crush her fancy party dress as he joined her. "Just what are you up to, Hannah-girl?"

Her eyes shone, drinking him in and making him feel all of ten feet tall. *You were gone a very long time. Where have you been?*

"Alaska mostly."

Her eyes widened into saucers. *Looking for gold? Did you find any?*

He chuckled, enjoying her exuberance. He gave a push with his feet to set the swing in gentle motion. "Some. Bears, too. Big black ones."

You are lucky to have so many adventures—see so many new places.

"You're pretty lucky yourself." He tilted his

chin toward the mansion behind her. "This looks like a big adventure in its own way."

Instead of agreeing, like he thought she would, her shoulders sank, the movement nearly imperceptible.

He hadn't intended to put a damper on the day. After all, it was her birthday party. "So how have you been, Miss Hannah?"

She blinked and seemed to shake off the mood. *Next week I'm going to see a man about my voice.*

Apprehension tasted sour in his stomach. "Thought you'd been down that road before."

She frowned. *I thought, of all people, you'd understand best.*

Great. He hadn't been here five minutes and they were arguing. "Understand what? Understand how many times you've had your hopes trampled? This isn't some endurance contest, Hannah. You were all broke up the last time when it didn't work like you hoped."

But this is different.

"How so?"

It's called hypnosis.

Coldness spread through his gut. "Like at a carnival? Some mind reader playing tricks with your brain?"

It won't be like that. He'd be doing it to help me, not to make fun.

"Sounds crazy to me. Crazy and dangerous."

She wilted at his words. Must have thought

he'd be as enthusiastic as she was. He felt bad—selfish even—for throwin' cold water on her hope. "I'm sorry I can't be more excited for you. I just don't want to see you hurt again. To my way of thinkin' you're fine just the way you are."

That's because you can read my hands. Not everyone can and... Her hands dropped to her lap.

"And what?" he prodded, knowing his voice was harsh and not caring. The gal would keep at this like a dog worrying a sore paw.

I...I... She squeezed shut her eyes. *Never mind. I'm sorry I spoke of it.*

Now he really felt like an ass. He just didn't want to see her hurt. "Go on. I won't laugh or give you any more grief."

She took a deep breath. *I want to sing.*

It was a dream any young girl might have—rich or poor. Taken by surprise, he grinned. "Guess I'd like to hear that myself."

You're just scared I'll talk too much once I learn how.

He smirked. That sounded more like the Hannah he knew—a bit on the sassy side. "Could be. But whatever happens—whether this hypnosis thing works or not—you're still Hannah to me. Nothing can change that." He said the words to convince himself. She *was* changing—right before his eyes, she was growing up.

A coyote howled in the distance, and the sound pulled him from his thoughts. The stars were popping out, too. Guess he best say what he'd come to say so she could get back to her party. He fished in his pocket and pulled out the leather pouch. "I…ah…have a little something for you—for luck."

Her eyes took on a sparkle. *A birthday present?*

"Call it that if you want. Been carryin' it for a while. It's not much." He handed her the pouch.

She loosened the drawstring cord and upended the bag. The necklace he'd had made slid into her waiting palm—a swirl of silver and abalone in the warm twilight. He watched for her reaction.

Her eyes opened wide in recognition.

She remembered. Unaccountably pleased, he said, "I've had that piece of shell with me ever since we found it on the beach. Been my good-luck piece. Figured it was your turn to have it."

It…it is lovely. Will you put it on me?

She handed him the necklace and flounced around on the swing, turning her back to him. The movement wafted her flowery perfume up to fill his nose. His gaze slid down the gentle slope of her neck and farther to her shoulders. He'd never seen so much soft, creamy skin. Queer sensations pooled in his stomach as he circled the silver chain around her head. A tendril of hair danced in the breeze where he needed to lock the clasp. He leaned close and blew it out of the way.

She inhaled sharply.

He smiled at her reaction and then leaned in to tease her. "Goose bumps?"

She didn't indicate she'd heard. In fact, she was mighty quiet. And goose bumps *had* formed on her upper arms. His fingers stilled in their task. He'd only meant to move the hair out of the way. After all, this was Hannah. He hadn't given any thought to his actions being more than that. Suddenly they were. Suddenly they seemed… intimate.

He finished locking the silver clasp and pulled back. "Done."

Hannah fingered the pendant as she turned to him. The gleaming shell rested just above the rose-colored satin neckline of her dress. He liked the way it sat there all shimmery on her smooth skin. "It's not emeralds…or pearls…."

I have those things. It… She stilled her hands and then started over. *This is special. It means a lot to me.*

She leaned up and kissed him softly on the cheek.

Drawing back, she stopped close enough for her breath to tickle his skin. Gray eyes, large and luminous, blinked up at him. Her nearness set his entire body to thrummin'—not exactly the reaction he'd expected.

"You're sure sayin' a lot for someone who can't talk," he mumbled, unable to look away. They were friends—practically brother and sister. And she was way too young to be lookin' at him like that. To give in to the urge forming—the urge to kiss her properly—would change things between them forever. He should get up and walk away right now, put some distance between them before he did something stupid.

Trouble was, his head told him one thing and his heart said another. And the second was drowning out the first. So he sat there like a dang fool, caught betwixt and between. Those pretty gray eyes of hers grew bigger, and she tilted her face up. His heart lurched to a new rhythm in his chest. Apparently the little lady was wantin' the same thing. A fool he might be, but he didn't need to be asked twice.

He slid his hat from his head, barely conscious of the motion. Then, leaning forward, he tested the waters—a quick brush of his lips to hers. When she didn't pull back, he took her by the shoulders and bent down to her mouth—careful to keep the kiss light. A birthday kiss. A sweet-sixteen birthday kiss. Gentle. Chaste. Her lashes swept down, and likewise he let himself enjoy the moment. She had the softest lips he'd ever felt, the smoothest skin he'd ever touched.

And she was an innocent. She trembled under his mouth, stiff and a bit awkward in a way only first kisses can be. That she'd chosen to share her first kiss with him humbled him. It was a gift—the gift of herself.

He broke contact and then brushed her forehead with a parting kiss, murmuring against her skin, "Happy birthday, Hannah."

When he pulled back, heightened color stained her cheeks, and her gaze was slightly out of focus.

Well, he was right there with her—in as much shock as she. Imagine that.

The tap of metal clicked on the flagstone path. "Hannah!" Dorian's harsh voice boomed through the garden.

Reluctantly, Caleb released her and stood to face her grandfather.

Dorian made his way toward them until he stopped three feet before them. Quietly, Hannah stood. Dorian took in the pendant she wore, took in her flushed face and cut a barbed look to Caleb before addressing his granddaughter. "You are ignoring your guests. Please, return to the house immediately."

Caleb glanced toward the front door. The partiers had wandered onto the open marble landing at the top of the steps and stared out over the railing, curiosity splashed across their faces. On the path behind Dorian, Rachel, large and awkward with child, hurried forward, followed by her husband, Stuart.

Rachel rushed up and hugged him fiercely. "You're here! When did you arrive? Did you stop at the house?"

He squeezed her tentatively, in awe of her changed form. "Hi, sis. Yes, I left my things there."

"Oh, it's been too long this time." She sniffled, and he saw the start of tears forming in her eyes.

Uncomfortable with the display of emotion, he turned to his brother-in-law, reading the dark bent of his expression. *Tread carefully,* it said. Rachel didn't need any worries, and an argument between him and Dorian wouldn't do her any good.

"Don't mind me. Really," Rachel said, blinking away her tears. "It's just something to do with being in a family way. I seem to cry at the drop of a hat."

He grinned at that. Seemed women could always muster up a good cry—sometimes in honest feeling and sometimes only to manipulate. He'd experienced both. "Guess I interrupted quite a party. I'll head to the house and you come on back when you're good and ready." Turning to Hannah, he resettled his hat on his head and tugged the brim down. "Your grandfather is right. Your guests are waiting."

Hannah pouted but moved her hands gracefully in answer. *Thank you for the gift. You'll come by tomorrow?*

Caleb caught the smoldering anger in Dorian's eye. "Sure. Tomorrow evening."

She smiled, reassured, and turned down the stone path to the house.

The moment she was out of earshot, Dorian

faced him squarely. "Please don't make contact with Hannah again."

"I'd say that's up to Hannah, Mr. Lansing."

Rachel's face blanched.

"You *will* honor my wishes with my grand-daughter." Dorian didn't raise his voice, but Caleb heard—no, he *felt*—the underlying steel. This was a man who got his way. "Hannah is young and impressionable, and she has been brought up to a finer style than one to which you are accustomed. I believe you would agree with me when I say that she deserves better."

Caleb nearly choked. The man was anything but tactful. "Our friendship goes back way before Hannah came here to live with you. Money doesn't figure into it."

Dorian raised his brows. "You'll find, Mr. Houston, that money has everything to do with her life now, the merchant business and her future."

Rachel gasped—a strangled, half-swallowed sound—and the corners of her mouth tightened, pale and drawn. Her hand clutched her bulging abdomen. "I…I believe I really must start home."

The way she said it, more than the words she used, had Caleb moving toward her to catch her by the arm. Stuart did the same, clutching her opposite arm in support. "Rach?"

Her attempt at a reassuring smile faltered. "We should be going."

"The midwife?" Stuart asked, looking at Caleb over her bowed head.

She shook her head. "It will pass. I need to lie down for a bit. Just overdid things today. That's all."

Stuart quirked his head. The look was subtle, but Caleb understood. He was to take Rachel home. Stuart would go for the midwife. It didn't matter that Rachel thought it unnecessary.

"Thank you for having us, Dorian," Rachel said. "Give Hannah our love."

Dorian stood aside to let them pass. Caleb could almost hear the thoughts swirling as the man assessed him one last time. "Mr. Houston. You'd be smart to remember what I said."

The challenge rang in the damp evening air. Caleb ignored it, but as he stepped away, flanking Rachel's side, he felt the man's gaze sear his shoulders. Dorian Lansing was not someone to turn his back on. He'd best remember that.

The guests were gone, the servants abed, the house quiet. Yet in one room, Hannah's sitting room, the gas lamp burned steadily. Hannah sat at her writing desk watching Grandfather stride the length of the apartment, his bow tie hanging loose at his collar and his face tight with controlled anger.

"I cannot believe that you left your guests, friends who had traveled considerable distances, to consort with that ne'er-do-well. Have you no pride in yourself? No sense of decency?"

Caleb is a good friend, too— Grandfather turned away before she could finish signing. She dropped her hands into her lap. She wasn't surprised. He had little patience for the way she communicated. Since the day she'd arrived ten years ago, unable to speak, she had been a disappointment. Each doctor she had seen, each professional opinion, each unsuccessful visit had frustrated him further. Yet she had no control over this wretched solitude. If only she could be the same as everyone else, if only she could force the words out, then everything would be righted. Grandfather would have to listen.

He stopped pacing. "Tonight's inappropriate behavior must be addressed. In view of what has occurred, I feel I must contain you to your room for the time being."

But she was supposed to see Caleb! Thoughts of his kiss came back full force. What a flood of sensations had come over her with that kiss. Was that what it was supposed to be like? One thing was certain. She wanted to talk to him about it. And she wanted another one.

But of that, Grandfather would not approve. She did, however, need to keep her appointment with the hypnotist. Opening her secretary, she withdrew a sheet of paper and dashed off the words *Appointment. Hypnotist. Ten o'clock.*

Grandfather frowned. "I haven't forgotten, but I regret now giving you leave to go. That man is not a physician. I find it distasteful to visit his establishment, to be seen in his part of town."

No! Grandfather mustn't change his mind! She had to see the hypnotist! Quickly she wrote Edward's name.

"It's not a matter of who will accompany you. This person is no more than a carnival charlatan—a waste of time. With further consideration, I cannot allow you to keep your appointment."

The thought flitted through her mind that he sounded much like Caleb had in his assessment of the hypnotist—a similarity she refused to dwell on at the moment. She had to go, had to try, no matter how slight the chance it would work.

"We'll talk more tomorrow, after you have time to consider your actions and how they've disgraced the family."

Grandfather was nearly to the door. She tugged at his arm.

He looked down at her, his mouth a firm line of disapproval. She'd seen that expression a number of times over the years since coming to live with him and Grandmother Rose. Nothing she did would change his mind.

Then, as she watched, the resolve on his face shifted.

She stepped back, unsure what this might mean.

"Your mother was the same, you know," he

said. "Impulsive. Headstrong. I had hoped you would not take after her in that regard."

Her mother? He never spoke of her. That he said anything emphasized how upset she'd made him. She'd been three years old when Mother drowned—and she had stopped speaking. At least that was what Stuart had told her when she was old enough to understand. As much as she would have liked to remember her mother, she couldn't. Her memories started at the lighthouse with Stuart taking care of her.

Grandfather sighed and patted her arm. "I don't wish to do this, you know—punish you like a young schoolgirl. Not at your age." He moved back to the window seat and sat, hands on his knees, and stared at the floor—a sign he was deep in thought.

The quiet between them filled with impending heaviness. Her breathing grew shallow, until the air in her lungs ceased entering or leaving. She dared not move. This was too important. Everything seemed to hang in the balance of what he would say next.

Finally, he looked up and narrowed his gaze on her. "Therefore, I have a proposition."

Three days later, Caleb knocked on the door of the estate and asked for Hannah.

"Wait here," the butler instructed. He didn't

bother inviting Caleb inside but shut the door in his face.

Caleb blew out a long breath. Guess he'd worn out his welcome in one fell swoop. Could be that the whales would start their trip south before he'd see Hannah now.

He paced along the top of the marble steps. Twice, he thought about leaving, despite the fact he'd thought of little else but Hannah for the past three days. It was that kiss. Whether he liked it or not, kissin' her had changed things between them. He felt—different now. A surprise, considering he'd known her all his life. Concerning, too. And he didn't want to think any further along those lines until he spoke with her.

He viewed the rose garden and lawn twenty feet below the low ornamental railing and re-signed himself to waiting as long as it would take. He'd meant to come by sooner—two days ago to be exact—but it couldn't be helped. Babies come on their own timetable without any consideration for the knots they might tangle in everyone else's schedules. His nephew, Lawrence, had squalled his way out and demanded every minute of his time while Stuart and the midwife tended Rachel. She'd had a rough go of it. Even now, thinking on it made his stomach clench.

The door hinge creaked and immediately he turned. "Hannah—" She wasn't alone. Her grandfather stood beside her, creating a chill in the air just by his presence. "Mr. Lansing."

Dorian didn't bother to acknowledge him.

"I couldn't come sooner. Rachel had a boy. She's fine—they're both fine." He stopped talking. Hannah looked as if she might be ill—or exhausted. There was a bruised, fragile look to her eyes, and she had trouble meeting his gaze. His breath left him in a whoosh of disappointment. She wasn't speaking. *That* was what the problem was. She'd had her hopes up so high. Too high.

He started toward her—not quite sure what to do, what to say. He wasn't exactly the "cry on my shoulder" type, but he had to do *something*.

She stiffened, clearly erecting an invisible barrier between them.

He stopped, curling his hands into fists at his sides to keep from reaching for her, whether to hug her or shake her, he wasn't sure. Hadn't he told her it was a long shot? Hadn't he warned her not to get her hopes up? "It didn't work," he said flatly.

She looked down to the slab of white marble at her feet.

He'd bet two shiploads of gold that she'd done this because of Dorian. The man steadfastly refused to learn the sign language. Over and over, Hannah put herself through agony because she wanted to communicate with him, and all the while Dorian didn't even try to understand.

A body couldn't keep warding off disappointment time after time without growing bitter.

Finally, she met his gaze. *I can't see you anymore, Caleb.*

That wasn't what he expected. "What's going on?"

She shook her head, a pained expression on her face.

Suddenly worried, he stepped toward her. "Did something happen at the hypnotist? Did he hurt you?"

She moved away until her back flattened against the great oak door. *No. I'm fine.*

Well, that was a lie. He waited for her to go on.

Things have changed since I saw you last.

It had to be that kiss. He darted a look at Dorian, a few feet away. It wasn't hard to figure that the ocean would turn red before that man would give them a sliver of privacy.

She twisted a handkerchief in her hand.

"I'll come back in a few days—when you are feeling better."

No. Don't come. I can't see you anymore, Caleb. Not ever.

He tightened his jaw. "You're not makin' sense. If it's the kiss that's botherin' you…"

You shouldn't have done that.

A slow burn started in his gut. "As I recall, you were the one doing most of the asking."

No. I'm sure you are wrong.

So that was how things stood. She couldn't own up to her actions. She was embarrassed about being forward, and instead of admitting it or dealing with it, she was trying to put the blame firmly in his lap.

He glanced at Dorian, wishing the man would disappear so he could talk easier with Hannah. Now, that *was* a fantasy. He swallowed. "This is how you want it?"

She nodded, not quite meeting his gaze.

He took one last considering look. They both knew she was twisting the facts, but she'd made her choice. He should have been ready for it. People he cared about had been leavin' him his entire life—first his mother, then his father, and then Rachel. This was just one more time.

"Have it your way, then." Slow and deliberate, he turned and strode down the front steps. Behind him, he heard the door quietly click shut.

Chapter One

Five years later

"I'm sorry, miss. I'll need payment up front for that."

Hannah stared at the thin, pimply-faced boy behind the counter for a full ten seconds. He shifted from one foot to the other, looking at any corner of the Cigar Emporium rather than back at her. He was new and hopelessly awkward in his new position. "You must be mistaken," she said, giving him the benefit of the doubt.

"No mistake. I'll lose my job if I extend more credit."

She stiffened, at the same time glancing over her shoulder to make sure no customers had heard. Across the room two men stood before a display of chewing tobacco and debated the merits of the three different brands. They appeared unaware of her situation, and she'd like to keep it that way. Only moments before she'd been thinking how she enjoyed the fragrance of the cherry-wood tobacco that permeated the small shop as a respite from the brine-laden air outside. Now she could barely think through her embarrassment.

Forcing a calm demeanor, she asked, "Is this a new policy? If so, I'm sure it doesn't pertain to my family." She pushed the hand-carved ivory pipe across the counter. "Please. I'd like it wrapped."

Still the boy hesitated, wiping his hands on his white apron.

"You *do* know who I am?"

He gulped audibly and fidgeted with the corners of the massive account book in front of him. "Yes, Miss Lansing. Your family has done business here for years."

"And half of the items in this shop arrived here by way of my grandfather's ships." She softened her voice. "This pipe is for his birthday. You wouldn't deny him his present, would you?"

"I...I... Your total has reached the limit."

"My grandfather pays the bill monthly. There must be a mistake." The ledger would prove her point. She reached for it to see for herself when a beefy hand splayed over the page, blocking her view.

"I'll take it from here, Toby. Go see to the other customers." The shop's owner, Mr. O'Connell, a heavyset Irish man with a handlebar mustache, turned the book back toward himself as the new clerk scurried away with a look of relief on his young face. "Can't have my other customers' tabs becoming general knowledge, now, can I? I'm sure, given your family's business, you understand, Miss Lansing."

What he implied stung. She wasn't one to manipulate such knowledge to her own advantage, though she knew those who would. She was only interested in the accounting of the Lansing total.

The two customers had stopped their discussion and listened intently now. Good gracious, but this was getting uncomfortable! Her cheeks heated. She never carried much money on her. According to Grandfather, it was unladylike. There had never been any problems in the past with putting items on a tab. Her gloved hands shook slightly as she loosened the blue ribbon cinching her purse and counted out enough money to cover a deposit on the pipe. "In the first place, I hadn't planned to have my grandfather pay for his own present, but it quite takes me by surprise that you won't extend credit to me. I shall return tomorrow with the rest. Good day, Mr. O'Connell." She made a stiff-backed, dignified exit—a Lansing exit. Grandfather would be proud—she hoped.

Once outside she stopped and took a deep breath, allowing a moment for her cheeks to cool and to put up her umbrella against the light rain. Down the wet street, her carriage waited. She had planned to stop at the milliners to check the designs for a new spring bonnet, but now she was uncertain. Would she run into the same predicament there as she had at the tobacco shop? Perhaps it would be best to first speak with Grandfather.

"Please, take me home," she instructed her driver when she arrived at the carriage. He jumped down from his seat and assisted her inside the conveyance. Only then, obscured by the dark velvet curtains from the curious stares of the few people who had ventured out in this weather, did she sink back into the plush cushions and consider what had just occurred.

It had to be a mistake. Grandfather was always punctual in paying his bills to the point of being regimental. For as long as she could remember, there had been plenty of funds from the shipping enterprise to cover incidentals whenever she'd wanted anything. Perhaps, with Stuart away, Grandfather needed a hand with the business. It couldn't be easy keeping track of everything with all that he had to do.

The carriage jolted into motion, but she paid no attention to the tree-lined city parading by. Absently she tugged on the pendant at her breast. Ever since Grandmother Rose had passed on, Grandfather had been happy to have her run the household. Although she was now proficient at throwing dinner parties and carrying on the conversation with business associates, Grandfather had maintained that the shipping business was a man's task. In the past five years he'd expanded it—adding two more ships. Had it become too much for him to oversee without an assistant?

The trip from the shopping district to the Lansing estate on Nob Hill took a matter of minutes. Once there, she hurried up the wide marble stairs and through the massive front door. The faint scent of lemon polish reached her as she deposited her cloak and umbrella into Edward's waiting arms. "Grandfather?"

"In his study, miss."

She headed down the hallway, untying her bonnet as she walked. The sound of her footsteps on the tiles echoed off the high ceiling and walls.

"Grandfather? We need to talk—"

His room was empty.

She sighed in frustration, spun around to search farther down the hall and then stopped herself. Something wasn't right. She turned back to the study. Papers and notes were scattered askew over Grandfather's massive desk. Totally unlike him. Neatness and order ruled Dorian Lansing and everything around him. He controlled his estate in the same manner he had once, as a young man of twenty-two, controlled his first ship—or so she'd been informed.

She hesitated in the doorway. Slowly, eerily, a moan issued, the sound coming from behind the dark Victorian desk. Her breath hitched in her chest. She ran to the far side of the furniture and found him lying prostrate on the parquet floor, his face pasty white.

"Grandfather!" she cried out, kneeling beside him. In the next breath she screamed, "Edward! Come, quick!"

A significant stroke, the doctor said. Upon hearing it, Hannah's heart plummeted to the pit of her stomach. Grandfather would need constant care and rest if he was to recover. After seeing the family's personal physician out, Hannah called the house staff together in the kitchen.

"Where is Tan Ling?" she asked. "She should hear this, too."

"Mr. Lansing discharged her last week, miss," Edward explained.

"Oh," she said, confused. Grandfather had neglected to tell her. Then she grew irritated. She should have been informed. After all, *she* was in charge of the household staff. It was her job to do the hiring and discharging. Tan Ling had been with the Lansings for the past three years. What of the letters of recommendation the young woman would need to find new employment? Had Grandfather considered them? Besides, more than any paperwork, she would have liked to have said goodbye.

She looked over the expectant loyal faces of those before her. "Mr. Lansing has taken ill and will require special care. A nurse will be attending him over the next few weeks while he recovers." *If he recovers,* she thought to herself, and then quickly pushed the traitorous idea from her mind. He had to get well. He just had to. "Please make her welcome when she arrives."

A burning sensation threatened behind her eyes. "This illness will be especially hard on Grandfather. He's…he's weak on his right side and unable to get out of bed. I'm sure you know how independent he has been."

Looks passed between the staff.

Hannah understood their trepidation. Dorian wasn't known for his patience or temperate disposition when he was in good health. What would the household be like now?

"That is all. Except, Edward? A word, please."

Hannah waited for the others to take their leave, and then turned to the butler. He had been a sailor on one of Grandfather's ships before coming to work at the estate. He'd been with Grandfather the longest and was a man she knew would answer honestly.

"What happened with Tan Ling? Was there an infraction of the rules?"

"No, miss."

"What, then?"

He paused, a discomfited look passing over his usually austere face.

"I have known you many years, Edward. Please, speak freely. I know you are cognizant of a great many things within the household and keep them to yourself."

"Very well, then." His brow furrowed as he chose his words. "I believe Mr. Lansing was concerned with conserving costs. The loss of his ships—"

Ships lost? She schooled her face to remain impassive. "Obviously it is worse than he confided to me."

Edward exhaled, believing her ruse that she was in her grandfather's confidence. "I believe so."

For the next three days, Hannah studied the Lansing Enterprises ledgers until numbers and cargo listings were leaking from her ears. Foul weather had claimed two of their largest cargos, not to mention the two ships, sinking both to the bottom of the sea. They had but one ship left—an older one that was in dry dock for repairs.

No matter how hard she stared at the figures, she couldn't come up with additional income. The majority of the balances had a minus before them. She longed to discuss it with Grandfather, but the doctor had said that any added stress might cause him to suffer a relapse. He was to be kept as calm as possible. She mustn't burden him with business.

Shuffling through the layers of letters and bills, she categorized them from most pressing to least—the most being a legal document from San Diego regarding the shipment of furniture and supplies to the Hotel Del Coronado, an establishment that was to rival the Palace in San Francisco. Apparently upon hearing of the downed ships, the owners had sent an immediate claim demanding compensation. She frowned. How considerate of them when Grandfather's health hung in the balance. Some things were more important than their gold-rimmed tea sets. She dropped the offending papers on the desk and then checked the time on the cabinet clock. Nearly noon. Perhaps his tray was ready. She rose to her feet and found Nina in the kitchen assembling Grandfather's lunch. "I'll take it to him," she said, picking up the tray laden with warm, mashed apples and cinnamon, a thin slice of cheese and clam chowder soup. "I'd welcome a respite."

"You'll be sick yourself if you don't rest a bit, Miss Lansing. You must take care. You can't solve everything in a day as much as you try."

"Thank you, Nina." She scooted out of the room. Nina would talk forever if given the chance. Her conversation was at times comforting, but right now Hannah needed solutions, not chatter.

She climbed the stairs and entered Grandfather's room. Upon seeing him sitting up in bed, surrounded by plumped pillows, she stopped short, nearly dropping the tray. "You're sitting up!"

A gruff "Harrumph" punctuated the expectant

pause following her words. He had no patience for people who stated the obvious. Quickly she handed the tray off to the nurse and hurried to his bedside.

"Are you well enough to do this?" she asked, worried that the strain might be more than he could handle.

He held his left hand out to her, and she moved to take it, letting him draw her to his side. She sat on the edge of the mattress and expelled a shaky breath. "You…you are stronger today?"

At his nod, she motioned to the nurse, who rose and stepped from the room. Hannah had made it a point to help Grandfather daily with his meals. So far, she'd managed to keep from pouring out her worries, but today would be doubly hard. The company lawyer had dropped by with a large packet, and the post had just arrived full of overdue bills.

She spread the linen napkin over his chest and scooped up a spoonful of soup. When she raised it to his lips, his gaze met hers.

"Whas wong?" he said, his words slurred.

Her smile was forced. "Hungry myself, that's all." She scooped up another spoonful, but he clamped his mouth shut.

"Whas wong?" he repeated and pointed to the lap of her skirt where she'd worried the fabric into a wrinkled mess.

She sighed. She'd never been able to get away

with anything with him. He could read people—her especially. The talent had made him a keen businessman—that and his innate stubbornness. People didn't call him Old Ironhead for no reason. He nearly always got his way. Perhaps it would be smarter to let him help her. Frustration at being kept in the dark would surely be worse than concocting a plan of action.

"I'll tell you if you promise to eat."

In answer, he opened his mouth, ready for another spoonful.

While he ate, she told him how she'd discovered the bills piling up. "Why didn't you tell me about the ships? Perhaps I could have helped."

Grandfather shook his head.

"But it affects me. It affects you and this entire household. You need to trust me with this."

Rather than acknowledge her, he indicated he was ready for another spoonful of soup.

Pressing her lips together, she held back the retort that threatened and brought the soup to his mouth. "It appears Thomas's company reimbursed for the first ship and cargo, but I couldn't find any insurance paperwork on the second ship. Does he have that at his office?"

Grandfather shook his head slightly and glanced out the window. Ignoring her? Or considering what to answer? She wasn't sure.

"Should I send a telegram to Stuart?"

It seemed the obvious solution to her. Stuart

managed his own shipping business now, but having trained under Dorian, he still partnered with him on an occasional run. Grandfather furrowed his brows.

"What, then?"

He grabbed the paper and pen from his bedside table. Moving them to his lap, he proceeded to write, left-handed and awkward.

"See? You should have learned to sign. It would help now," she said, teasing lightly while he scribbled. He grunted, apparently not flattered by her suggestion.

"Here. Let me take a look." She picked up the note and deciphered his squiggly handwriting. "Accept Thomas's offer?" Her gaze flew to his. "Marriage? You think the answer is for me to marry?"

He frowned at her with only half of his face, took the paper and wrote again. *He'll take care of you.*

She couldn't believe what he was suggesting. For years he'd said Lansing Enterprises was her legacy, and now he was asking her to turn her back on it? She rose to her feet and paced in the small confines of the room. "But…what about the business? Families we employ depend upon Lansing Enterprises for their livelihood. What about them? I cannot consider only myself."

With the pen, he carved the words in the paper, tearing it in the process. *You need a secure future.*

"But I thought… I believed…" She searched for the right words. He'd led her to believe she would inherit the company. "This is just a temporary setback. We'll build the business back up. We'll press on. That's what you always say."

He pressed his lips together on the one side of his mouth, and wrote, "Thomas knows what to do."

That was not how she'd envisioned her life. She'd thought she would assume control of the company. She'd made plans…. "Grandfather," she began, sinking back onto the bed. She closed her eyes, took a big breath and then opened them again. "This illness has scared you. You're acting like…like you won't get better. But you will. Look how much improved you are today compared to yesterday." The alternative, she could not bring herself to contemplate. He'd always been there for her, even when they disagreed. She couldn't lose him.

His glare only reinforced her words. A week ago he'd encouraged her to consider Thomas Rowlings's proposal. Grandfather's business associate was a pleasant sort and rather dashing for a man twenty years her senior. His insurance company was prosperous. She'd want for nothing.

It *was* a viable solution. She didn't expect— didn't *want*—a marriage based on love. That emotion led only to disappointment and heartbreak. Yet why did she suddenly feel as though she couldn't breathe? "I know you are thinking only of my good…"

Grandfather's gaze never wavered from her face.

She had to get away, had to take time to consider things. She rubbed her forehead. "You truly believe this is the best course?"

He nodded once, slow and firm.

She dragged in a shaky breath. "I see. Thomas is due back from Sacramento in one week. I'll… I'll give him an answer then."

In the study, Hannah sat numbly at the large desk, staring at the piles of papers without really seeing them. Marriage… It seemed so final…like an iron door closing. And although she respected Thomas, he hadn't shown any interest when she'd mentioned her desire to start a school for children who couldn't speak. He'd simply smiled, rather patronizingly she thought, and changed the subject.

She gathered the stack of ledgers and deposited them in the third drawer. As she started to lock the desk, she noticed a packet from the lawyer and the pile of bills still sitting out. Although she trusted Edward, it wouldn't do to have the other servants learning the extent of their circumstances and gossiping to others in town. She stuffed the papers into the drawer, yet one envelope refused to fit tidily in. She pulled it out and then recognized Stuart's careful penmanship.

He'd taken his ship south several weeks ago and should be returning any day now. He seldom made long trips anymore, always anxious to return to Rachel and his children. Years ago he'd had a falling-out with Grandfather. Other than an occasional business dealing, they no longer communicated. So this wouldn't be a personal letter. As acting owner, she had the right to read it. She drew the silver letter opener across the seal.

Dorian,
I trust this letter finds you and Hannah well.

While finishing business here in Los Angeles, I've discovered information that may prove useful to you.

Wares from your last shipment have appeared on the open market here—without evidence of ill use by the sea. My records show that the *Margarita* stopped in San Diego and disappeared shortly thereafter. I shall see if I can learn anything more before starting home.
Stuart

She stared in shock at the note. This changed things. If the merchandise was turning up in Los Angeles—and in salable condition—that meant the ship hadn't gone down due to rough seas. It meant something entirely different altogether. Could it be the ship was somewhere else—possibly across the border in Mexican waters?

Visions of the lighthouse where she had once lived filled her mind. Even now she could hear the cry of the gulls as they glided effortlessly on the updraft created by the sandstone cliffs.

Shaking off the memories, she read the letter again. Nervous energy built inside, a fine tension that ricocheted through her. If she could find out what had truly happened, perhaps it would be possible to fix things enough to save the business. That would solve everything! She wouldn't have to marry Thomas—at least not on his terms.

This was not something she could hand off to someone else. She needed to keep control. Only then would Grandfather believe she could assume leadership of the business. She must prove herself. She shoved the letter into the drawer and locked the desk.

It was simple. She must go to San Diego. There would be some maneuvering involved—particularly regarding Grandfather. He couldn't know until she was safely away. She'd have to leave a note for him. The staff—Nina—could give it to him after she was well on her way. Time enough later to explain things.

She tucked a wayward strand of hair behind her ear and realized her hand was trembling. Excitement coursed through her even as she tried to tamp it down. This was impulsive and perhaps a bit foolhardy, but if she considered every angle and prepared for difficulties, then surely she would get her answers. To sit and wait for Stuart to return or Grandfather to get well wouldn't accomplish anything!

She'd need an escort. Edward could accompany her. *Oh, think again, Hannah! Edward will go straight to Grandfather.* The butler's loyalty was commendable, but in this situation could only hinder her.

What about Caleb...?

The thought stopped her midflight, and she plopped back onto the chair.

Her gaze darted to the drawer that held the small address book. No. She couldn't. She'd given Grandfather her word.

Besides, with Caleb's penchant for adventure he could easily be in Timbuktu by now. Yet the thought refused to leave her. Caleb knew about the currents and tides—things she didn't. After all this time, would he still be in San Diego? And more than that—would he even see her after the way she'd treated him?

She looked back at the desk drawer. At one time, back when they'd been friends, she'd written his name in that book. She fisted her hand. She shouldn't. She really shouldn't. She'd been so good. Tried so hard to please Grandfather. He would never approve of this.

Caleb even knew the shipping lanes and the crosscurrents.

Barely breathing, she reached out and pulled on the drawer. She withdrew the book…flipped through the pages.

Harrison…Heinrich…Houston…

Exhaling, she stared at her own childish penciled handwriting. Grandfather hadn't updated the entry. In fact, he'd crossed out the name with bold slashes of indigo ink, nearly obliterating its existence. The action spoke of suppressed anger… possibly fear, but he had nothing to worry about. A promise was a promise—and for a Lansing, it held even more weight.

And because of it, Caleb was no longer a part of her life. She wasn't proud of herself for what she'd done that day; in fact for many years she'd done her best to put it from her mind. It hurt to remember. But she'd kept her promise to Grandfather. That was the important thing. Her friendship with Caleb had been the price. Caleb would never forgive her, which was as it should be. She didn't expect his forgiveness—didn't deserve his forgiveness.

Her throat constricted. She couldn't have it all. A choice had to be made and she'd made it. Selfish? Yes. Purely and wholly selfish—wanting to speak, wanting Grandfather's approval, wanting…Caleb. She smoothed her fingers over her lips. To this day she remembered how his kiss had felt, how it had made her feel.

Suddenly angry with herself for dredging up a past she'd knowingly formed, a past that couldn't be changed, she slammed shut the drawer. It had been a crush. Puppy love, perhaps. And it had died years ago.

She would still keep her promise to Grandfather. If Caleb was in San Diego, she'd hire him for his expertise—and that alone. She wasn't going there to see him. That part of her life was over. What mattered was the business. Only the business.

Chapter Two

Southern California, 1888

Keeping a steady hand on the reins, Caleb maneuvered his gelding past a sprawling pear cactus and then up the muddy slope from the river delta. With every step forward, the gelding slid halfway back through the soft muck. For the past three days, rain had drenched the earth, swelling the creeks and splattering the brown landscape with patches of green. The sparse vegetation needed it—for that matter, the people needed it to survive through the dry months.

He hiked the burlap sack higher on his saddle, tying it securely to the horn. Thoughts of the three coastal quail he'd shot made his mouth water. Bit by bit, with each mile that passed, the peaceful feeling he'd absorbed while hunting disappeared. Hardly came as a surprise. Solitude fit him. Always had.

He glanced at the horizon. The sun hovered

just above the ocean. Wyatt would be looking for him. Putting the mudflats to his back and leaning forward in his saddle, he urged his mount into a rocking gait toward town.

When he entered the saloon on Fourth Street, his boss looked up from analyzing the ledger in front of him. His gaze landed on the heavy burlap sack in Caleb's hand and a slow smile grew beneath his dark handlebar mustache.

Caleb tossed the bag to Yin Singh, Wyatt's personal cook. "There's three. I'll take the biggest." The cook grinned and bowed, and then disappeared under the stairs and into the kitchen.

A cursory survey of the room found two customers at the bar and another three at the gaming tables. The evening was just getting started, and so far things were quiet. It wasn't until later that the whiskey and tanglefoot loosed inhibitions and tongues—not to mention fists. Jim Avery, the barkeep, stood behind the counter, and with his meaty hand methodically polished the waxed countertop with a cloth, making it glow a deep honey color while he watched the goings-on. Jim nodded, acknowledging Caleb's entrance.

"Stop by your land?" Wyatt asked from his seat at the faro table.

"I'm still ponderin' about buyin' that particular stretch."

"I'm surprised someone hasn't beat you to it with the length of time it's taking you to decide."

Caleb shrugged. The stretch of river valley was choice grazing land—hunting, too. He had the money—had saved it up over the past five years, but each time he headed for the land office, something made him stop. He wasn't the "settling" type. And owning land sounded more like an anchor than an investment.

"Ya sliced it, mister!"

A young man—boy more likely, judging by his spare frame—hollered at two men playing billiards. When they ignored him, he bellied up at the end of the bar, tried to hook his boot heel on the rung of his stool and missed. Another attempt and he sat square, grabbed his Stetson off his head and slammed it on the counter. His unruly red hair, matted with sweat and grime from the confining band of his hat, sprang up in shock at the sudden freedom. He beat his fist on the bar, motioning to Jim for a beer.

"Haven't seen him here before," Caleb mentioned to Wyatt. The kid couldn't be a day older than seventeen.

"First time would be my guess. I believe that young man is on his way to a whale of a headache come morning."

"One's all it takes with someone his size," Caleb said, pushing away from the bar and sauntering toward their object of discussion. The boy stopped guzzling and faced him with the reckless bravado and glassy gaze liquor could bestow.

"Had enough?" Caleb said.

"None of your business how much I drink. My money's as good as the next man's." The boy took a defiant swig of beer and turned back to the bar.

"I can see that. Hard earned, too, I'll bet." The kid was nothing but stringy, corded muscle held together with sweat. "Which ranch you ride for?"

He didn't answer. Probably didn't even hear Caleb, the way he was caught up in his attitude—nursing some wrong with a heavy dose of anger. Suddenly he blurted, "Took six months! Six months of slavin' for her daddy only to find out she planned to go back East to finishing school and catch herself a dandy."

Acid roiled in Caleb's gut. He wasn't going down this trail. "What's your name?"

"What's it to you?" A belch rumbled out, and with it some of the boy's bravado evaporated. "I might as well be a flea on a rock. Why'd she even treat me nice in the first place? Got me thinkin' 'bout her all the time, thinkin' about us. It was all a lie. Big sinkhole of a lie."

"Best chalk it up to a lesson learned the hard way."

"Sure bet! I'll be a whole lot smarter from now on. Won't no pretty skirt fool me again. I'll take me another beer, barkeep!"

Jim's gaze slid to Caleb. "Older and wiser," Caleb murmured with a nearly imperceptible shake of his head. "Startin' now.

"'Fraid you've had enough to drink, Rusty. Time to head home while you can still sit your horse."

"You can't tell me what to do."

Caleb wasn't fooled by the belligerent tone. The kid was heartsick and slidin' toward misery. Caleb preferred anger. "Matter of fact, I can."

"Just try it, mu—ister."

On the last word, Caleb grabbed the boy's upper arm so tight he figured he'd kill off some fingers—whose he wasn't sure—but he wasn't going to let the boy stay and drink himself to the floor. Better for him to throw a punch or two and get some of his feelin's out.

Rusty flung a weak hook with his free arm. His fist stopped just short of Caleb's jaw, caught in another firm grip. "Leave it!" Caleb ordered, and twisted the boy's arms behind him while at the same time forcing him toward the door.

They stepped outside, and Caleb could have sent him sprawling into the street easily enough. Would have without a second thought if the boy had been a man—a man should know better—but the kid had had enough damage to his dignity in one day.

"Go home. Count yourself lucky you found out early on she was a gold digger." He let go of the boy's arm.

"But she weren't. It was her daddy."

"One and the same."

Rusty met Caleb's gaze. The young whelp still wanted to challenge him! Unbelievable. And stupid. Caleb raised one brow. When the boy swung, Caleb blocked with his forearm and jabbed his other fist into the kid's gut, striking quick, like a snake. The blow knocked the boy down two steps, where he lost his balance and sprawled face-first in the dirt.

Caleb followed and stood over him. When he didn't try to stand, Caleb reached down and yanked him to his feet. "I'm doing you a favor, kid. Take it. Make a move other than heading out of town and you'll be sorry." He picked up the boy's hat, slapped it against his thigh once to knock off the dust and handed it over.

The boy curled the brim before stuffing it on his head and meeting Caleb's gaze. "Name's Josh. Not Rusty."

It took a slice of humble pie for a boy this age to admit defeat…and a scrap of respect for authority. Caleb took the offered olive branch. "Caleb Houston. See you around, Josh."

The boy nodded, found the reins to his horse and climbed on. Caleb figured he'd get about halfway to his ranch before spewing out the liquor that sloshed around in his belly.

"Well," Wyatt said, standing up when Caleb re-entered the saloon. "You handled that with more perception than usual."

Caleb ignored him.

Wyatt slipped on his wool coat and bowler hat. Didn't look much like the lawman who had cleaned out Tombstone, but anyone who crossed him knew those looks were deceiving. "Keep things quiet tonight. I need to check on my other properties."

Caleb raised his chin in acknowledgment. Earp ran into more trouble at his other gambling halls. Caleb should know—he'd worked at both, the worst on the edge of the Stingaree district. A rougher brand of men with fewer rules and even less restraint frequented that establishment. After surviving a year, Wyatt had offered him the job here. Caleb looked over the waxed and polished wood of the bar and tables. Here in the center of the business district the glassware was finer, the clientele classier and even the brawls more refined—if that was possible. Oh, they happened— the arguments, the fights—but they started out subtle, creeping up on a body with only a look or a word before suddenly turning deadly.

Once Wyatt left, Caleb slid onto the closest bar stool. "Make it black, strong and hot," he called loud enough for Yin Singh to hear in the kitchen. Lowering his voice, he turned to Jim. "Newspaper come yet?"

Jim reached under the counter, pulled out the most recent weekly and dropped it beside the steaming mug of coffee Yin delivered.

Caleb grunted his thanks and started to skim the front page.

"I signed for this, too. Hope it ain't bad news." Jim slipped a telegram on the bar.

Caleb stared at the paper. The only person who'd send him a telegram was his sister. His gut took a dive. He grabbed up the official-looking transcript. If anything had happened…

Hannah arriving in two days. Please look out for her—for me—for Stuart. Love, Rachel.

Hannah? His thoughts raced back to the last time he'd seen her—a time he'd buried deep and refused to think about.

"You look like you got the wind knocked out of your sails," Jim said. "Someone die?"

"More like resurrected," Caleb mumbled. It had been years since he'd seen Hannah Lansing. Five years and five hundred miles. He'd figured San Francisco was far enough away that he'd never again see her in this lifetime. That had been his plan. What was she doing coming here?

"Ghost from the past?" Jim eyed the telegram with growing interest.

Caleb crushed the paper in his fist, left his coffee untouched and slid off the stool. "Doesn't matter. I don't aim to find out."

Chapter Three

Hannah stood just inside the lobby of the Horton Grand Hotel and breathed a sigh of relief. Her heartbeat slowed to a steadier rhythm as she noted the large display of flowers on the central table. The Horton Grand Hotel appeared to be the essence of respectability—an oasis in a town of gambling halls and smaller businesses. The walk from the train station had caused her no small amount of anxiety. She wasn't used to being so totally on her own, especially in a strange town. Halfway here, she'd seen three men on horseback racing through the main street of town, whooping and yelling and kicking up a minor dust storm. She'd known when starting her journey that this was no San Francisco, but it was a wilder town than she'd expected.

Not for the first time did she consider that her flight here may have been a bit impetuous. She hadn't thought the trip completely through, and now those things she'd taken for granted in San Francisco—things like getting from Nob Hill to the docks, a trip usually made in a carriage with a servant accompanying her—seemed difficult and worry laden.

She had picked the Horton specifically for its location. The Florentine would have been a safer choice for a single woman, but Rachel had said Caleb worked at the saloon across the street. That would make him more accessible should she need him. She strode through the lobby past a middle-aged couple sitting in overstuffed leather chairs and placed her reticule on the ornate oak-and-brass front desk.

A short, round, gray-haired man looked up from studying the ledger. "May I help you?"

"I'd like a room."

He surveyed the lobby behind her. "You're alone? I'm afraid the Horton does not—"

"I'm Miss Hannah Lansing," she said quickly before he could deny her accommodation. "And here on official business for my company."

The clerk straightened, a small Napoleon at attention. "Of Lansing Enterprises?"

She nodded. "I'll be attending the grand opening of the Hotel Del Coronado."

He looked confused. "But you are staying here? Rather than there?"

It did sound suspicious. Those who'd helped finance the hotel had seaside rooms for the celebration. Grandfather hadn't wanted to invest. It wasn't any of this clerk's business, but she felt she had to give him a plausible explanation. "I will be meeting with a few friends and business associates while here. It seemed simpler to stay in town rather than out on the peninsula."

"Then, on behalf of the Horton, I am delighted you chose our hotel for your respite." His hand hovered over the ledger before printing her name.

She relaxed somewhat. The first hurdle was behind her. She'd made it safely this far.

He swiveled the ledger so that she could sign her name, and then snapped his fingers. A tall, thin man appeared from the back room. "Jackson can show you to your room."

"Thank you. My trunk is at the train station."

"We'll see to it, miss."

She followed the porter up the staircase. On the second floor, Jackson opened the first door in the hallway. A bouquet of flowers adorned the table in the center of the room, filling the space with the scent of orchids. Along the wall, an oak buffet table held matching brass candlesticks on a delicate lace table runner. Walking to the adjoining room, she found a four-poster bed and canopy. An ornate, full-size pedestal mirror occupied one corner near the foot of the bed, and a stand with a gold-rimmed china bowl and pitcher stood in the opposite corner.

Jackson lit the gas wall sconces in both rooms

before closing the drapes at the two tall windows. "I'll be about retrieving your trunk now. Dinner is at six."

She *was* hungry, but she was tired, and the thought of eating by herself in the dining room with others speculating about her aloneness was more than she wanted to endure tonight. "Thank you, but might I have my meal brought up?"

Jackson nodded and turned toward the hallway. She closed the door behind him, released a pent-up breath, whipped off her hat and tossed it onto the settee, saying a prayer of thanks that she'd not been denied a room. That would have been a setback she hadn't considered. Thank goodness the Lansing name was known here.

She pushed a loose strand of hair back into place, securing it under her twisted bun, and then walked to the window and peeked through the drapes to look out over the town. With the descending twilight, colors were fading to shades of gray. Three tall brick buildings towered over the others—their signs indicating a bank, Marsten's store and a gambling hall. The first two appeared closed for the day, but directly across from her hotel room, the saloon was lit up like a sparkler on the Fourth of July. Golden light and occasional raucous laughter spilled out on the boardwalk along with a light tune someone played on a piano.

Grasping the pendant of silver and abalone

at her neck, Hannah searched through the fancy etched windows of the saloon. Somewhere inside Caleb went about his duties. Rachel had been curious as to why she was asking after him, and Hannah had made up a story about mailing the necklace back to him. Apparently Rachel had believed her ruse for she hadn't alerted Grandfather, and no one had tried to stop her departure.

Would Caleb even want to see her after all this time? She swallowed hard. Most likely he wouldn't. It didn't matter. It couldn't. She'd made a promise to Grandfather. Although she might be skirting it a bit in contacting Caleb, she had to have an escort, and once she learned more of what had happened to the ships, Grandfather would understand—and hopefully forgive her. After all, he'd always put the business first in his life. Surely if she did the same, he could only be proud. She intended to keep her promise—a Lansing *always* kept a promise.

The memory of Grandmother Rose's thin, reedy voice trilling in her ear came to her. *It is paramount that in all things your conduct be above reproach. You are a Lansing. Your reputation must be above speculation or gossip of any kind. Believe me, any correction or chastisement that I give will be minimal compared to what society will bestow.* At the time, Hannah had chafed against the rules of etiquette. They'd felt like a binding, an iron corset. But now, hearing the raucous music from across the street, they felt safe and secure—something that framed her existence.

She dropped the drapes into place and turned toward the small writing desk against the wall. First thing to do would be to send a missive to the port authority agent requesting an audience as soon as possible. Then a second note to the manager of the Hotel Del Coronado informing him she'd be present at the grand opening and would like a word with him. When Jackson brought her supper, she would give them to him for delivery by courier in the morning.

After eating a succulent supper of lamb, she sat down again at the secretary. It was time she wrote a short letter to Grandfather. If she posted it tomorrow, it would take a week to arrive at the house in San Francisco. By that time, perhaps she would be heading home. He'd be angry when he learned of her quest—angry when he found out she'd left San Francisco—but if the end result were the answers concerning the ships' disappearances…

Putting the finished note aside, she stared at the new blank page in front of her. Time for one more note—and the most difficult. She swallowed hard and then picked up the fountain pen once more.

Mr. Houston. I'm in town for a short visit.
Please feel free to call this afternoon. Hor-
ton Hotel.
Hannah Lansing

Caleb fingered the impression in the wax
seal—a curled, elaborate HKL. Leave it to a
Lansing to use fancy paper. He read the note
again. The Horton. Not the best, most expensive
place in town but pretty near to it. And way too
close for comfort. He glanced through the open
doors of the saloon and across the wide, dusty
street to the Horton's entrance. Acid churned in
his gut. Miss High and Mighty. What was she
up to? They weren't exactly on speaking terms
any longer.

"You say this arrived at noon?"

"Seems I mentioned that." Jim narrowed his
gaze at Caleb's tone. "It ain't my job to come
lookin' for you. You're good at makin' yourself
scarce. One minute you're hunting quail up to
Tecolote Canyon and the next thing I know you're
hauling in a string of fish."

Caleb ignored him. Right now, fishing off the
point sounded like a fine place to be until Miss
Lansing left town. Maybe he'd camp there.

"Ain't you goin' to go see her?"

In answer, Caleb walked around the counter
and deliberately poured himself a shot of whiskey.

"You're not foolin' me."

Caleb scowled. "Leave it, Jim. It'll take a lot more than her crooking her finger for me to drop everything and look her up."

Jim shook his head as if Caleb were dense. "I'll say it plain, then. You're not one to drink this time of day, and suddenly a note from this woman has got you doing it."

Caleb looked at the amber liquid, swirled it around in the glass before shoving it toward Jim. "Save it, then." Whatever Hannah wanted—if anything—she would have to ask a whole lot nicer for him to mosey over to her hotel. Pushing thoughts of her from his mind, he walked over to the Bradison brothers' weekly poker game.

Chapter Four

Caleb stared at the fancy stationery as if it was a stray cat with a piece of dynamite strapped to its back. The envelope, all gussied up with a black satin ribbon, had arrived from the Horton just after supper. He'd been eyeing it for the better part of two hours. He should set fire to the thing, but another part of him wanted to march across the street and tear up the note in front of Her Highness, dropping the pieces at her royal feet. It wouldn't appease what happened between them, or Dorian's slight of Rachel and Stuart, but it would sure make him feel a sight better.

Instead of taking either trail, he slid his pocketknife along the paper, breaking the ties, and opened the envelope.

Mr. Caleb Houston,
I find I am in need of your assistance. Please

meet me at the Horton Hotel at your earliest
convenience. The sooner the better.
Your friend,
Hannah Lansing

Well. That was a sight more cordial than the
previous note. So she needed his help—not that
he planned to give it.

His sister's request nagged him. He didn't want
to "look out for Hannah." He didn't want to get
that close. It would muddy things, and right now
he was doing just fine with the line he'd drawn
between them. But Rachel asked so little of him
now that he was grown.

Maybe a quick check wouldn't hurt—just to
appease his conscience. He'd only make sure
she was safe and sound, send the information to
Rachel and then go about his business.

He had to admit, he was kind of curious as
to what Hannah looked like now. How had the
years changed her since she was sixteen? She'd
been pretty back then—just starting to fill out.
He couldn't imagine her any more so. Too bad
her beauty was only skin deep.

He slipped off the bar stool.

"Where you agoin'?" Jim asked, straightening.

"Got a score to settle, and for the first time I'm
holdin' a full house." He stuffed his arms into his
leather jacket and straightened his collar. "Won't

take long. I'll be back for some of Yin's stew before Clyde plays another round on the piano."

He strode to the road, his gaze locked on the front door of the Horton. Two doors down a dog snarled from the shadows and then barked incessantly at a passing rider. Caleb shut out the sound, intent on getting his first look at the woman who had been the hull stuck between his molars for the past five years.

He entered the hotel, absently noting the rich interior, and then without a pause in his steps, zeroed in on the front desk.

The man behind the counter took one look at Caleb as he approached and raised his nose in the air—an interesting position since the clerk was the shorter of the two.

"I'm lookin' for Han—Miss Hannah Lansing," Caleb said. Guess they weren't on a first-name basis anymore. Not after the way things had set between them. The clerk muttered something about waiting while he notified her.

Caleb sauntered over to the fireplace. A woman like her would take her time coming to see him, no matter that the meeting had been at her request. She'd make some kind of a grand entrance.

The heat from the cracklin' logs took the chill from the damp night air. He rubbed his hands together, blew on them a time or two and then turned around to give the same consideration to his backside. A flash of light glanced off his eye—light reflected off a woman's dangling gold earrings.

She spoke with the desk clerk. There hadn't been enough time to fetch Hannah, so it couldn't be her. This woman wore a quality deep red traveling suit that hugged her waist. A fancy matching hat, swathed with black netting and three large black feathers, hid her features, although anyone with eyes could tell she'd be a looker just by the confident way she held herself. She tapped the toe of her polished boot, obviously not pleased with what she was hearing. Rich people always thought the world spun around them.

She turned from the counter, twisting her handkerchief in front of her waist. He stopped short in the middle of blowing on his cold hands. Memories flooded him of a little girl crying over her puppy, practically strangling her pinafore. It couldn't be…

The woman looked straight into his eyes. Beneath the black netting, her dove-gray eyes widened against pale, creamy skin. Her jaw slowly opened before she seemed to remember herself and closed her mouth. She tucked a wayward strand of blond hair over her ear and then checked the fancy twist at her neck, a move that unconsciously showed off her figure in that formfitting jacket and full skirt.

Caleb might as well have been sucker punched, the way his gut twisted into a knot. It wasn't enough that she was rich and confident—she also had the looks to match. Like fine wine in elegant crystal, she outsparkled the chandelier. His mouth went dry. He counted it significant that he remembered to remove his hat.

It didn't change one thing, though. He still planned to speak his piece.

And in that moment her face became a mask of perfect, controlled alabaster. Slowly, she walked across the room and stopped before him. "Mr. Houston. How good of you to come. I...I feared you might not have received my message."

He froze—and couldn't draw another breath. Hannah Lansing...speaking?

He'd never believed it was possible after so many years of silence. And yet here he was, hearing her voice with his own ears! The rich, cultured cadence held him mesmerized. He'd never given it much thought—her speaking like everyone else. Didn't actually believe it would ever happen. She'd been young and not much more than a baby when she'd lost the ability to speak. How had she gotten it back? And when?

It took him a moment to come back to his senses and realize that although her words were polite enough, her tone was formal—distancing—like being doused with a bucketful of cold water. He sobered instantly. She might be talking, but she hadn't thought enough of him to inform him. That only pounded the nail of truth deeper about their lack of any real friendship.

Now, what had she said? Something about her note?

"It came," he said. "They both did. Just took a while to decide if I'd answer."

That seemed to shake her up. She looked down, away from his face, and swallowed hard. "I see. Then, I thank you for deciding to come."

"Didn't figure we had much to say to each other after so long."

She blinked. "I suppose I deserve that. *Touché*, Mr. Houston."

He was baiting her, punishing her for the way she'd left things between them. He'd thought he was over it, that he'd buried the bitterness a long time ago, but seeing her now—well, guess it wasn't buried deep enough after all.

She looked him over, starting at his boots. He could sense her cataloging everything as her gaze touched on him. Boots—leather, dusty. Denim jeans—worn, serviceable. His hat in his hands—a tan, weather-beaten Stetson. Cotton shirt. Leather vest. Neckerchief tucked at his collar. She stopped when she reached his face. He didn't look his best, but he wasn't plannin' on changing up just because she'd ridden into town.

"Your sister will be gratified to know you are looking well."

"I get by all right."

She twisted the handkerchief again, obviously uncomfortable with the awkward gaps in their conversation. Guess his attitude didn't exactly inspire small talk. He had one foot trampling on everything she was sayin' and one foot already headin' for the door. It wasn't like him to be so cantankerous, but she just seemed to bring out the worst in him.

"So you've taken your grandfather's name," he said, trying halfheartedly to remedy his mood. "Where is Dorian?"

"He didn't accompany me."

That brought him up short. "You're traveling alone?"

"Of course not. My valet and maid have accompanied me. However, there have been some complications. It has put my business here behind schedule."

So he hadn't been a thought in her head until she'd run into trouble with her *schedule*. Guess that told him where he stood. He chewed on that notion and grew angrier with the chewing.

"Believe me," she continued, "this is as uncomfortable for me as it is for you."

"Somehow I doubt that."

Her mouth pressed together in a perfect seam.

"I take it you are representing Lansing Enterprises now. Congratulations. Although I gotta admit I'm surprised Dorian eased up on the reins enough to give you a position."

"Yes…well…he did."

He had to know but hated to ask the question, hated to let her know that he'd wondered about her at all. "So when did you get your voice back?"

"It's been a while."

"When?"

"Four years ago."

So—she'd had plenty of time to send him a letter and hadn't. Well, what did he expect? She'd made it clear enough they weren't friends any longer.

"I'd like you here tomorrow at nine to accompany me."

He raised his brows. He didn't care to be ordered about. "Now, hold on, Hannah—Miss Lansing." The formal name didn't roll off his tongue any easier this time, but he'd remember to use it if it killed him. No way would he forget the way she'd treated him. Calling her by her proper name would just cement the fact. "I haven't said I'd do anything."

"But you're here. I thought that meant…"

"Go on. Spit it out. What's this all about?"

The desk man approached. "Is everything all right, miss?"

She nodded. "I'm fine, Mr. Bennett." She waited for the man to leave and then pressed her hand against her temple. On closer examination, purple smudges tinted the skin beneath her eyes. He hadn't noticed those right off.

"Can you stay for supper?" Her eyes—surrounded with those long lashes—looked up at him all expectant and hopeful. Five years ago that look had gotten him into hot water and changed the course of his life. He didn't relish a repeat performance.

"Caleb?" she asked again.

"I've got a job to get back to. I've been gone too long as it is."

"I hoped at the least we could have a cup of tea. And…and talk."

"Tea? That's what this is about?"

"No. Of course not."

She said it too quickly, worryin' that handkerchief again. At this point, he was surprised it hadn't been torn to shreds. "I'm not believing any of this. One minute you say you didn't plan to see me at all, and then the next you want to have tea. You're not making any sense. Level with me, woman. What exactly is going on?"

Her eyes widened at his sharp tone, and her chin raised a notch. "All right, then. I'll be blunt, as that is what you prefer. The Hotel Del Coronado opening ceremony is tomorrow. I am in need of an escort."

She had to have a fever. "Me? If you remember at all, I'm not much for crowds. It sounds like a pretty fancy shindig for the likes of me. Shouldn't you be attending with the mayor or one of his lackeys? Someone closer to…"

Her brow furrowed delicately. "To what, Mr. Houston?"

"Look—" He turned to block their conversation further from the interested desk man. "Pardon me for being confused, but the last time I saw you, you and Dorian made things very clear. I don't owe you a thing."

Frustration flashed through her eyes. "You are not being fair. I had no—" She took a deep breath. "You don't understand anything."

"Then, explain it to me."

The way her brow wrinkled up, she looked as if she was in pain. It surprised him. Lansings were tough as old cowhide, in his estimation. But then, she could be quite the actress. He had believed what he'd felt in that kiss so many years ago. He wasn't plannin' on playing the fool a second time.

"I'll pay."

"Now, that sounds like something your grandfather would do. Why me? Why don't you save some money and have your valet go with you? He's already in your service." He shoved on his Stetson. He'd heard enough. Too bad the only remembrance he'd have of her voice was this conversation. It left the taste of sour pickle juice in his mouth.

"Double."

He paused.

"I'll pay you double what you make at the saloon."

A hint of desperation had crept into her voice. The money would come in handy, but it was something else that tugged at him, a feeling that there was more going on that she wasn't saying.

"Mr. Houston…I really want you to be the one escorting me."

Maybe he could make himself stand being near her in short doses—for the money—and because it would salve his conscience concerning his sister. "How long?"

"Two days. All I need is two days of your time."

His gut told him to stampede for the door. He should listen to it.

"Please? I really need your help."

There it was—she'd finally come around to asking him. Now was his chance to squash her the way she'd squashed him. So why wasn't he throwing it back at her like he'd planned? "What time did you say this ribbon-cutting happens?"

Something glimmered, lighting her eyes. Hope? "The ceremony starts at eleven."

"Guess I could see my way to doing it for the money. Long as we are clear on that." At least that was what he was telling himself. "I'll be by at ten."

"That will make us late."

"Half past nine, then."

She stretched out her hand. "Agreed."

He hesitated. It was how business deals were

made, although usually it was man-to-man. Touching her seemed a might more personal than he wanted at the moment. He kept his hand stuffed in his pocket. "Agreed. Two days."

Slowly she pulled her hand back. "Yes. Thank you, Mr. Houston." She turned toward the stairs.

He could handle this. Two days would pass quick enough. Long as he kept the upper hand, it would be easy money. He could tell her off later. Feelin' a bit ornery, he decided to let her know who was in charge. "Miss Lansing?" Her proper name rolled off his tongue easy enough.

She stopped. "Yes?"

"I'm not much for waiting."

A slight hesitation was the only indication he'd unnerved her before she replied, "Neither am I, Mr. Houston. I'll see you in the morning."

She spun her trim backside on him and walked to the stairs. He watched the swaying movement of her burgundy skirt as she mounted each stair until she stepped out of sight on the landing. A queer feeling rolled in his gut that had nothing to do with the absence of food there.

Turning toward the door, his gaze collided with the desk man's. The man watched until Caleb stepped through the ornate entryway to the street and let out a long—*long*—breath.

Heaven help him. Hannah was all grown up.

Chapter Five

Hannah woke early the next day, her thoughts on last evening's encounter. Dressed and ready, she waited at the sitting room window, watching for Caleb to emerge from the saloon.

He hated her. She felt it to her bones. What she'd done years ago had ruined any hope of friendship between them.

She raised her chin. It didn't matter. This wasn't a social visit. Paying him would keep things businesslike and proper between them. He was the right man for the job. Although it hurt deep inside that he wouldn't do it out of the goodness of his heart. He would have—*before*. But obviously, things had changed. *He* had changed.

She thought back to the first look she'd had of him in the lobby. He was as tall as a ship's mast, and, though lean, he looked solid, as though nothing could move him from the path he set. The day's growth of whiskers and the simple clothes

he wore had only enhanced his ruggedness. And
the gun belt—low on his hips… He carried a gun
now. Years ago he'd only carried a knife.

How much more had he changed on the inside?
Was it a fantasy of her own mind that she even
knew him at all?

If only things were different. If only she hadn't
been forced to make a choice. The ache in her
breast deepened, and she tugged on the pendant.
But no. She hadn't really been forced. She'd done
what she had to do. The stark reality was that, at
sixteen, she'd wanted to speak more than she'd
wanted anything else, even Caleb's friendship,
and so she'd made that vow to Grandfather—a
vow that existed to this day.

Absently she twirled the long gold fringe on
the heavy draperies. Caleb had been lanky then.
That wasn't the case any longer. Last night she'd
noticed his stance that guarded their privacy.
How his wide shoulders had easily blocked out
the curious stares of Mr. Bennett and Jackson.
He'd fairly cocooned her in a corner of the lobby.
The thick red hair of his childhood had darkened to the color of a rich brown cherrywood
color, and his face—always a bit angular—was
now square-jawed and firm. A man's face. She
swallowed. The boy she'd caught sand crabs with
on the beach was gone, and in his place stood
a compelling stranger. A compelling—*brood-
ing*—stranger.

A polite knock sounded on her door. She opened it to Jackson.

"Mr. Houston is in the lobby."

Hannah nodded her acknowledgment and shut the door. She walked to the bedroom and stood before the full-length mirror to smooth her skirt. For the third time that morning, she puffed the sleeves on her blouse and repositioned her blue velvet hat just above her chignon. "What Mr. Houston thinks is not my concern," she told her image. "It's the manager at the Hotel Del that I need to impress." She took a deep breath, grabbed her parasol and started for the door.

In the lobby, the sight of Caleb waiting for her, holding what looked to be a new black Stetson, had her gripping the handle of her parasol a bit more tightly than necessary. He'd been busy. He'd shaved, which brought the strong line of his jaw into view. His hair hung wet and slightly wavy where it brushed his white shirt collar. Instead of the bandanna he'd had on yesterday, a dark gray bow tie circled his neck. He wore a dark gray vest and black pants. And his boots… He'd polished them recently—this morning? Caught off guard by the sudden butterflies inside, she pressed her hand snug against her tummy.

He walked to the base of the stairs, looking her over in much the same way she'd just appraised him. "Mornin'." He took her cloak from her arms and draped it over her shoulders.

Edward had done the same for her numerous times over the years. So why did Caleb's closeness and his clean, soapy scent stir those butterflies in her stomach into a frenzy? He picked up a black wool coat lying on the wing-back chair and, with a crooked finger, slung it over his shoulder as he escorted her through the lobby and out the door.

"You're mighty quiet," he said once outside.

"I…I expected the same person I met last evening. You…you clean up well."

He huffed. "I'll change if that's what you want. You *are* paying me to accommodate you."

"No. Of course not. I'm…more than pleased." She opened her parasol and propped it on her shoulder. For all his surliness, he sure watched her closely.

"Don't see those much around these parts."

"I burn easily." And she needed something to keep her hands busy. With so many years of signing her thoughts, her hands retained the connection of the words and motions—a weakness should she suddenly forget herself and start signing in the midst of her confrontation with Mr. Barstow today.

"Hmm. Well. Let's get a move on."

He accepted her answer easily enough. She had the urge to explain further, but already he'd started down the boardwalk. She picked up her pace to catch up to him.

"We'll walk to the docks," he said. "It's not too

far. Word is there are carriages arranged on the other side to take us from the ferry to the hotel."

She stopped suddenly. "We aren't taking the Coronado line?"

"No."

"Why not?"

"They're still laying track. Won't be done for another two months or so." When she didn't move, he arched one dark brow. "Something wrong with the ferry?"

She swallowed. "I...I just thought... The hotel is on a peninsula, isn't it? I thought we would take the train or...perhaps a buggy?"

"We'd never make it in time for the ceremony."

"Still—there must be another route...a short-cut perhaps?"

He smirked. "Other than a hot air balloon ride over the harbor, this is your only option."

His sarcasm irked her. "You needn't be condescending. I'm well aware the sea breeze would send a balloon toward the foothills—not toward the peninsula."

"I'm not tryin' to be—" He stopped talking. The puzzlement on his face dissolved into speculation. "Wait a minute. Are you saying you're afraid of the water? Miss Lansing, heir to one of the largest shipping enterprises on the West Coast—is afraid to get on a boat?"

Her cheeks warmed. "Of course not. That would be silly."

"Then, what is the problem?"

"I just prefer land travel to water. Always have."

His expression sobered. "It's a short ride on the ferry. You can see the other landing from here. No waves, no swells. I'm not taking a buggy twenty miles out of my way just so you can keep your boots dry. We either take the ferry or we don't go."

Hannah rubbed her forehead. This was unexpected. She had to talk to the two owners of the Hotel Del Coronado, or at least the manager. They'd all be at the ceremony today. "There must be another solution," she said, although her voice carried none of its previous strength. "I...I really must attend."

His green eyes hardened. "It's the ferry or nothing."

She gazed longingly at a carriage passing by. It had been years since she'd last boarded a boat. Perhaps it wouldn't be so bad now. Perhaps, if she forced herself, she could overcome her discomfort. "Very well. It seems I have no choice. The boat it is."

They turned the corner and passed a grocery with boards on the windows and then, farther down the street, a sad-looking milliner's storefront with nothing but empty hat stands in the windows.

Her steps slowed. "I was informed business was doing well here."

He glanced sideways at her. "A month or so ago land prices started coming down. Your stake in the Hotel Del might not have been timed the best. People 'round here are selling out and leaving."

She nearly told him the truth then—that there was no money invested, although it had been her wish to advance a small sum. Grandfather had refused. In the end, she held to her own counsel and let Caleb assume what he would. Better too little information than too much.

They walked a while before he spoke again. "So are you going to tell me anytime soon how you got your voice back?"

It was inevitable he'd ask. She had prepared an answer—enough to satisfy his curiosity and no more. It was the "more" she wanted to avoid.

"You said it had been a while," he prompted.

"Nearly four years ago." She could see him calculating back. "It was the hypnotist. I saw him for over a year, going back weekly. Grandfather was not happy about that—he thought him a charlatan at first. But the man, Mr. Donniger, was adamant that it would take more than just a few visits, that each session built on the last. And something…I guess a small change, a small insight each time, made me keep going back. Six months into the therapy, I uttered my first word."

Caleb blew out a low whistle. "So it worked

after all. I was of the same mind as Dorian about the hypnotist."

"I remember."

They stepped around the corner of a brick warehouse and the sea air swirled around her skirt. Quickly she clutched her bonnet, tying the ribbons more securely beneath her chin. The strong odor of fish filled her nose. They were close to the wharf. Another block and the sparkling harbor water greeted them, along with one tall sailing ship and a steamer vying for a place at the long dock. Halfway down, passengers crossed over a slanted gangplank to board a ferry. Along with the people, several buggies were lined up to make the trip.

"What a hullaballoo," Caleb muttered, and then startled her by grabbing her arm and pulling her out of the way of a man with a large barrel over his shoulder. With a surly look, Caleb let go as quickly as he'd gripped her. She nearly stumbled after his release. Glaring at his back, she followed in his wake as he maneuvered through the crowd on the boardwalk and led her out onto the wooden pier.

At the base of the ferry's ramp, Hannah hesitated while Caleb continued up to the deck. The rocking of the boat brought back images she'd rather leave tucked away for good. Her heart started a scattered pounding in her chest as she gripped the railing with one hand. It had been her constant hope that she could escape this type of situation. A foolhardy hope, especially in her line of business, but a hope nonetheless. Even Grandfather had never suspected her fear, and here she would expose it to the one man she needed to appear strong before.

She stepped onto the wooden planks, forcing herself forward. First one foot, then the next. *Concentrate on your breathing. Don't look down. Act natural. It will be over soon.*

Her heartbeat rushed in her ears. Her stomach roiled, and then a wave of dizziness hit her with the force of a northern gale. Halfway up the ramp she froze and locked both hands to the railing. Her knuckles whitened. Ten feet below, harbor water lapped steadily against the pier pilings, drawing her, pulling her. She felt all over again her mother's arms letting go, releasing her…then the water swirling, pulling Mother away.

"Hannah?" Caleb's deep voice came from far away.

She couldn't answer. Couldn't break whatever had a hold on her. This was a mistake. She had to get to solid ground.

Turning abruptly, she hit a wall of satin-covered muscle. Caleb stood so close she could feel his body heat. His hands grasped her upper arms, steadying her. She stared at the shell button on his vest directly in front of her. "I…I don't feel well," she mumbled through numb lips.

"Can't say all this hoopla thrills me either, but this is your party." He grasped her elbow and put his other hand to her back, spinning her around to face the ferry. "Come on, Miss Lansing. Show some of that grit the Lansings are famous for."

She swallowed hard, feeling the insistent push of his fingers against her spine.

Ten leaden steps and she was on the boat. Without taking a breath, she walked briskly to the center of the ferry and grabbed on to a solid-looking pole. Her heartbeat slowed to a more recognizable rhythm as she sucked in a deep, steadying breath.

Caleb studied her intently from a few feet away.

"Brute force is not your best attribute, Mr. Houston," she said, trying to regain her composure. She brushed off an imaginary piece of lint from her skirt to keep from meeting his gaze. When she felt sufficiently recovered, she looked up again.

He had the gall to smile. To smile! It was small, barely a hint of an upturn at the corner of his mouth, and then it was gone. "What was all that?" he asked.

"I already explained. I prefer land travel."

His gaze hardened, and she had a feeling she'd stirred a hornet's nest. He wanted more than a pat answer, more than a brush-off.

"You dropped this." He held out her parasol.

Feeling foolish and embarrassed, she took it.

He *was* looking out for her, she supposed, and she was grateful for that. The small steamer let loose with its shrill whistle, making her jumpy all over again.

"Boats never used to bother you. What happened?"

"Nothing happened."

"I don't buy that. Not when I see you huggin' that pole like a starfish hiding from a barracuda."

She clamped her lips together. She knew precisely when things had changed—the day she'd first spoken. Somehow, when the hypnotist had unlocked her voice, he'd also unlocked the memory of her mother's drowning...and the overwhelming fear Hannah had felt at the time. It seemed she couldn't have one without the other.

He didn't press further for an answer, but his gaze remained contemplative. She closed her eyes and concentrated on the scent of brine and feel of the breeze on her cheeks. The ship's steam engine whined and clanged as it propelled the vessel across the harbor. She took comfort in the sound. As long as she heard it, she'd reach the other shore safely, even if the ferry was moving at an abysmally slow crawl.

"I won't let anything happen to you."

His words washed over her. Safe. Comforting. She opened her eyes to find him watching her, the sea reflecting in his eyes, deepening the green. It would be nice to believe him, nice to be able to rely on him as she once had, but she knew she couldn't. He was only with her because she was paying him.

She pressed her lips together and turned, staring over the whitecapped water's surface to the far dock, willing the shoreline closer, closer, closer....

Caleb shoved his hands into his front pockets and let out a low whistle. He stood on the fourth-story balcony of the Hotel Del and gazed over the long stretch of beach and vast expanse of ocean before him. At this height, the wind muted the sound made by waves crashing against the shore. Far below, a few men and women had wandered from the crowd near the front steps and made their way to the beach.

On the other side of the harbor, on the far peninsula, the old whaling port lay derelict and abandoned. High above it, the lighthouse stood like a lone sentinel against the blue sky. The lighthouse... He'd shoved the memories to the back of his mind over the years. Didn't make sense to dwell on what used to be. But now with Hannah on his doorstep, he couldn't seem to stop thinking of that winter long ago.

She'd been six when Rachel, the town's new schoolteacher, had agreed to tutor her at the lighthouse. Stuart had been the light keeper and had refused to put Hannah in school with the other children. At first, Caleb had thought it was because Stuart worried the children would make fun of Hannah since she couldn't speak. Only later did he discover Stuart was hiding Hannah from the authorities along with himself.

Hannah's constant shadowing had been a nuisance, and at first Caleb had tried his darnedest to evade her. But something had changed along the way—*he'd* changed. He'd had one foot in trouble his entire life, always looking for adventure, or the next harebrained idea. With Hannah watching, he'd had to rethink his actions—be accountable. In a short time he'd learned to "read" her. The sign language had been like learning a secret code—fun for him and, at the time, essential for her.

He huffed and turned away from the view. None of that mattered anymore. Money had changed her into someone else entirely, and he wasn't sure he liked the woman she'd become— distant, cold. Chalk it up to Dorian's influence. Her fancy hat with the netting, her gloves and parasol—it all seemed like armor to ward off anyone getting too close.

I won't let anything happen to you.

Where had that come from? She was no damsel in distress; she was a Lansing. His impulse had to have come from seeing the fear on her face on boarding the ferry. She'd been scared to the tips of her toes and trying desperately to hide it.

Course, she had every right to be scared considering she'd been there when her mother drowned. But it hadn't been an issue when she was little. Why now? What had happened to make her so afraid of the water? It didn't add up.

Guess as much as he wanted to understand her reaction, he wasn't about to ask her again. The less he knew of her and the sooner she returned to San Francisco, the easier it would be for him to get on with his life.

For the better part of an hour, the two of them had toured the hotel along with a large group of sightseers. When the owners called the investors for a private tour to areas blocked off to the general public, Hannah excused herself to use the privy. Odd timing on her part. In her place, Dorian probably would have demanded special treatment—and at the least, his name mentioned in the opening speech.

So here he stood, the ribbon ceremony over, the tour concluded and Hannah nowhere in sight. Heading down the wide staircase, Caleb stepped out on the expansive veranda. Men and women milled about, drinking tea and eating fancy miniature cakes. He scanned the crowd, looking for a flash of dark blue among the black suits, top hats and derbies. No such luck.

Turning, he headed inside, intent on finding her. He entered the dining room and stopped. Even though this had been part of their tour, he was once again amazed at the sight. No expense had been spared. The room was large enough to shelter a whale. No pillars, no columns obstructed his view to the long windows that looked out on the ocean. Gleaming redwood panels and bisecting beams crisscrossed the cathedral ceiling, the like of which he'd never seen. While he stood there taking it all in once more, he heard Hannah's voice.

He crossed the parquet floor, slowing and listening as he neared the half-opened kitchen door.

"I ordered that wood from Brazil over a year ago," a man said, his voice raised.

"The matter is being looked into...."

"That's not good enough!"

Something slammed against wood. A fist? The sound jolted Caleb, propelling him closer. Did she need help?

"Please, sir, let me explain."

Hannah's voice sounded controlled—perhaps in an effort to calm the man. Through the crack in the doorway, Caleb saw a stout gentleman pacing back and forth, mopping sweat from his brow with an oversize handkerchief.

"This is all very odd," he mumbled. "Very odd."

I agree, thought Caleb. What was going on?

"My grandfather had sufficient reason—" she began again.

"He should be here himself! Not send someone

else to deliver this kind of news. A woman has no business sense whatsoever in this sort of thing. Does he think that by sending you I'll be lenient? That I might hesitate to call in my lawyers?"

Hannah took a deep breath before continuing, "Captain Taylor is investigating the situation as we speak."

"That's all well and good, but considering the shipment is already paid for, it is you who should be worried. I expect to be compensated."

"And you will. I've just told you…my grand-father has taken ill. As soon as he recovers—"

"*If* he recovers, you mean."

Dorian sick? Caleb inched closer.

"Mr. Barstow, I act in my grandfather's stead. Surely you can allow me the courtesy you would show him."

Silence followed her words.

"You *will* give us time to find out what happened. Rest assured, we are not trying to deceive you. Lansing Enterprises has a sterling reputation."

"That reputation will buy you one month, young lady. You have one month, and then I'll go to the authorities."

"They are already aware of the situation."

"That sounds like a Lansing," Barstow said. "Dorian probably has the sheriff in his back pocket. Still, you've already had more than enough time. Someone will pay, and it won't be me."

The door swung open with a bang and the man strode through, unaware of Caleb's presence off to the side. A few seconds later and Hannah walked out, heading to the main entrance.

He followed her onto the veranda, noting the slump to her shoulders despite the fact her back was as straight as a mast.

Dorian ill? And Stuart investigating something? So his instinct had been right. There was more going on than she had let on. Interesting little puzzle. "Miss Lansing."

She spun around, the ocean a deep blue backdrop to her pale skin and blond hair. Suspicion clouded the air between them.

"You disappeared on me," he said. "Missed the tour."

"Oh…the tour. Yes." Her eyes cleared. "Are you enjoying yourself, Mr. Houston?"

He shrugged, fingering the brim of his hat in his hands. "I've had a look around. Impressive place. Swanky water closets. Fancy everything."

"Yes. Yes, it is." She relaxed slightly.

"What was that all about back there?"

Startled, she quickly shuttered her expression. "I'm not sure I know what you are talking about."

Oh, she knew, all right. "By that you mean I don't have the right to ask questions."

She didn't answer—which was an answer in itself. He should have known. After all, he was just a hired hand here.

The silence between them lengthened. She glanced at the ocean, then the hotel, and then fidgeted with her parasol.

He wished she'd just throw the contraption away. He liked a little sun on a woman—much more than the pale, bloodless look she wore now.

"I realized—" she began with some difficulty "—rather belatedly this morning, that today is Valentine's Day. I…uh… Will you need to be back at a certain time?"

So that would be the way of it. Keep to the surface. Keep to her rules. Well, he'd give it right back, then. "Are you asking if I am going to work after this? Or is that a roundabout way to find out if I have a lady friend expecting me? Because I would have to say that it's none of your business." He plopped his hat on his head and started down the steps toward the beach.

She put out a hand to slow him but then stopped just short of touching him. "I don't mean to pry. It's a special day to some. I simply wondered if you had other plans."

"Doesn't matter. I agreed to do this."

Her lips thinned into a solid line. "For the money."

"Can't cat walk around the facts."

The wisp of a frown marred her brow. Apparently she didn't care to be reminded about the business nature of their arrangement, even though she kept throwing it up to his face.

"You're nearly thirty now," she said. "A man. For all I know, you could have a wife and children tucked away, waiting for your return."

"I could, at that."

Her hands went to her hips.

A familiar stance. She'd stood just so when she was frustrated, and she'd been frustrated a lot when she was young, mostly because no one could understand her. Well, he understood her just fine, and he wasn't going to give her an inch. "Hannah, you set the rules a long time ago. As far as I know, they haven't changed."

Her mouth dropped open. "A long time ago… You're talking about San Francisco."

"If the boot fits…" She'd severed things then. She didn't have a right to ask him questions of a personal nature. But then a small part of him liked that she'd tried—a part he wasn't ready to acknowledge still existed. "Take a different tack, Hannah."

He led her away from the gathering of townies and the orchestra playing a rendition of some high-falutin' song from some European songwriter and onto the expanse of white beach. They skirted a pile of smelly amber kelp washed up and drying on the sand.

Silence stretched between them. Though they were but two feet apart, it may as well have been five hundred miles. She sighed. "Do you need to be back for work or have you taken the day off?"

He stopped walking and faced her, irritated and tired of the game she kept playing. "Jim will cover for me if I'm late. Clear enough?"

She frowned at him and then looked toward the small cluster of carriages waiting to convey patrons to the ferry landing for the return trip to the town. "Perhaps we should start back."

His frustration was growing by the second. "Seems neither of us is getting the answers we want."

"I want…" She lifted her gaze.

And he was struck by the intense sadness reflected in her eyes. Unable to answer it, let alone have a coherent thought, he chose the wise thing and silently waited for her to continue.

She swallowed. "I want only what we agreed to—your company for today and tomorrow."

Her answer didn't fool him one bit. There was a lot more than that going on, and it wasn't just business. He'd get to the core of it. Eventually. Before she left. "If you are ready, we can head back to town."

She nodded, avoiding his gaze, and fell into step with him.

"Something else puzzles me," he said.

"If you don't mind, I can't handle much more today, and I still have the ferry ride back. Can we call a truce of sorts? Just…not talk for a while?"

She did look done in. Which, in his opinion, was a good time to push for answers. "Well, think on this, then… If I looked over the hotel's roster of investors…"

She closed her eyes, resigned to hearing him out.

"Would I see the Lansing name?"

Chapter Six

That evening, Hannah allowed herself a moment to think about the events of the day. Thoughts of Caleb tugged at her, and she walked to the large window to peek between the heavy drapes at the street below. He stood there in front of the saloon with another man, their bodies silhouetted against the light coming from inside the establishment. He was easy to distinguish—tall with those impossibly broad shoulders. And strong—so strong when he'd grabbed her arm.

Neither of us is getting the answers we want.

His words had been on her mind the entire evening. The main answer of course, was that she needed to learn about the missing ships. *But what about the other?* Her conscience goaded her. It was something she hadn't let herself consider before this trip. It had seemed too far out of reach, too much an unrealistic wish.

Absolution.

She didn't deserve it, but that didn't make it any less wanted, any less desirable. If only he would forgive her, maybe then she could begin to live with herself. Maybe then she would stop seeing herself as the cold, heartless creature she'd become.

A knock came at the door. "Your supper, ma'am."

She released the drape. Moving to the door, she allowed Jackson entry. He set a tray on the table and quietly let himself out again.

Sliding onto her chair, she removed the silver dome. The aroma of baked fish with lemon, onions and stewed tomatoes wafted up. Despite the feast laid out for guests at the Hotel Del, she hadn't been able to eat earlier. Her stomach had been tied in knots, what with the ferry and then bickering with Mr. Barstow. Perhaps now she could enjoy her food.

A folded piece of paper lay on the tray near the china cup. She opened it and glanced over the desk clerk's script. Mr. Webberly, the port authority agent, had stopped by while she was out. He would return first thing in the morning. Hopefully, her encounter with him would go better than her confrontation at the Del.

Mr. Barstow… Things hadn't gone very well. Although she'd tried to stay calm and in control, in the end he had had the upper hand. She let out a sigh. She must improve with these business dealings. She must or risk losing the company altogether. Even if she married Thomas, she wanted to retain control of Lansing Enterprises. It would be hers. It was the only thing she would have that was completely hers.

The next morning, Hannah dressed in the last thing she had packed—a deep green skirt and cream-colored blouse. The lace collar and large malachite stone brooch set off her neckline. A bit of a softer look than yesterday's suit, perhaps, but still appropriate enough for a business meeting. She gathered her long hair into a chignon at the nape of her neck, securing any flyaway tendrils with a hairnet and modest mint-green bow.

"Miss?" Jackson spoke through the solid door. "Mr. Webberly has arrived. He waits in the lobby."

"I'll be right down."

She checked her appearance in the standing mirror and then started down the stairs. On the landing, she slowed to compose herself. She must play this out rationally, the way Grandfather would, calculating just what to say and when. Her future very well could depend on how well she handled this conversation.

Descending the remainder of the stairs, she noticed a slight, bookish man with thinning hair and thick spectacles pacing the length of the Persian carpet. The moment he turned toward her, she sensed his agitation. Not exactly the mood she'd anticipated. Still, in her experience, graciousness could overcome many a questionable beginning. "Mr. Webberly? Thank you for coming. Won't you have a seat?" She indicated a brocade chair.

She sat on the settee opposite him, separated by a small tea table at their knees. He fingered the rim of his bowler hat, a disgruntled frown on his face, glancing over the luxurious furnishings before focusing back on her.

"May I offer you tea or coffee?"

"No, thank you," he said in clipped tones. "I cannot be away from my desk long. You requested an audience?"

"Yes, I require your services."

He frowned.

She leaned forward, perplexed. "Have I done something to offend you, Mr. Webberly?"

"What is this all about, miss? I am not accustomed to being called out from my office this way."

"Your office?" she said, perplexed. Grandfather always conducted his business meetings at the estate, either in his office or his library. In lieu of that, she considered the hotel lobby appropriate. She certainly could not entertain him in her room! *Press on,* she told herself. "I would like to check the records regarding my family's ships— Lansing Enterprises."

He straightened in his seat. "You're connected with the shipping magnate?"

At least she had his attention now. "As I'm sure you are aware, two ships along with their cargo have recently gone missing. The last port for the *Rose* and the *Margarita* was San Diego. You can understand that I am quite concerned."

When he didn't give any indication one way or the other that he recognized the ships' names, she hesitated. "You are familiar with the names? One spring and one just two months ago, before the New Year."

He steepled his fingers. "Before we discuss matters, I must know... Do you have a note of authority?"

"A note?"

"At the risk of sounding indelicate, before I can talk about any of this with you, I will need Dorian Lansing's written authorization."

That hadn't even been on her mind when she'd packed. "I'm his granddaughter and heir. I assumed I wouldn't need one." When that received no response, she added, "I help run the business."

"So you don't have it," he said flatly.

Realizing that she had leaned forward, she pulled back, hoping she hadn't appeared too anxious. "No. Grandfather is indisposed and asked me to follow up on the situation."

"As a businessman, he would have known to give you some kind of documentation. It is standard procedure."

She hadn't expected this. Usually the Lansing

name got her whatever she wanted. She rubbed her brow. "In my hurry to arrive in time for the opening of the Hotel Del Coronado, I neglected to consider this before leaving San Francisco. My grandfather really is not feeling well. Normally he would take care of such details." She cringed inwardly at her tone. Already she sounded defensive.

He studied her a moment, his gaze considering. "Well, I'll need some form of identification before we can move forward."

She removed a few letters from her reticule and laid them on the mahogany table. "Will this do?"

After looking through them, Mr. Webberly handed them back, his demeanor only slightly more cordial. "I'm sorry if I offended you, Miss Lansing."

"I understand. You must be careful in your line of work. Can we proceed now?"

He took a moment to adjust his spectacles. "If, as you say, he is indisposed, it does make one wonder why you would leave him to attend something five hundred miles away."

"How…?"

"It was in today's newspaper—your appearance at the Del's opening."

She barely controlled her gasp. He questioned her motives! And he didn't even try to disguise it. If she were a man this would not be happening. She clenched her teeth, biting back the retort forming on her lips. It wouldn't do to lose her temper. She needed his services if she was to find out anything. "Mr. Webberly—"

"It wasn't for the hullaballoo, if that's what you're implying," Caleb's deep voice interrupted from behind. How long had he been standing there? How long had he been listening?

His presence overshadowed everything else in the room as he removed his Stetson and stepped closer to the settee. The move felt protective and proprietary all at the same time. The fringe from his leather jacket brushed her left shoulder, tickling her skin at the collar. "Good morning, Mr. Houston," she managed.

Mr. Webberly looked from Caleb back to her, his gaze questioning. She stiffened. This was not the type of help she needed—especially since a nervous fluttering had established itself inside her rib cage.

Smoothly, Caleb continued, "Lansing Enterprises had business dealings with the owners of the Del that needed to be addressed—*in person*."

Mr. Webberly rose to his feet. "I wasn't questioning her loyalty."

"Oh, I think you were," Caleb retorted.

"Caleb...really," she said. "I can handle this."

Mr. Webberly frowned. "Miss Lansing, who is this man?"

Belatedly she realized she'd used Caleb's given name. This was not how she had anticipated the conversation going. "He's a…friend of the family."

The words fairly stuck in her throat. Did either of them consider the other a friend? She had sold that right long ago for the price of a voice. Caleb had made that clear enough yesterday when he'd refused to answer any personal questions. Obviously he didn't trust her anymore. No. She wouldn't call them friends. For now, though, she needed to gain the upper hand. "Mr. Webberly, how can we address this so that we are both satisfied?"

He glanced from her to Caleb and back. "How long will you be in town?"

"Only a few da—"

"For as long as it takes," Caleb inserted smoothly, flashing a warning look to her.

"Yes, of course," she said, backtracking. "It is highly suspicious to have lost two ships due to inclement weather within six months. Lansing Enterprises wants answers. *I* want answers."

"These things happen, Miss Lansing. You aren't the first merchant to lose a shipment."

"But never before with my grandfather's business. And never two so close together. We will not risk any more ships coming through this port until we are satisfied with the safety of the route. I'm sure you can understand how that would affect business here. The railroad companies certainly haven't positioned themselves to help this community as we have." There. That sounded definite. Authoritative. Surely he would grant her request now.

"We would hate to lose your business. Your family has provided extensive commodities in this area for nearly thirty years." He removed his spectacles, folding and then tucking them away into his vest pocket. "Very well. I must verify all this with Mr. Lansing. Once I get the release, you may look over the reports in my office. I'll send a telegram immediately."

Her breath caught. "The letters aren't enough?"

"I'll clear everything through him first."

She rose to her feet, a protest on her lips.

Caleb grabbed her arm. His expression revealed nothing of the rough pressure he exerted on her skin as he met the port agent's gaze. "You do that. We'll stop by your office tomorrow to go over everything."

Mr. Webberly nodded to both of them and headed for the lobby doors.

As soon as the agent was out of hearing distance, Hannah jerked from Caleb's grasp. She rubbed her upper arm. "You had no right to interfere."

His green-eyed stare took on the sheen of hard jade. "You didn't tell Dorian you were coming. He doesn't know anything."

She glared at him.

"And I'll bet if I tried to find your valet, I

wouldn't find his name on the hotel registry, or your maid's. Level with me, Hannah. You're here on your own, under your own steam, aren't you?"

The desk clerk looked up from his papers as the volume of Caleb's voice increased. He stared at the two of them.

"Please," Hannah hissed. "Keep your voice down. It won't do to have the help knowing my business."

Caleb clenched his jaw. "The help," he said flatly. "Does that include me? A family friend?"

"Don't be sarcastic. I was simply waiting for the right opportunity to explain things."

"Let's pretend I believe you on that. But go on. I'm listening." He folded his arms across his chest—waiting.

She couldn't organize her thoughts with him glaring at her like that. "What are you doing here anyway? I was handling things with Mr. Webberly just fine. I didn't need your interference."

"Funny. I thought I was helping."

"What made you think that?"

His smile held no humor. "Maybe the look of delight on your face when I walked up."

She had forgotten how much he could irritate her with just a turn of a phrase. "I didn't want Grandfather involved. He's going through a rough patch with his health. I didn't want him to worry. Now, unfortunately, he will worry twice as much.

Caleb snorted. "Appears it's too late to stop that now."

"Thanks to you.

"Enough, Hannah. No more games. It's high time you tell me what's going on."

"You're saying I should lay my cards on the table? Unload all my little secrets? Why would I do that? To satisfy your curiosity? You only promised to assist me for two days, remember? And that only with the outlay of cold cash." The last two words she bit off sharp and angry.

"Maybe I'll change my mind."

That stopped her. Was he teasing? Or serious? By his tone, she couldn't be sure. "Why would you do that? For more money?"

His face was a mask of granite, his thoughts as difficult to discern as the shifting sandbars beneath the ocean's surface. "Fine. Have it your way, then." He plopped his hat on his head.

He couldn't leave! She needed him one more day!

She reached out. His forearm yielded nothing but firm muscle and sinew under her fingers. He looked pointedly at her hand on his arm and then raised his eyes to hers. Immediately she let go. Her skin felt singed with his heat—whether from his arm or his gaze, she wasn't sure.

There was no course left open to her but honesty at this point. She had nothing more to offer. "I...I can't pay you. Not more than I've already promised." He'd walk away now. She was sure of it.

He stared hard at her. "Hannah, this doesn't have anything to do with money."

Hope—just a wisp—uncurled inside. "Then, what does it have to do with?"

"Trust. It has to do with trust—a thing that used to go unsaid between us."

She plopped down on the settee, a barrage of misgiving whirling through her. She was honor bound to keep her promise to Grandfather. It was the fact that she *wanted* Caleb's help that frightened her...*wanted* his nearness, his security.

But could she trust *herself?* That was the problem. She met his gaze, trying to be objective. He was older now, mature. And if yesterday's trip on the ferry was any indication, he was someone she could count on. She *could* do this. She would. And leave at the end of the week with the answers she needed and her promise kept.

"You could be a huge help, Caleb. Your knowledge of the ocean, of its moods and rhythms..." He waited, looking wary of what she was saying. Wary of her. She closed her eyes and made her decision. "I would ask for your discretion."

"Now, who would I tell? We don't exactly travel in the same circles."

Hannah flinched.

Whatever was going on, it was obvious she

wanted to keep it to herself. Was she in some kind of trouble? He sighed, realizing he'd answered his own question. How could it be anything but trouble that had her so far from her home? "Seems lately we are always throwin' darts," he mumbled.

She twisted the handkerchief in her hands.

"I heard some of what you said to that man at the Del yesterday," he admitted. "You can start there."

"You heard?" She glanced down, her expression defeated. "I thought so."

He placed his hand over hers, stopping her worrying of the fabric, and felt a slight tremor go through her.

She pulled back and tucked the cloth into her satchel, and continued in a calmer voice, "Then, I believe you heard part of the situation. Almost a year ago, Mr. Barstow ordered numerous items for the Hotel Del to be delivered by Lansing Enterprises. They were to arrive on the *Margarita*. I spoke with him yesterday to find out if he received any of them, and if so, how. You heard a portion of the conversation."

"He didn't exactly try to keep his voice down."

"No. It wasn't the best of situations."

"So I take it he didn't get his order."

She sighed. "Last March, Lansing Enterprises lost a merchant ship—the *Margarita*. It sailed from New Orleans to Cuba, then around the southern tip of South America, making several stops along the coast of Chile to trade. The last place it docked was Ensenada, Mexico."

"Just south of here," he murmured.

"Last spring had violent weather, so when Grandfather heard about the loss of the ship and crew he attributed it to a storm."

"What did the report say?"

"It was vague, but said weather was a factor. The captain was a good man, seasoned, and well liked by his crew. His record spoke for itself. That was the first loss for the company in fifteen years."

"Dorian's been fortunate, then. Go on."

"Then, before the New Year, a second ship was lost."

"Let me guess…same place?"

The look she gave him confirmed it. "This has been quite a blow. My grandfather has only one ship left, and it is docked for repairs. He also recently had an investment go sour. He… *We* are worried that the business will not recover. It cannot survive a scandal or breach of contract. Not now."

That caught his attention. As far as he knew, the company was strong enough to weather any problems. Caleb took a slow breath. "What does your father have to say?"

"Stuart?"

He frowned. "He's your father—or at least you used to consider him your father."

"It's…awkward between him and Grandfather—at least regarding me. In a way, Grandmother Rose was the buffer. Now that she is gone…"

No wonder he'd heard less and less from his sister regarding the Lansings. They led different lives now. He could understand how it put Hannah in the middle. "Dorian has always been a hard one."

She stiffened. "I love Grandfather. Remember that."

In other words, tread carefully. "He's never done me any favors. But I'll try to remember that I'm talking to a grown woman with blinders on."

"What happened between Stuart and Grandfather doesn't have anything to do with what's going on with the ships."

"Maybe not." But he wasn't convinced. Over the years, all their lives seemed to intersect at crazy moments—moments like this. "All right. Then, what about the second ship? What happened to the *Rose?*"

"Named for Grandmother. I'm convinced losing that ship prompted Grandfather's illness. The *Rose* was his oldest ship, and dearest. He started the business with it."

He didn't like seeing anything Dorian's way, but he understood. "I can see why that would be a hard blow. So about his health… What happened to him?"

"Apoplexy. His illness has affected the muscles on his right side. He can hardly open an envelope or sign a paper. And so I took over…without giving him a choice in the matter. As I looked through his desk, I became aware of unpaid bills, back orders, things that told me the business was in difficulty."

"Knowing Dorian, that had to be tough on him. He probably hadn't told you anything."

"He has been impossible at times. Grouchy. Horribly difficult."

"He does like total control, but I bet you have done just fine."

With his compliment, her cheeks flushed an interesting shade of pink that he found peculiarly fetching. As she talked, she became more animated, more the Hannah he knew. Yet the way her gaze skittered to the side said something more. There was still more to the telling.

"If I am ever to take over the business as he has said I will, I need to understand it—all of it. While going through the mountain of mail on his desk, I came across a letter from Stuart saying he'd found evidence of wares from the *Margarita* in the outdoor market. They were in excellent— or at least salable—condition."

The news jolted him. He glanced around the room, making sure no one was in hearing distance of their conversation, and lowered his voice. "That changes things significantly."

She nodded.

"Where did he find them?"

"Los Angeles. He was in port with his own ship dropping off lumber from up the coast. Likely he's on his way back to San Francisco now."

"Does Stuart think that you're in Frisco?"

She hesitated before answering, "Yes."

He stared hard at her. She'd taken a huge risk. "Does anyone know you're here?"

"There is Edward."

A knot the size of a half-hitch bend tightened in his gut. "Who is Edward?"

"I told you before—remember? Our butler."

"Ah, yes. Dorian's gatekeeper. He should have stopped you."

"He wasn't aware of my plans. I left him a note."

"No one else knows?"

Again she hesitated. "Mr. Webberly said this morning there was mention of my attending the Del's opening in the newspaper. I don't know how anyone found out. I did not talk to any newsmen."

He wanted to shake some sense into her. What she'd done was this side of crazy. "You should have waited for Stuart—or got word to him."

She frowned. "I am the one who must learn what is happening to the shipments. It is my business—and Grandfather's."

"Who else have you spoken to since you arrived in town?"

She looked bewildered but answered. "No one other than Mr. Barstow at the Hotel Del Coronado and Mr. Webberly today. And of course the clerk at the Horton knows I'm in town."

"You haven't mentioned anything to the sheriff?"

She shook her head. "There's hardly been time. But to tell the truth, I hadn't thought to involve him unless it was necessary."

He sank onto the wing-back chair in the corner, piecing together all that he'd learned, filling in the blanks as much as he could. She needed a bodyguard. She was an heiress, which meant the risk to her immediately quadrupled. It didn't matter that her fortune might have dwindled. Others wouldn't know that.

"I realize what I've done is a bit impulsive." She read the look on his face. "All right. It was very impulsive, but it is done now. All that remains is to gather the facts and return home. Then Grandfather can decide what to do. Please—I know you have knowledge of the shipping lanes and the currents along this coast—things I don't know. You…you could be an immense help. You already have been. I don't expect you to work for nothing. I will pay you—eventually."

"I don't want your money, Hannah. That's not why I'm here," he said in a low voice. "You have no idea what you're getting into. And when Dorian finds out—well, he won't care for the fact that I'm involved. He'll want me strung up by the yardarm of his last vessel. Not that I care what he thinks."

Her eyes were big with worry. "But you had nothing to do with my decision to come here. I came because it is the last place the ships were sighted."

"Dorian won't see things that way. And Stuart won't either. If I hadn't been here, you wouldn't have ventured this far. Maybe you don't see things that way, but they will."

"But it's not true! How could they?"

"That's how I'd see it, if I were them. And if I was smart, I'd pack you on the first train back to Frisco." His mind whirled with the few options available.

"But…what about the ships?"

"I couldn't care less about Dorian—his ships or his money." He was worried about *her*. His stomach roiled. He was in trouble. He should be walking away. Fast. But he couldn't. He knew he couldn't. And it wasn't because he owed his sister anything either.

"Grandfather is very sick, Caleb," Hannah said earnestly, leaning toward him. "Really. You have nothing to worry about from him. The doctor said the least alarm might…might…"

She was getting herself all worked up. Even

if he couldn't stand the man, he had to appreciate her affection for her grandfather. She was loyal to family, and that counted for something by his reckoning. He started to reach across the short distance to hold her hand, but then thought better of it and stopped. "Dorian is tougher than you give him credit for. And I know you wouldn't have left if you thought he was on his last leg."

"You haven't seen him lately. This situation with the company has aged him. He's not the same."

He smiled slightly. "I have a feeling that won't stop him from giving orders from his bed. When he gets Webberly's telegram, he'll be sending someone to fetch you immediately."

Abruptly, she stood. "Which means I must find out what happened to the shipments as quickly as possible. And you are right about the sheriff. I must speak with him." She picked up her reticule from the settee, opened it and pulled out gloves.

"Hannah…slow down." He waited for her full attention before continuing. "You can't run all over town chasing information on your own. It's not safe."

"This is *my* worry, Caleb."

She was using his given name more and more and didn't even realize it. "Mine, too, now."

"Are you saying you'll help?"

He nodded once, deliberately. "I figure I'm in up to my knees with both boots."

"What about your job? The hours you keep? I heard music from the saloon carrying on until just before dawn this morning, and here you are at barely ten o'clock. You must be exhausted."

His lips twitched.

She stiffened. "And what is it you find so amusing?"

"Just the fact that you were thinking of me before drifting off to sleep."

Her gray eyes flashed. "This is serious."

The fact crossed his mind that he'd been thinking about her at nearly the same time. He kept that to himself as he searched her face. She really was beautiful—beautiful and way beyond his reach. It would be good for him to remember that fact. "Don't worry about how much sleep I need. I'll sleep when you head back to Frisco." The words came out as more of a growl than he'd intended. He took a deep breath. "There's one thing more to consider if I'm going to help you."

She waited.

"We do this together. No more early-morning meetings without me."

She opened her mouth.

"I want your word on it."

Her lips pursed.

He would have been amused if he hadn't been so dead serious. She didn't have a choice, as much as she wanted to believe she did. "You're not going to win this one, Hannah. I realize you like calling the shots, but I'm not backing down. Not on this. You're…you're too important."

Her eyes clouded over at his words. "Very well. You have my word," she said softly.

He let that settle between them.

"And…Caleb?"

He paused in sliding on his Stetson.

"Thank you. So much."

Her voice stroked over him like a caress. He liked hearing her talk, liked the smooth cadence of her words, but he couldn't let himself forget where he stood with her—a hired hand. That was how she really saw him.

He tipped the brim of his hat to acknowledge her thanks. "Now, grab something to keep warm. We'll send Dorian a telegram of our own and then stop by the sheriff's."

In ten minutes she was back in the lobby with a dark green cloak covering her shoulders. He was glad to see she'd left the parasol in her room.

"I've thought about the telegram. It's a good idea. At least Grandfather will know you're assisting me. Perhaps his mind will be at ease, knowing that."

"Don't bet on it. No reason for him to trust me now any more than he did five years ago." Caleb opened the door to the street. "What about you? Do you trust me?"

Clearly startled, she met his gaze and then quickly glanced away. "I'm not… I don't…"

What had made him ask that? He was convenient, that was all. He blew out a breath. The sooner she got the answers she wanted, the sooner she'd leave and his life would get a whole lot easier. "Never mind. Let's get this done."

Chapter Seven

What about you? Hannah couldn't get Caleb's question out of her thoughts as they left the telegraph office. Did she trust him? To a point, she supposed she did. She felt safe with him in a way she'd never felt with anyone else. But there were things she could never let him know. And trust—real trust—had to go both ways between people, or it was an illusion.

If she was honest with herself, she *was* glad to see him again. It was there in the way her hope expanded beyond her common sense when he'd agreed to help her. It was there in the casual brush of his sleeve against her arm, and the weight of his hand at the small of her back as he ushered her down the boardwalk.

She didn't want to feel this rush of...of emotion. Being with him brought back memories that were better left buried, memories that hurt in their sweetness. To acknowledge them meant she had to face the bargain she'd made that day with Grandfather.

She stepped away from his light touch, out of his reach. A small move, but with it her head cleared and she breathed easier. He'd said she was important. Was he only helping her because of her status as a Lansing? Or was it possible he still felt something for her? The second the thought took shape, hope started to grow—hope that they might find their way back to the easy friendship they'd had once. At the same time she felt like a traitor to her name.

After sending the telegram they stopped at the sheriff's office. Unfortunately, he was away on a call to a nearby ranch and not expected back for several hours.

"What next?" Caleb asked, standing on the wooden boardwalk outside the law office.

His question took her off guard. She appreciated the fact that he was asking for her direction. It wasn't something Grandfather had ever done. There was plenty of daylight left. The sun was at its zenith, a cool, pale circle of light behind a thin sheet of clouds. "I'd like to check the newspaper reports of the accidents."

At the *San Diego Herald,* the strong, pungent odor of ink permeated the room. In one corner, the pressman rolled new ink over the tray of raised letters, readying the press for duty. He stopped when he saw them enter, rubbed his hands on his apron and stepped out from behind the press. "What can I do for you folks?"

"We'd like to see old copies of the paper—the second of January of this year, and March of '87 if you have them," Hannah said.

He moved to the opposite side of the room where the wall was lined with deep shelves from floor to ceiling. He slapped his beefy hand on two short stacks of newspapers. "That'll be here and here. Just keep 'em in order."

Caleb dug through the piles and pulled out the papers dated the week before, during and after the time the *Rose* was lost and then the *Margarita*. She removed her cloak, hanging it on a nearby peg, and then sat down at a large oak table near the front window.

She expected him to sit across from her; however, Caleb seemed to have other ideas. He dropped the newspapers in a pile on the table and then moved over and stood behind her, bracing himself with one large hand to the table and his other to the back of her chair as she spread out the papers. His breath tickled her neck just above her collar, and the faint scent of soap and leather swirled about her, nearly overwhelmed by the odor of ink in the room.

A tingle raced to her toes. This was impossible! She'd read the same sentence four times and still didn't know what it said. She couldn't concentrate with him standing so close. Closing her eyes, she tried to take hold of her senses and bring them under tight rein.

She read the sentence again. Twice. And gave up. "Do you mind?" she asked, hearing a slight edge to her voice.

He straightened, his gaze stabbing her. "Don't believe I do," he said, then deliberately bent over and began reading again.

Her cheeks warmed. What was he about? He must realize he was disturbing her. She drew in a slow, deep breath. If this was some kind of a bid for the upper hand, she would not allow him to see that he was playing havoc with her concentration.

"Are you finished?" His baritone voice rumbled over her shoulder.

How long had she been staring at the paper? Her cheeks heated. Quickly, she turned the page and focused on the next section. A small corner article mentioned the loss of the *Margarita*. The second, more recent, article mentioned the *Rose,* commenting briefly that it was Lansing Enterprises' second loss in as many years.

She sighed, disappointed, and closed the paper. On the back page, a different article mentioned calm and sunny weather for the entire week. "That's odd," she murmured. "I thought the loss was due to a storm. That's what we were told." She read over it once more, and then handed it to Caleb.

"We'll know more once we see the official port reports."

"I'd hoped for more information. For such a major event in my life, it seems like very brief news coverage."

Caleb straightened. "I'll ask around. Grease some throats or palms."

"What do you mean?"

"Use a little liquor or money to loosen tongues. There are those who would trade information for cold cash."

"Where will we find such men?"

"Along the wharf."

"Sailors?"

"Possibly. Or just dockhands. They're the ones who would know something."

A shudder ran through her. She'd noticed such men before in San Francisco and yesterday on the pier. Foulmouthed. Rough. "They might say anything for the money. How can we be sure they would tell the truth?"

"We can't."

She digested that bit of news. He obviously wasn't worried about dealing with such men, but it made her nervous. Of course, she would never admit that. She would see this thing through. Scooting her chair back, she stood. "All right. What time will you come for me?"

"What are you talking about?"

"So that I can go with you."

At his dumbfounded look, she reminded him, "You said we'd do this together."

He frowned. "Now, hold on. Not this, Hannah. The places I'll be going are no place for a lady. Whether you are there or not won't make a difference to what I find out, and it might just hinder me."

"What do you mean?"

"Might make people clam up—quit talkin' with you there. You aren't exactly the type to go unnoticed. You're too…too…"

"What?" she said, narrowing her eyes. "I've been in plenty of strategy meetings with Grandfather. I know when it's prudent to keep my mouth shut."

"That's not it." He scowled. "You're too…much of a *woman!*"

"Oh!" She had no reply for that. "Oh," she repeated as heat crept up her cheeks, and she knew they were turning a bright pink. "Well, there's not much I can do about that! But this is my worry. I should be there."

His eyes narrowed. "I'm not giving you a choice."

Rigidly, without looking at him, she organized the papers and placed them back on the shelf.

"Not much fun, is it?"

"Now what are you talking about?"

"Being kept in the dark."

She frowned. "I'm only trying to do my part."

"Naw." He studied her face, his head cocked to one side. "You can't stand the fact that you might have to wait in your room while I fish for information."

It was the truth, but she hated to admit it. She didn't like to give up control. Guess she had a little of Grandfather in her after all. "Well…how can I be sure that you'll tell me everything?"

His hard stare made her take a step backward. "Look, Hannah. You've come this far. You've asked for my help. Now, you can either trust me with it…or you can go home." He took her cloak from the peg on the wall and shoved it toward her. "Put this on. You're going back to the hotel."

Caleb stormed back to the saloon, his thoughts swirling like a dust devil over the desert. That stubborn streak of Hannah's had him so riled that a week of fishin' sounded mighty nice at this point. She was determined—he'd give her that much. Years ago that determination had nearly got her killed when she'd chased after her puppy and then the both of them had been trapped in a cave by the tide. She'd nearly drowned.

He entered the saloon to find the usual customers plus a few new ones. The Bradison brothers had their weekly poker game going with two unsuspecting cowboys. The brothers were hard at it, playin' no-holds-barred against each other. They enjoyed the game—sometimes too much, getting rowdy and whoopin' up a storm when they fleeced another at the table, but then usually they let the yokel win most of his earnings back. They didn't want sour feelings—just an entertaining game.

At the faro table, Wyatt tipped his chin to Caleb. Wyatt had long since given up on the two Bradison brothers ever making it as serious gamblers. Caleb figured the two brought more goodwill to the saloon than any amount of liquor could accomplish.

Lola, wearing a dress the color of deep rust, leaned over Tom Bradison and whispered teasingly in his ear. Jim emerged from behind the bar to slap four ales in front of the players.

All in all it looked like any other weeknight in town.

Caleb headed down the short hall to the kitchen, splashed the day's grit off his face and neck and dried off with a dish towel.

"Surprised to see you back," Jim said, coming to his side while Caleb poured himself a draft at the bar. "You took off in a hurry. Been reminiscing with that lady friend of yours? Showin' her the sights?"

"Some," he said noncommittally.

"She heading back to Frisco soon?"

"Turns out she's got a few more things to do."

Jim eyed him sharply, with one bushy gray

brow peaking. "Don't sound like it bothers you as much as it did when she first got here."

Caleb grunted. "The shock has worn off some."

Wyatt stepped up to the far end of the counter. Caleb waited while Jim poured him a whiskey before approaching his boss. He leaned one elbow on the polished wood counter. "Where's Josie?"

"Not singin' tonight."

"She all right?"

"Got a stomachache."

"Too bad. She always draws a nice-size crowd." He'd hoped to increase his odds for gathering information.

Wyatt grinned. "She does, at that." He turned his back to the room and took a swig of his whiskey. "So tell me what's happening with Miss Nob Hill. Has she taken you to high tea or to meet the mayor yet?"

Caleb scowled. So Jim had been talking. Wyatt would have a party with it before this was over. "She's not like that."

A wide, slow grin split Wyatt's face.

"Let that go. Seems there is more going on than I figured."

Wyatt smirked, but he held back the *I told you so.* "Often is the case when it comes to women."

Caleb steered clear of that comment. "Remember that ship going down off the coast last month? Originally from San Francisco, but on its return trip from New Orleans."

"Sank right after Christmas, I recall."

"The ship belonged to Miss Lansing's family."

Wyatt set down his glass with a jolt and gave Caleb his full attention. "Your lady friend is a Lansing? Now, how'd I miss that the first time around?"

"Didn't mention it."

"Okay. So how'd you come by knowin' her?"

Caleb blew out a breath. "Long story. She lived here a while before going north to Frisco. We were kids together out on the point. She came back for the Del's opening. Since she was in town, she decided to ask around about the ships. We checked the newspaper account earlier today."

Wyatt took a drag on his cigar and then blew the smoke rings across the bar. "Anything there?"

"Not much."

"What about the port authorities?"

"We tried. Webberly won't let us see the report until he has the go-ahead from her grandfather. We sent a telegram today."

"Bureaucrats…" Wyatt said, disgust filling his voice. "You know, this Miss Lansing might be a big help in getting that land you been looking at."

"I don't need her help. Don't want anything from her but a swift return to Frisco."

Wyatt's brows hiked up a notch at Caleb's tone.

"About the ship," Caleb continued quickly. He didn't want any speculation about his relationship with Hannah. There wasn't one. "Thought I'd ask around the Stingaree. Men there know what happens even before the devil does."

Wyatt straightened. "They play for keeps there. But I guess you know all about that. Watch your back." He shoved away from the counter.

"Tomorrow night okay with you?"

"Don't discount what I said about the land. She could be your ace in the hole." With a cloud of cigar smoke circling his head, he headed back to his place at the faro table.

The saloon was lively for a Tuesday night. Caleb spoke to a few men about the ships. No one had any more information.

"You callin' me a liar, Swede?"

Caleb moved toward the two men trading insults. Lola stood between a tall blond and a regular customer named Franklin. They each had a hand on her arm and looked ready to split her in two.

"Lola," he said. "Scoot on outta there."

She tried, but neither man let go.

"Franklin, what's this all about? You know Wyatt don't allow fightin'."

"Then, tell this big oaf to keep his hands off my gal."

Caleb raised his brows. "First time I heard you say that about Lola."

"Well, I don't like him looking at her or touchin' her."

"I haf just as much right as you," the Swede said, his eyes blazing blue fire.

"She got your ring on her finger?" Caleb asked Franklin, knowing Lola had no such thing.

"Don't matter."

"How 'bout you?" he asked the Swede.

The man didn't budge.

"Then, I'd say neither one of you has a claim. It's up to her who she talks to."

Lola wrenched from their loosened fingers and stepped away from them. She rubbed her reddened skin. "I ain't a thing to be pawed at! You can both go back to wherever you came from and leave me alone."

At the dressing-down, Franklin grumbled something under his breath and stomped off, catching up his hat and heading out the saloon door.

The Swede took advantage of that fact and headed right back to Lola, who apparently had gotten over her stewing. She appeared downright friendly, teasing and flirting with the man right up to closing time.

"Hoosten?" The Swede looked him over on his way out of the saloon. "You the one askin' aboot the ship?"

Caleb gave him his full attention.

The man studied Caleb. "Why?"

"Got a friend who wants information."

"Your friend should do his own asking," the Swede murmured.

"Sounds like you might know something. I'm willing to pay for information—solid facts."

"Got no more to say." The large man slammed out through the swinging doors.

Caleb strode after him, but the Swede disappeared around the corner by the bank. He retraced his steps, and, locking the saloon door behind him, he trudged upstairs to his room. Not much to report back to Hannah. She needn't have worried so much that he'd hold out on her. He flopped down on his bed, laced his fingers behind his head and stared at the ceiling.

He'd tolerated the time he'd spent with Hannah today. Wasn't as bad as he'd thought it would be. She had a good head on her shoulders, and he'd seen glimpses of the girl within the woman—the girl he'd once liked. He blew out a long breath. Seemed he liked the woman, too.

Good thing she'd be leavin' soon.

Chapter Eight

The next day, Caleb repeated the Swede's words to Hannah during their walk to the port authority office. He had barely set his backside to the outer bench in the waiting area before they were both greeted and ushered into the office.

Mr. Webberly rose from behind his desk the moment they entered. "Good morning. I've been expecting you."

"I take it you heard back from Lansing," Caleb said, noticing a change in the man's demeanor.

"Yes. And I've taken the liberty to obtain the files for you." He pointed to two folders on his desk. "Take your time looking through them. If you have any questions, I'll be just outside the door."

So Hannah's position had improved some since yesterday. Caleb wasn't used to such treatment. More often it was a cursory glance, along with a man staying in the office to keep an eye on him.

When Mr. Webberly had exited and closed the door, he turned to Hannah. "You always put up with that?"

She moved to the desk and flipped open the first file. "What do you mean?"

"The way he treated you just now, compared with the way he acted yesterday."

She concentrated on the pages before her. "It happens," she murmured. When he made no move to join her, she looked up. "I can't change how people react, Caleb."

"So you learn not to trust anybody."

She shrugged and went back to reading the report.

That explained a few things. Like why he felt she still wasn't telling him the whole truth. When everyone treated you differently once they knew you had money, how did you know who your true friends were?

The small glimpse into her life as it must be on Nob Hill rattled him. He'd imagined days full of shopping and nights full of fancy dinner parties, but with people she could have fun with—people she could trust. That didn't seem to be the case. Was she ever lonely?

None of my business, he told himself.

He pulled a chair up beside her and started reading through the official reports of the two ships. The fragrance of roses drifted up as he leaned closer to her shoulder. He inhaled, deep and slow, letting her scent fill his senses.

The pages trembled in her hand.

He glanced up. She stared at him with those fathomless gray eyes. He'd seen that look before a long time ago. He thought he'd be over it, be stronger somehow, but it still had the power to pull him in, to captivate—even more so now that she was all grown up. With conscious effort, he broke from her hold and, with his gaze, followed the curve of her cheek to her lips. She didn't move—barely seemed to breathe.

Then she blinked and drew her brows together, tilting her head slightly before turning back to the report.

He'd closed the space between them to mere inches. Suddenly aware of it, he backed away. He had a job to do, and he'd best get on with it. The sooner she got her information, the sooner they could both get on with their lives—a litany that played through his thoughts more and more.

The three pages on the first ship didn't have much in the way of new information for them. The perfunctory reporting was straightforward, with the times the loss had been noticed and the declaration of the end of the search attempt. It concluded that turbulent weather and rough water farther out to sea were the deciding factors in the loss of the ship. Ditto for the second ship.

"A storm at sea," she murmured and closed the

report. "That is the same information Grandfather received." She let out a frustrated sigh, straightened the file and then laid it down square on the desk. Funny, he'd never noticed how long and slender her fingers were before. He was noticing a lot of things he shouldn't be noticing about her.

"This could be a fool's chase," she said with a sigh. "Sometimes when there's nothing there, it's simply because nothing is there."

He scraped his chair across the wood floor as he stood. "But with what the Swede said, I don't think that's the case anymore. Sometimes you have to look between the lines." Staring into her troubled gray eyes, he found his thoughts more muddled than ever. "The ships... That *is* what you're talking about...."

"Of course. Caleb...I... We..."

Mr. Webberly opened the door. "All finished?"

Hannah started. Recovering quickly, she cleared her throat and rose from her chair. "Yes."

"I hope you found everything in order."

She nodded briefly. "Thank you for the use of your office. We'll be going now."

"Glad to be of service, miss," Mr. Webberly said, stepping aside to let Hannah pass through the door.

Once outside, Hannah opened her mouth to speak. Caleb glanced back to the building they'd just come from. Webberly stood at the open window, a frown on his face.

"Not here," Caleb warned in a low voice, and took her arm, urging her up the street. "We're being watched."

Something was bothering her. It showed in her slower pace in spite of his hand pressed to her lower back. It was as if her thoughts took up all her concentration. She passed the storefronts without a glance inside, without even realizing they were passing them.

At the hotel's entrance, rather than hurry into the lobby, she stopped. A milk wagon, pulled by two long-eared mules, rattled past. She paced restlessly back and forth on the boardwalk until the noise diminished.

"What is it?" he asked.

"The news account didn't say the same thing."

"You caught that." He tipped his hat down against the early-afternoon sun. He'd wanted proof—something more than what she'd been telling him. He had it now. Maybe not enough to convince the sheriff to look into it again, but it put to rest his own doubt.

"Well," she pressed on in that determined way he'd come to expect of her. "The newspaper didn't mention the weather as a contributing factor. I would have thought it would."

"They said it was cool, sunny weather. No mention of a front coming in."

"Could it have been an oversight? Just poor reporting?"

"Here? The weather is calm to the point of boring here. Usually the least little rain shower gets written up as if it's a life-threatening squall."

"So you believe the newspaper account."

He nodded.

"And the port authority report is wrong."

"Whitewashed, if you ask me. Too perfect."

"Then—"

"I know where you are going with this, Hannah. Let's keep things in perspective. Something could have happened on the ship—a fire started from cooking, or lightning striking the supply of gunpowder on board."

"With one ship—yes. But not with two. According to the paper, the ships disappeared without a trace—not even a puff of black smoke on the horizon."

"The only hard evidence we have is that the merchandise turned up in Los Angeles—"

"And the fact that the two reports contradict each other."

He removed his hat and shoved his fingers through his hair. This was all starting to sound a lot more involved than he'd first suspected. And a lot more organized. He looked down the street. Two men loitered at the entrance to the general merchandise store while the owner swept the boardwalk. Another man smoked a cigarette on the saloon's front steps. If more than a few men were involved, then the risk increased exponentially. Hannah could be stirring up a nest of snakes.

"Caleb?"

Hearing his name jostled him from his thoughts. He resettled his hat. "There's reason to doubt the report. I'll know more after tonight."

"You believe me, then."

He nodded. "Yeah, I believe you."

She smiled and then stared up at him with those winsome gray eyes. "Thank you."

And again, he was captivated. He should head back to the saloon. Put some distance between them before he did something he'd regret. She'd made it clear he was just filling a needed job.

Her lashes swept down as her gaze darted to the door of the hotel. "I…I suppose I should go in…."

He didn't care for the fact that he wanted her to stay. "I've got a few things to take care of before tonight."

"Of course. I realize that I've been monopolizing your time. Before you go, I…I want to speak to you about what happened earlier."

That was about the last thing he wanted to do. "There's nothing to talk about."

"But there is. There's…a history between us. One that—"

He knew all about their history, and he wasn't about to repeat it. He'd learned his lesson. "Like

I said—there's nothing to talk about. I'll help you out for the time that you are here. That's it."

"But about what happened back there at the port authority office. You need to know—"

"Hannah, so help me…will you just leave it? Nothing happened. I know how things stand between us. You've made that clear from the start."

She stiffened at his words. "Oh. Then, we understand each other."

"We sure do."

Warmth crept up her collar. Whatever attraction she'd felt in the office must have been one-sided. How like her to let emotions rule her—just like when she was sixteen.

The heavy hotel doors opened and the desk clerk called out, "Miss Lansing, I thought you would want to know immediately. A telegram has come for you."

"Thank you, Mr. Bennett." She caught Caleb's expression at the man's deference. She opened the telegram.

"Contacted Stuart for immediate escort home. Grandfather."

Succinct. And full of controlled anger. Dorian's implacable face swam before her. Suddenly her time here was finite. She crushed the paper in her hand.

"What is it?" Caleb said from behind her.

"Grandfather." That one word explained everything. "He has contacted Stuart to fetch me home."

"When?"

"Immediately." Her entire world turned on the missive. Disappointment weighted her shoulders.

"It's for the best, Hannah."

She frowned. "No, it's not. I need to have answers. If I go back now, before I have anything substantial, all this will be in vain."

His dark brows drew together. "Then, send him your own telegram. Tell him what you just told me—that you need more time."

"He won't listen. He only sees things one way—his way. I can't bargain with him."

"We have time. It will take at least four days for Stuart to travel south from San Francisco."

She let out a sigh. "I wish that were true. However, Stuart isn't in San Francisco. He's in Los Angeles."

That made him pause. "Then, he could be here as early as tomorrow. We would only have tonight."

She nodded. Everything was unraveling. "It depends on how sea-ready his ship is."

"Knowing Stuart, it was ready yesterday."

"I don't want to stop now. We're getting close. I can feel it."

"I figure we have twenty-four to forty-eight hours before Stuart arrives. We'll keep at it until he shows up. For all we know, he may even help."

He watched her closely, his face shaded by the brim of his hat. "There's something you're not telling me. Let me see it."

She handed over the telegram. Caleb knew how Dorian was. There was no point in hiding anything from him. The telegram said absolutely nothing more. Nothing. No endearment, no caution for her to be careful. Why she hoped that after all this time it might…

He read it for himself and then glanced sharply at her face.

She tried to explain. "He's angry with me. And Grandfather has never been demonstrative. Not in actions or words."

Caleb snorted. "He's the last man I'd hang the word *warm* on."

She swallowed, her throat thick with the struggle to squash her disappointment. It was a weakness—this urge to cry. This overwhelming need for Grandfather's approval.

He touched under her chin, lifting her gaze to his. "Don't give up just yet. There's still time. I'll find out what I can tonight."

Her breath caught. He offered hope. Yet her reaction to his look, his touch, was way out of proportion to his words. "And you'll contact me first thing in the morning?"

He lowered his hand, nodded and then strode across the street.

She watched him until he disappeared into the

saloon. It was as if he'd seen all the way into her soul to the very thing she tried to hide, the thing she shared with no one. Could it be he still knew her better than anyone, even after all this time?

Caleb turned up the collar on his leather coat against the damp night air and trudged toward the Stingaree district of town. He couldn't get his thoughts off Hannah—not that he was trying very hard. Her loyalties were to Dorian and the Lansing name now, and he had to respect her for that.

Yet the look on her face when she'd read Dorian's telegram troubled him. She'd looked... vulnerable. And then she'd straightened her shoulders and, transforming before his eyes, become an impenetrable block of stone, the invisible armor clinking into place as her face toughened with resolve.

Dorian had hurt her. Oh, not physically—but somewhere inside. And this hadn't been the first time by the way she dealt with it so quickly. How many times had she had to rally herself against his coldness? What kind of a life had she really had in San Francisco?

The only answer that came to him was the one he didn't like—a life that she wanted to return to.

He had to stop thinking about her like this. Just get the questions about the ships answered and get her out of his life. That was best for both of them.

Heading down Market Street, he passed warehouses of every shape and size that lined each side of the street. In a corner building, a single yellow light shone from an upstairs back room. The black hand-painted sign over the door marked it as a Chinese laundry. Caleb turned the corner. The street narrowed, grew darker.

Overhead, a thick cloud bank had rolled in from the sea and obliterated the stars. Foreboding wrapped around his chest. He pulled his Stetson lower on his head, hunkered into his coat and stretched his stride. He felt for the familiar handle of his gun at his hip.

He hadn't come this way in years—purposely. The Stingaree district was the devil's own playground. Rough and squalid, filled with opium dens and prostitutes, brawling and knife fights— not exactly the same clientele he ran into at Wyatt's place.

Here, unless he paid for it somehow, no one would be forthcoming with information. It was the "somehow" that worried him. Could be money, could be blood, could be both. These men stuck together and were suspicious of anyone from the outside. They preyed on strangers. Tonight, he was the stranger. His only hope was to drop a few hints and then wait for someone to come to him with answers—preferably in bright daylight tomorrow.

He stopped in front of the Iron Tub. The faded sign on the darkened front facade bragged of the best whiskey from Ireland. Setting his shoulders, he entered the dimly lit saloon and waited for his eyes to adjust. A smoky brown haze filled the room and hovered over the tables with enough kick to it to sedate a horse. Not exactly regular tobacco.

Caleb counted two customers sitting at the far end of the bar and three at a table playing poker. The card players glanced his way, dismissed him and quickly returned to their game. He walked between a few tables and stopped at the bar.

"What'll ye have?" the barkeep asked. He was a man as wide as he was tall, with jowls to match and frizzy white hair that shot out in all directions from his head.

"A beer will do." He plunked down a coin on the worn counter.

The barkeep nodded to him as he finished wiping out a glass.

Candles burned on every table, and a gas chandelier in the center of the room lent light to the place, yet still it seemed dark. Caleb stared into the shadows. Why was it so dark? He looked up and froze. Spiderwebs laced the ceiling and beams, so thick a man couldn't see through to the wood behind. The entire atmosphere created an eerie coziness.

"I see you ain't been here before," the barkeep said, puffing out his chest—a nearly imperceptible move considering his width. He slammed a mug full of ale down in front of Caleb. Beer sloshed over the mug's side, but the man took no note of it and made no move to clean it up. He sucked in air between the crack in his two front teeth. "Takes you back a bit when you first come in, don't it?"

Caleb checked his drink for any eight-legged creatures floating on top before taking a gulp.

The barkeep grinned. "Took me twenty years to build this. Saw a place just like it in Frisco back in '68. A real emporium it was. Then and there I vowed I'd have one meself one day."

Caleb figured the man wouldn't appreciate any criticism—not after twenty years. "Unusual," he murmured.

"That it is!" The barkeep grinned and moved away to answer another customer's request for ale.

The man, a gaunt-looking fellow with yellow eyes and brown, stringy hair, had entered the saloon after Caleb. He studied Caleb a wide moment before leaning one elbow on the counter and stating, "You ain't a regular."

Caleb waited. If he acted too eager to join into conversation, the man would back out of it.

"But you got a familiar look to ya." The man stepped closer. "You one of Wyatt's boys?"

Caleb had the sudden urge to pull away from such foul breath, but he checked it. The man's curiosity was a good thing. At least Caleb wouldn't have to take the lead and bully himself into a conversation with someone. "Just happened to be in this part of town and got thirsty."

"Just happened to be, eh? Don't take me for a fool, mister. With your job, you can get all the free beer you want."

The barkeep and several of the other customers had stopped talking. A glance their way told Caleb they listened—a little too closely.

"So what brings you to this part of town? You wouldn't be here unless you wanted something... more," Yellow Eyes continued, his gaze skeptical.

"Careful, now. The barkeep might take offense if you talk about his establishment that way." Over his shoulder he noticed two more men entering the saloon. Four men—whiskered and mangy—played poker now, and three tough younger bucks stood at the far end of the bar. One wore a gun, but the others had knives sheathed at their hips. "But you do have a point. There *is* something I want."

Yellow Eyes smirked.

"Information."

When that statement met a wall of studied indifference, Caleb plunged ahead. "The answers I'm looking for can be found here. Nothing comes in or out of the port without somebody here knowin' about it."

Yellow Eyes grunted.

Not the most encouraging sound. There was nothing to do but keep going. No point in tiptoeing. "In the past six months, two ships have gone down off the coast. I want to know what happened to them."

The barkeep glanced over Caleb's shoulder, then moved down the counter, washing it off, his eyes intent on his business.

Caleb noticed the others got the message as loud as he had. "I'm willing to pay." Money might be the only incentive that would override pack mentality here.

Yellow Eyes raised his brows. "Pay, you say? That type of information could cost a pretty penny."

"Nobody knows nothin' around here."

The new voice, gravelly and belligerent, came from behind Caleb. He turned and faced a dark-haired bruiser—one with biceps the size of tree trunks and a face with pox scars that only a dog could love. Black eyes glittered from beneath heavy, thick brows. The other men cleared a space for him.

Caleb moved his hand from the bar to his thigh, in closer proximity to his gun, just to be ready. "I'm not looking for a fight. All I want is information. Like I said—it's worth something to me, enough to pay."

A sneer split the other man's face. "Well, ain't that just a relief to me mother."

Caleb set his jaw.

"I don't care what you want. You'll finish your

beer and be on your way." The bruiser's grin turned evil.

Rankled, Caleb stood his ground. The only things these men respected were guts and stubbornness. One sign of weakness and they'd attack—a feeding frenzy of sharks. "I only take orders when it benefits me."

"Can't fault you for that, but if you value your skin, you'll do as I say."

A flash of silver caught Caleb's peripheral vision. He reacted in one smooth sweep, stepping back and grabbing the man's hand. He squeezed, at the same time twisting around so that the man's body was between him and the others. Chairs scraped the floor as the men scrambled to their feet. Caleb squeezed harder. The knife clattered to the plank flooring.

Outrage filled the bruiser's face. "You've done it now, masher!" he growled under his breath.

Caleb released slightly on the man's arm. It was a common hold—one he had used before at the saloon. It was also an effective one. "I think you know something you need to share."

Something cold and hard shoved into his back. Then he heard the sound of a trigger being cocked.

"Time for you to leave, mister," the barkeep said. "I don't want no trouble here."

Knives were one thing, but getting himself

killed wouldn't help Hannah. He let go of the bruiser, who stumbled away a few feet.

He'd done what he came to do. Now he just had to wait for word to spread and hope someone desperate for money would come to him. A look about the place told him that could be anyone here.

He whipped up his hat from the counter, ignoring the dark look from the bruiser. He was absolutely sure now that there was more to the ships being lost at sea. Someone was hiding the truth and wanted it to stay hidden. And he'd just stirred the pot. Something would float to the surface. He strode out of the saloon.

A moonless sky greeted him as he headed back to Fourth Street. Hannah was too close in proximity to these men. If they had any inkling she was the one wanting answers, she'd be at risk.

To his right, a door creaked open, and two men spoke in muffled voices. He moved his hand to the handle of his Colt .45.

Another three hundred yards and quiet surrounded him again. Glancing about, he saw nothing but dark buildings and shadows. He was getting jumpy. He relaxed his grip and pulled his hat lower, firmer on his head.

Good thing Stuart was on his way. If foul play had caused the loss of the ships—and it was beginning to feel as though that was more and more the case—he wanted Hannah out of here. She wouldn't like it, but he couldn't be worried about her while he investigated. When Stuart arrived, he'd hand her over.

A boot pounded the dirt behind him.

He grabbed his gun. At the same time a sharp pain exploded through his head. He sank to his knees. Stunned, unable to react, he noticed the two gas lamps in front of him gave off starbursts of light and then went out. A man grunted behind him, just before something hard slammed between his shoulder blades. Out whooshed his breath. His hands tingled—then went numb. His gun clumped to the dirt.

"No! Don't kill him yet…."

The ground rushed toward him.

Chapter Nine

Hannah stirred sugar into her second cup of tea and then settled her spoon in the gold-rimmed saucer. She'd chosen her seat for breakfast in the hotel's small restaurant in order to see Caleb when he emerged from the saloon.

The ornate, gold-plated clock on the mantel in the dining room chimed once. Half past ten. Surely he was awake by now. He wouldn't sleep until noon, would he? Not when this might be their only chance to compare notes before Stuart arrived.

"Is there anything I can get for you?"

Startled out of her thoughts, she met the waiter's gaze.

"Perhaps more biscuits?"

"No, I'm fine." She settled into the straight-backed chair again. A moment later, she plucked the mutton sleeve on her shoulder and then folded her hands in her lap with a conscious effort to keep from further fidgeting.

Taking a sip of tea, she thought back to yesterday and the port authority office. She'd thought Caleb had wanted to kiss her. That awareness had shut out everything else—the men working in the adjacent room and the barked orders of dockhands on the wharf outside. It had also shut out the promise she'd given Grandfather. There'd been wanting in his gaze. Once before he'd looked at her with that same intensity. Bittersweet memories of her first kiss washed over her. Her heart had raced then, too.

She'd felt the pull. No one else made her feel like that—so alive. Only Caleb. Why him? Only him?

But he'd denied it. Had it all been in her head?

No matter. It was over. In the past. And there it would stay. She glanced again at the clock.

Eleven.

Oh, this waiting was interminable! No matter the hour, he should be awake by now. If he didn't step through that door in the next ten minutes, she'd march across the street and demand to see him. It wasn't such a huge undertaking. Proper etiquette might be stretched a bit, but it wasn't as if this town was San Francisco.

Caleb would probably be disagreeable anyway—especially if he had imbibed last night. It would also explain why he hadn't yet appeared. She tapped her fingers on the marble tabletop.

Eleven-ten.

Enough. She took a deep breath and stood. Drawing on her straw bonnet, she tied the ribbons at her chin with a determined jerk. She would not be held captive by her promise to remain here at the hotel—not if he slept off a liquored drunk. From the doorway, Mr. Bennett watched her movements, curiosity on his face. Before she could change her mind, she nodded to him and then strode through the door and out to the street.

Another deep breath and she mounted the step to Brannigan's Saloon. She tried the double brass handles. Sealed tight. She knocked on the outer doors. No one came immediately. Wonderful. A good thing Grandfather couldn't see her. She felt awkward standing there on the boardwalk in front of a saloon. Grandfather would be outraged.

A scraping noise came from the other side of the doors, and then a key jiggled in the lock. The door opened a crack and a man's face appeared. A thick silvery mustache coated his upper lip and drooped down on each side of his mouth, rather magnificent in its length. After an undignified yawn, his watery blue eyes fixed on her. "What can I do for you, ma'am?"

"I'm looking for Caleb Houston," she said. "And it's miss."

A salt-and-pepper brow shot up, and he looked

her over more closely. "So you're the one he's been dropping his chores for lately. I've been doing double duty since you showed up."

"I...I know he works late. However, we had an agreement this morning. He was to meet with me."

"'Fraid I ain't seen him. Though that's not saying much. He usually don't make an appearance until noon."

Couldn't the man check for Caleb in his room? At least make sure he was here? "I'm sorry I've taken him away from his work. I won't be in town much longer, so you have little to fear that it will be a permanent change. He has been a great help to me already, and he speaks highly of you." She shut out the warning inside at the small fib.

Her words brought a reluctant grunt and a slight quirk to one side of the man's mustache. "Has he now? Don't see what he could be a-sayin 'bout me."

Footsteps sounded on the boardwalk behind her, reminding her of her predicament. No self-respecting woman would be caught peeping into a saloon at this hour or—for that matter—at any hour. Suddenly she very much wanted to be off the street. "Might I wait inside for him?"

He opened the door wider. "If'n you want. Name's Jim...Jim Avery."

"Thank you," she answered, and stepped inside, shutting the door behind her. She looked around, curiosity getting the better of her. She'd never been in a saloon before. Why, it was nothing more than a restaurant—a restaurant with an exceedingly long bar, gaming tables and lots of bottles. The way the bottles were positioned against the large mirror, it appeared there were twice as many.

A huge picture above the mirror caught her attention. In it, a voluptuous woman reclined on a dark couch with a come-hither smile on her lips. She wore a Grecian robe that draped casually over certain well-endowed parts of her anatomy—leaving little to the imagination. "Oh, my!"

Jim radiated pride. "Ain't she a beaut?"

"Ah...yes. She's lovely."

"Been here as long as I have. Name's Rosie. Short for Rosalind."

"That's...ah...lovely."

"Like in Shakespeare," he added.

"Of course. From his play, *As You Like It*."

Perhaps she'd passed some kind of personal test because suddenly he said, "I didn't see Caleb come in last night. Must have been late—or early, depending on yer point of view."

"But he *is* here?"

"Purty sure he is. That's his hat on the table there. Not like him at all to leave it there. He tends to keep the few things he owns close."

"Hmm," she said, peering up the stairs to the

open hallway and the row of doors. Which one led to Caleb's room?

"Well, now," Jim said. "I got chores to do. Caleb's room is the last one on the left. You can see the door from here."

He expected her to go up? Just like that? "I…I believe I'll wait here."

"Suit yourself. I got a pot of coffee on, should you want any." Jim disappeared into a room under the stairs, presumably to get the coffee.

She walked to the table with Caleb's Stetson and sat down to wait. Looking around the large room a second time, she noticed things she hadn't before—the high luster on the wood of the bar and the fancy brass knobs and hardware on each of the cupboards. Row after row of cut glassware sparkled on the long shelf. With the early-morning sunlight on them, rainbows of color danced throughout the room. She hadn't expected such refinement. It reminded her more of the Nob Hill Gentleman's Club that Grandfather frequented rather than what she thought a simple saloon would look like.

Mr. Avery returned with a cup of coffee at the same time she picked up Caleb's hat and turned it over. A dark splotch of color on the inner brim drew her attention. She pressed her finger against it. Damp. Foreboding filled her as she drew her hand away and stared at the stain left on her skin. It looked like blood—fairly fresh blood. "On second thought, Mr. Avery, I think I will take the coffee up to Caleb after all."

"Sure thing. But he don't take to being spoiled like that. Ain't used to havin' anyone fuss over him. Course, he might treat you different than he does me. He's like a bristly boar to me most the time, especially in the morning."

She took the cup with saucer and started up the stairs. It could be nothing, she told herself. She could be jumping to conclusions. Her hand shook slightly, and the china cup rattled. The Stingaree district—hadn't he mentioned that it was quite rough? He hadn't wanted her with him because of it.

The closer she came to his door, the more she had second thoughts about charging into his room. It seemed too…personal. What would she find? Would he take offense at her intrusion? With her hand on the smooth oak banister, she hesitated. "Mr. Avery? It seems a bit forward of me to barge in on him. Perhaps it would be best if I wait here while you awakened him."

"Guess I could do that." He mounted the stairs, inched past her, and ambled down the hall to the last door. He knocked, and then leaned in toward the door to listen. "Caleb! You in there? You got company awaitin' on you."

A grumble came from inside the room. She strained to hear, but couldn't make out the words.

"Well, it's your high-falutin' friend, and I don't

think she'll take kindly to that as an answer." Jim shot a sheepish look her way. "No offense meant, miss."

A moment later the door swung open. Jim's body blocked most of her view, but she heard Caleb's low rumbling voice. Unable to make out his words, she climbed two more steps until she saw him plainly.

A large purple bruise spread over his right cheek, and his eye had swollen shut. Dried blood stained his chin. His dark hair stood on end, tousled and messy. She gasped and dropped the cup.

At the sound of breaking china, he glanced her way and frowned—at least she thought he frowned—his face was such a mess, she wasn't sure. He shook his head at Mr. Avery and then drew back into his room, firmly shutting the door.

What in heaven's name had happened to him? "Caleb!" She raced up the stairs. "No! Don't shut me out!"

Mr. Avery turned to block her path, his back to the door like a deputy guarding his prisoner. "He ain't taking visitors just now, miss."

She would not be put off. "He'll see me."

"You got to understand…he wants to clean hisself up a bit afore he sees anyone."

She fisted her hands and shoved them on her hips. She understood plenty. Caleb had been fighting and was probably sleeping off a head full of sour mash. She didn't have the time for such foolishness, but even as angry as it made her, she had to know that he was all right!

Staring down the determined look on her guard's face, she said, "The only thing that would keep me from entering that room right now is if there is another woman in there with him. Barring that, I'm going in, so you may as well move aside."

"Miss—now, don't get yerself all het up. He's all right. He just needs a minute to wake up. I'm sure if you wait—"

"Step aside, Mr. Avery. Or…or…"

Suddenly, Jim's eyes crinkled at the corners. "Or what, young lady?"

"Or…" He was rather large for her to shove aside, but she was determined.

"Let the lady by, Jim."

A trace of disappointment flashed in Jim's eyes. "Well. All right," he grumbled. "I'll back off. Guess I'll let Caleb fight his own battles—not that, by the look of him, he wins." He stepped aside.

She pushed open the door and stopped.

Caleb sat on the edge of his bed, elbows on his thighs, holding on to his head as though it might fall off if he moved. The same clothes he'd worn yesterday—the tan canvas pants and muslin shirt—were now wrinkled and unkempt on him. The covers lay helter-skelter on the mattress behind him.

She stepped over his gun and leather holster curled carefully on the floor between them. "You've been drinking! How could you! How could you?"

"I'm not drunk," he said quietly.

She took stock of the small room—a dresser, a bed, a washstand and a chair. Plain. Functional. Two books sat neatly stacked on the dresser, the spines carrying titles about business and finance. She sniffed. No odor of liquor. And there wasn't a bottle in sight. She looked again at the neatly coiled gun belt. It lay just so—with the gun angled and ready for quick defense. Maybe she had jumped to conclusions.

She squatted to eye level, concerned more about his injuries than anything else. "Let me have a look."

He didn't move. "It looks worse than it feels."

"Somehow I doubt that." She took him by the wrists and gently pulled his hands down. At the same time he raised his face, giving her a good look at his swollen eye, the purple bruise and the shredded skin of his scraped cheek. A trail of blood had clotted on his upper lip to form a scab. Her chest ached at the sight of him. She looked away to collect herself.

"Oh, Caleb." She took in a shuddering breath.

"I'm okay. I mend quick."

"I hate to think what that says about your lifestyle."

A tight smile emerged for a second, looking more like a grimace. "Means I don't turn my back and I don't give up."

"As long as you take care to pick your battles. I don't recall that discernment was your strong suit when you were younger."

"Thanks for the vote of confidence. Now head downstairs and wait for me there."

She ignored him, instead calling over her shoulder. "Mr. Avery? Would you be so kind as to bring a glass of water for Mr. Houston? And if you have it, ice."

Caleb scowled. "I'll be all right. Give me a minute to wake up. Scoot on out of here."

Instead of minding his orders, she examined his hands, noting the location of the scrapes. "This didn't happen in a barroom brawl. It couldn't have. You have dirt embedded in your scrapes." She hoped he'd prove her wrong—that this had been due to his job and not because of her. Please, she prayed silently, not because of her.

"Maybe the floor was filthy."

She turned over his hands. How foolish did he think she was? "Your knuckles are not scraped or bruised at all—only the palms. You didn't throw a punch."

She waited, but he didn't offer any further explanation.

She stood up. "Oh, Caleb. I never should have involved you in this. I'm so sorry. I feel awful!"

"*You* feel awful?" He started to shake his head and then stopped, wincing. "Like I told you—the Stingaree isn't safe. I was alone—an easy target. It could have been random."

"I wish I could believe that, but I don't."

He sighed. "Didn't think you would. And I guess I agree. This was a warning—a bit more persuasive than the Swede."

"I should have never let you go by yourself."

His one undamaged brow quirked up. "And what could you have done about it?"

"I don't know." She walked the length of the small room. "Something."

"Thought you didn't care. That this is a business arrangement."

She glared at him.

"Please, Hannah. Stop pacing. You're making me dizzy. Just…just sit down somewhere."

She stopped abruptly. She hadn't meant to make him feel worse than he already did. Glancing about the room, she saw only the one straight-backed chair. She scooted it close to his bed and sat down.

"I knew what I was doing," he said, serious now. "But there were just too many of them."

"More than one? Oh, Caleb. How many?"

"Two men."

"Did they want money? Or you?" She was almost afraid to ask—worried about the answer.

"Both."

"Before the…fight…were you able to find out anything?"

He grunted. "Enough to know the loss of the ships are not due to a storm at sea."

"I think we've established that. One ship might have been an accident, but not two. And now… this attack on you…" It struck her then that she cared less about the ships, about the cargo, than she did about the fact that he'd been hurt.

"Did anyone see you walk over here?"

His abrupt change of subject confused her. "What do you mean?"

"I think it's past time we got a lot more careful. And it's past time we let the sheriff in on this. Way past."

Just then Mr. Avery entered with a glass of water and a bucket. "No ice, miss. But I brought some warm water and a cloth." He set the glass on the bedside table and the bucket on the floor at Caleb's feet.

"Thank you," Hannah said. She leaned around Caleb and plumped the pillow against the wall. "Now, sit back."

He didn't make a move.

"What is it?" she asked, straightening. When he didn't answer directly, she chalked it up to his bleary state of mind and turned to wring out the washcloth in the warm water.

His gaze flicked to Mr. Avery, who stood in

the doorway. A comical grin split the man's face. Caleb looked back at her. "What are you doing?"

She thought it was obvious, although for some reason her hands wouldn't stop shaking. "I'm trying to make you comfortable and clean you up."

"I'm a big boy, Hannah. I'll be fine."

She pursed her lips. "I know what I am doing. I've taken care of Grandfather before."

Mr. Avery cleared his throat. "I'll just leave you in good hands."

"Jim, don't you leave," Caleb said, a warning in his voice.

"Oh, no. I think your lady friend has things well in hand."

The amused lilt in the man's voice irked her. "Mr. Avery, would you see to some breakfast for Mr. Houston?"

"I'm not hungry," Caleb grumbled.

She ignored him, turning to Mr. Avery to make her point. "Perhaps some porridge?"

His grin broadened under that generous mustache. "Yes'm."

"And please leave the door wide-open." She almost added, "for propriety's sake," but thought the reasoning was obvious.

She waited for Caleb to adjust himself. A bit of a staring match ensued—a battle of wills. She would have been amused had she not found the entire situation worrisome. Finally, with a grunt, he swung his legs, one at a time, up onto the mattress and relaxed back against the pillow. He kept his arms crossed over his chest. "I can take care of myself."

"I know," she said, softening her tone. Carefully she dabbed at the blood on his face. "It's just…I need to do this. I can't help but think you took this beating because of me. I'm so sorry. I had no idea what we were up against."

"Quit apologizing. It's not your fault. I knew what I was doing." He followed her every move with a wary expression.

"We must inform the sheriff. It cannot wait a moment longer."

"Glad you agree, 'cause I already spoke to him."

She stopped her ministrations and stared at him. "You went without me? When?"

"Last night when I dragged the fellow who did this to me to the jail."

Her mouth dropped open. "I thought you said there was more than one?"

"The other got away. Soon as I'm cleaned up, we'll pay a visit to Sheriff Cramer. Maybe he's learned something from his overnight guest."

She rinsed the dirt and blood from the cloth in the warm water. At least he was including her. She dabbed at some crusted blood on the corner of his mouth. His upper lip, though slightly swollen, still curved in a way that made her heart flutter. A queer sensation spread through her, curling and uncurling.

The touch of his gaze on her face never wavered. She felt it on her skin, but couldn't make herself meet it, too afraid he'd see her thoughts pooled in her eyes. Thoughts that were growing too large to contain. Thoughts that shouldn't be there, and definitely shouldn't show.

He took her hand, drew it away from his face. "I think I'm clean enough."

Where his fingers touched hers, her skin tingled. She pulled out of his gentle grasp and plunged the cloth into the bucket, hoping the water on her hands would somehow cool the warmth of her cheeks. Why did he have such an effect on her, even now after all this time?

She cleared her throat. "You never did tell me how you ended up in Alaska in the first place."

He didn't answer immediately, and the silence stretched between them, a silence that was heavy with unspoken thoughts. She looked up to find him studying her quietly.

"When you came to my birthday party," she said, hurrying to fill the awkwardness. "When I was sixteen. You said you'd been in Alaska."

"I remember."

"Well?"

"You haven't told me about your voice."

"But I did! The hypnotist. Remember?"

"Yeah, I remember all that. But I want to know how it happened. How it came back. How it felt."

"All that?" she said with a weak smile. Her attempt at humor fell flat.

"Actually more. I'm curious who the very first person you spoke to reacted."

"Why?"

"Because it should have been me."

She couldn't answer, couldn't speak for the truth of his words. And beneath those words she heard more—she heard his hurt. "Caleb, I—"

"Remember Sam?" he interrupted. "Sam and I became friends after I pulled him from the ocean."

"I remember you saving a boy's life. That's all." She didn't know why he'd changed the subject so quickly either, but she was glad of it. He was getting too close, tugging on strings that held her life together. If he tugged too hard, the entire thing might unravel.

"There was a girl he was sweet on just south of the border. He wanted to see her, but he was nervous about the reception he'd receive from her family, so I went with him. After the dance, he walked her home. With Sam there was no tellin' how long he'd be, so I joined a poker game in the cantina to pass the time. That's all I remember until I woke up, a day later, ten miles out to sea and on my way to Alaska. I've been more careful ever since."

"Until last night."

"I wouldn't say that. I was careful last night. There was a lot for one man to handle."

She took a deep breath. "This is why you did not want me asking questions on my own."

"Yes. Now it's your turn."

It took her a moment to realize he expected her to tell him about her voice—what had really happened. She swallowed, not knowing where to start, how much she should say—if she should tell him at all. His steady gaze mesmerized her. She'd always liked his eyes—light played off them in varying green shards of color, reminding her of the colors of the ever-changing sea.

As swift as lightning, he grabbed her wrist—this time with a determination that took complete control. "Hannah. Stop."

Jarred out of her reverie, she stammered. "I'm sorry. I didn't realize…"

"What? Didn't realize what? That you were staring at me the way a woman does who wants—" He stopped abruptly and shook his head. "This is craziness. Get out of here. I'll finish on my own."

What had he seen? Too much, the answer teased. "But, Caleb…I feel…responsible. There must be something I can do."

"You can leave," he said.

"But…"

"What are you playing at, Hannah?" He pushed

away, leaning back on the pillows. His chin jutted out. "You're the one who set limits. I'm just upholding them."

She pulled in a shaky breath. "You're right. I'm…I'm sorry." She was letting her emotions get the better of her. Always, always, they waited to make a fool of her.

"Look. I promised to help you and I will, but I won't put up with this…" His words trailed off. "Wait downstairs for me—or better yet—back at your hotel. We'll talk there."

"I—I am only trying to help. I want to be friends again, and friends look out for each other."

"Call it what you want, but what I feel for you is not entirely friendship," he said, his voice harsh. "I'm not sure what it is at this point."

She struggled to regain her composure and then stood. "Every time we are together…it's… it's not like it used to be. What has happened to us, Caleb?"

Fleeting pain washed over his face before he covered it. "You grew up. We both did. And we can't go back."

Her chest tightened with an ache so profound she thought she might stop breathing. "I…want to go back," she whispered. She could hardly believe she was admitting it after all this time. "I miss what we had. I miss the easiness we shared."

He pressed his lips together before answering, "It can't ever be like that again."

His words struck misery to her core. "Then, I ruined everything, didn't I? You'll never forgive me."

"What are you talking about?"

She couldn't tell him, couldn't ask. A Lansing didn't do that—didn't show weakness that way. A Lansing—

"Guess it doesn't matter now," Caleb said, interrupting her thoughts. "I don't want it to be like it used to."

He wasn't making any sense. "Then, what do you want?" she demanded, frustrated. She couldn't turn back the clock any more than he could.

"I want more."

She stared at him, the cloth wadded and forgotten in her hand. "More?"

"And there's the crux of it," he continued, his jaw tightening. "Because you don't see me like that. You can't see me like that."

She didn't know what to say, how to answer him. Did she even know her own mind anymore? San Francisco, Grandfather... All seemed so far away and part of a different life.

He took the cloth from her. "Go back to the hotel, Hannah. Wait for me there."

"Yes," she said softly, stunned by his admission. "Perhaps that would be best. I'll...I'll be at my hotel."

Leaving the room, she closed the door behind

her and turned to head down the hall. Mr. Avery blocked her passage.

"I don't do this for just anyone," Mr. Avery said, a chuckle in his voice. He was carrying a tray with the porridge.

It felt like aeons ago that she'd made that request. She had to leave, had to get outside where she could breathe, where she could think.

He caught the look on her face and stopped smiling. She couldn't explain—didn't know how to explain—so she simply squeezed by him and descended the stairs.

Chapter Ten

"Mind telling me why that pretty young gal is near tears?" Jim said, barging into the room.

Caleb snorted. "A Lansing near tears? It never happens. Don't let her fool you."

"Didn't look like she was trying to fool anybody. You must have been pretty rough on her."

It had to be the hit he'd taken on his head last night. Hannah had said she was nursing him, just like she had done with Dorian. *He* was the one imagining things that just weren't there—like the tenderness in her touch and the sheen of tears in her eyes. She thought of him like a friend. That was all. Nothing more. Guess it was a step up from being a hired hand, but not nearly enough, in his estimation. "I asked her to leave. Politely, I thought."

Jim set the tray at the end of the bed. "You were getting along real good when I left. What happened?"

"None of your business."

Jim's face hardened. "Fair enough. All she was trying to do was help."

"I don't want her kind of help," he muttered. "It sucks you in like a dust devil and then flings you out ripped to shreds. I don't need the aggravation."

Jim studied him with way too much interest.

"Now what?" Caleb demanded. He hadn't meant to upset her. He just couldn't stand having her close. Her touch, so gentle, made all his senses collide inside. Every part of him wanted to forget that she was a Lansing, pull her against him and kiss her senseless. But the minute he did, the minute he gave in to his wants, his needs, she'd reject him, and push him away like yesterday's breakfast. In the end, he wasn't up to her standards. He didn't fit in her life, and he didn't need the painful reminder.

"I'm beginning to understand," Jim said.

"There's nothing to figure out."

Jim shook his head. "You both can't see what's plain in front of you."

"You're out of your mind."

"Oh, I got a good mind. And I'm a'usin' it right now." Jim studied him a moment more and then motioned to the tray. "Don't expect me to repeat this type of thing. I was doing it more for her than for you anyway—'cuz she asked so nice."

Caleb stared at Jim's departing back, then rose

and swung the door shut. He glanced at the porridge. Jim had even put cream and butter on it—
something he never did even for himself. Made
Caleb feel like a heel for his sharp retort.

Best clean up and go try to smooth the waters
with Hannah. He grabbed a bar of soap from the
dresser and started washing up in earnest. Without a mirror to check his face, he ran his palm
over his raw jaw and cheek. By the feel of it,
the skin over his right cheekbone was swollen
to twice the normal size. Guess a shave was out
of the question. He combed back his hair, finding the raised lump where he'd been hit—most
likely with the butt of a gun. It had gone down
some since last night. He tucked in a clean shirt
and then pulled on his boots. The last thing he
added was his holster and Colt .45.

With the cobwebs clearing from his head, he
strode across the street to the hotel. It was obvious someone didn't want him snooping around,
and if they found out it was Hannah wanting the
information, she'd be in danger, too—and an easier target. He couldn't implicate her in any way.
Unfortunately, enough people already knew she
was in town.

Hannah liked to control things—he'd figured
that much out about her. The fact that he did some
things his way didn't fit into her perfectly ordered
plans. But like it or not, the roughing up he'd just
received was a warning, and her plans were due

for an abrupt change. Even if it made her as mad as a queen bee over its territory, he wouldn't be changing his mind.

He arrived in the Horton's lobby as she slowly descended the wide staircase to the landing. She was wearing a deep green skirt and cream-colored blouse and a vest that fit snug at her small waist, something he couldn't help but admire. *Look, but don't touch,* he told himself. She stopped on the landing and didn't come any farther. That was when he noticed her expression—pale, drawn, with wide, frightened eyes.

He hadn't done that—no matter what Jim said. Something was wrong. He took a step toward her. Then another.

She opened her mouth, but no words came out. She looked fragile…shaken.

Alarmed, he dashed up the half-flight of stairs. "What is it?"

My…my room. She mouthed the words.

He looked up the stairway to an open doorway. "Wait here."

Bounding up the stairs two at a time, he stepped inside her room and stopped. Cushions lay strewn across the floor from the settee. Beside them, a chair was turned on its side. Clothing lay scattered on the tabletop, wrinkled and apparently pawed through. A familiar flowery scent filled the room—its source an upside-down bottle of perfume, the liquid spilling over the edge of the table and soaking into the swirled design in the carpet.

"Son of a…" Caleb clamped down on his oath.

Hannah appeared at his side. "The door… The lock…was broken."

She started to move farther into the room, but he threw out his arm, stopping her. "Let me make sure no one's inside." He drew his gun and strode into the adjoining bedroom. A quick survey assured him no one was lurking behind the door, in her wardrobe or under the bed. He checked the window. Grit on the outer sill had been disturbed. He returned to Hannah. "Whoever did this is gone."

She looked so vulnerable, so scared, with her gray eyes wide and shocked. She crossed her arms over her midsection, hugging herself as if she'd break into a million pieces if she didn't hold herself together. Then she began to shake.

He closed the space between them in four strides and enveloped her in his arms. "I guess we can safely say that someone does not want us combing through old records or asking questions. And they know we are working together."

"Who would do such a horrid thing?" The words trembled out of her. She clung to his vest with both hands, burrowing her face into his shirt.

In response, he held tighter. "It'll be all right, Hannah." He hated to see her so shaken up, so fragile.

After a while, she pulled back and looked into his face. "I don't have anything worth taking here. No money. No valuables. What were they looking for?"

"Could be this is a warning. Or something to scare you so that you won't dig any deeper. We can stop here, Hannah. You don't have to continue." Her small frame went rigid beneath his hands. Okay. So quitting still wasn't an option in her mind.

"I can't stop. I can't run back to Grandfather like a coward. There's too much at stake."

"Nothing is worth you getting hurt. Even Dorian would agree to that. You have the other ship. You'll be able to build your business back eventually. It's not the end of the world."

"No. I can't let this stop me."

Usually he admired her determination—but not about this. "Let the sheriff handle it, Hannah. And although I hate to contact Dorian again, he needs to know, too."

She nodded slowly in agreement.

He stepped to the door and tugged on the bell-pull. Within minutes, Jackson arrived, followed immediately by Mr. Bennett.

The desk clerk's eyes narrowed at the sight of the room. "What has happened here?"

The subtle accusation in the man's voice had Caleb stepping between the man and Hannah. "Miss Lansing has been away all morning, and she returned to find her room turned upside down."

Mr. Bennett focused on Caleb for the first time, eyeing his swollen bruised face. He pursed his lips. "We run a respectable hotel, Mr. Houston. I don't know what you and Miss Lansing are up to, but obviously it has spilled over into this hotel."

Hannah frowned. "Exactly what do you mean by that? Are you implying that somehow this is my fault?"

She wasn't going to change anyone's mind here, Caleb realized, but at least she didn't look frail like she had when they'd first walked into the room. As a matter of fact, she appeared to be gathering momentum the way a wave swells before it crests and breaks.

She glared at Mr. Bennett. "I'd like to know if any other room is in similar disarray or if it is just mine. Or if anyone noticed a noise or unusual activity. Would you mind checking?"

He hesitated a split second before turning to do her bidding. They followed him. The rest of the doors remained locked, or the occupants were inside and hadn't noticed a disturbance. "Seems your suite is the only one disturbed, Miss Lansing." His tone dripped with accusation.

Hannah's brow furrowed. "If you would call for the sheriff, I wish to log a complaint."

The desk clerk's attitude shifted immediately,

his face blanching. "That won't be necessary, miss. We can handle this quietly."

"I need to report this."

"This is why you didn't stay at the Hotel Del! You're here to ruin this establishment and me along with it."

Hannah's jaw dropped open. "I did no such thing! I wouldn't! I'm as upset as you are...even more so! It is *my* things that have been scattered about, *my* things that have been pawed through."

Caleb had had enough. Hannah shouldn't need to defend herself. "You heard the lady," he cut in.

"Horton will fire me over this. I don't want trouble."

"Afraid you've already got it." Caleb turned to Jackson. "Get the sheriff. Now. Or I will."

Jackson looked once at Bennett, who finally nodded his consent. "Please, not a word to the newspapers," Bennett said. "You do understand the delicacy here. Bad publicity will ruin this hotel. Times are hard enough, and I've got a family to feed."

Caleb was of a mind to tell the entire city, but that wouldn't help Hannah's situation. He hadn't cared for the desk clerk's attitude the entire time, and his sniveling only served to confirm what he thought of him.

"Yes. Of course I understand," Hannah said, placing a hand on Caleb's forearm. Had she read his thoughts about the man that easily?

"I won't be informing anyone other than the sheriff," she continued. "In return I trust you will have a care with your words should my name come up in conversation. And certainly neither one of us is anxious to bandy this to the newspaper." She walked over to the table and righted a straight-backed chair, then sat down to wait for Jackson's return, relieving Mr. Bennett of further attention.

Sheriff Cramer gave a long, low whistle as he surveyed the room, stepped over the cushions on the floor and strode into the bedroom. There he gave another long, low whistle and checked the sliding and locking capability of the window. Coming back to the parlor area, he studied Caleb's face before speaking. "You're lookin' a sight worse today. Must be plenty stiff."

"I'll live," Caleb said, choosing to ignore Bennett's gaze of surprise that the sheriff was already involved.

"Your friend didn't have any company during the night."

"Has he said anything?"

"Not as yet." He whipped out a small pad of paper from his vest pocket. "Now tell me about this. Anything gone missing?"

Hannah answered him. "Not that I can see."

"Any idea what they were after, Miss Lansing?"

She shook her head.

"Could have been a simple robbery, but I'd have to rule that out based on the information about the ships." He wrote something more on his paper, and then shoved the pad away. "Looks like they were out to find something or scare you."

"They succeeded." A tiny tremor shook her voice. "I don't suppose there is another room available that I might move to?"

"I'm sorry, miss," Mr. Bennett said. "The others are either taken or too far from the desk for an unaccompanied woman."

After the sheriff and desk clerk left to check the perimeter of the hotel together, the mantel clock chimed one o'clock, and then the suite was silent. Hannah walked into the bedroom. Caleb followed. She stooped and picked up her dark red jacket—the one he'd seen her wearing that first night. A tear slid down her cheek and plopped on the garment, turning the material nearly black. For a moment, she seemed at a loss as to what to do with the thing. Finally, she tossed it aside on the four-poster.

"You all right?" The words seemed inadequate, but they were the only things he could think of.

She didn't answer. Instead she picked up a cotton nightgown and folded it, then cuddled it close in her arms. "Somehow, knowing a stranger went through my things…has touched them…" She expelled a shaky sigh. "I want to burn them all."

He had a hard time understanding her. As long

as her things were all here and hadn't been torn or ruined, what did it really matter? And why, if she wanted to burn it, did she cradle the darn thing in her arms? But something told him just to let her talk. Let her get it off her chest.

More and more slowly, she put away clothing and righted the lamp, moving as if the weight of the ocean was crashing down on her shoulders.

Caleb watched silently. She wasn't safe here. Not anymore. He should put her on the first train to San Francisco. But he couldn't be sure if someone would follow her onto the train. For now, he didn't want to let her out of his sight. Stuart would be arriving soon enough to take over. He'd wait for that.

"We're getting out of here."

She looked up. Startled. "What do you propose we do?"

He hadn't a clue at the moment. "We'll take a ride."

"But your injuries…"

"I'll be sore whether we go or stay, and I don't want you hanging around here. You'll only be miserable, which is what whoever did this wants you to be. We won't give him that satisfaction." He grabbed a dark blue shawl from the floor and draped it over her shoulders.

"Where are we going?"

"First off, to the livery to rent a buggy."

The scared expression on her face shifted a little, though her eyes still looked haunted. Something constricted in his chest. He started to walk over to her, but then stopped himself. She'd felt too good in his arms before. If he held her once more, he was in serious danger of losing his common sense. This feeling—as strong as it was becoming—wasn't something he was going to act on. He'd promised to help her, and he'd do that, but she'd be going back to San Francisco and her rich life—and he'd stay here. His future was here, and she had no part in it.

Maybe if he told himself that often enough, he'd start to believe it.

But whatever was going on inside him, he couldn't let her be alone. Not after this. And he wasn't going to give her a choice.

He smoothed his palm over the butt of his gun handle, noting the way her gaze followed his movement.

Worry clouded her eyes. "And you are sure you want to travel? With your injuries?"

His head pounded and his shoulder ached, but he could still move. "I'm not six feet under. I'll manage. Look, if you don't want to go, just say so. I think it would do us both good to get out of town. Maybe it would give us a new perspective on things."

She pulled into herself even more, avoiding his eyes. "All right. It's only for today. Stuart will be here tomorrow. He'll have me on his ship and heading home before another day passes. You won't have to babysit me much longer."

Where had all that come from? He stared at her. "That's not how it is with me."

"I'm not a fool. I know you weren't happy to see me. You've thought this entire time that I had no business pursuing answers." She surveyed the room once more.

He didn't like that the fire had dimmed in her eyes, but her safety was of utmost importance, so in one aspect, she was correct.

"I didn't expect it to come to this," she said softly.

"There's foul play going on. Just what did you expect?"

"I don't know—just not this."

He waited, but when she didn't explain, he slipped on his Stetson. "Let's go, then. We can sort things out on the way." He didn't offer his arm, didn't touch her in any way. She seemed fragile at the moment—brittle—as if she might shatter should he touch her.

She was silent on the way to the livery. Within fifteen minutes they'd passed the last house of the community and put the dust of the town behind them.

Chapter Eleven

Caleb flicked the reins, urging the horse into a quick trot. He wanted to get Hannah out of town before anything else happened to her. He wanted her out where he could see someone coming from a mile away. At least he could protect her then. He sat to her right side. That way his body shielded her and anyone who might try to hide in the hills and canyons they passed. To her left the open harbor provided safety. A steamer chugged past, heading toward the long public pier.

By the time they reached Old Town, his stomach was growling. He stopped at the local cantina and bought some warm buttered tortillas, keeping three for himself and handing two to Hannah. She ate them in silence as they rode past the schoolhouse and the children playing in the treeless yard. It was only after they crossed the mudflats, forded the shallow point in the river and started down the dirt road to the end of the peninsula that he finally started to relax.

Beside him, Hannah sat like a stone statue. Even over the bumpiest of ruts she kept her hands clasped tightly in her lap, as if she might fracture into sharp pieces if she relaxed. He felt her tension most in the quiet after the creak of the buggy's hinges and again after the keening cries of the gulls overhead.

"There's talk of channeling the river here," he said, hoping to ease her into conversation. "The road washes out every spring during the rainy season."

"Mmm." The answer, noncommittal, enveloped them in silence for another two miles. He tried again.

"How long has it been since you came this way?"

"Ten years and three months."

He darted a glance at her, surprised that she'd counted the months.

She wrapped her arms around herself again. "We don't have time for this, Caleb."

"Well, I'm not taking you back to town. Not until I sort through a few things. It's safer out here."

She huffed. "No place is safe." Pressing her lips together, she turned her gaze back to the road.

It was another mile before she spoke. "Caleb... this can't be all right with your boss."

"Wyatt will get over it. I'll be back in time to work the late half of my shift. Besides, I need to be there. Last night I left word that I was willing to pay for information."

"What if you're hurt again?"

"Jim will watch my back. And we don't know for sure that my roughing up had anything to do with me asking questions. Might have been someone going for my money."

She frowned. "You don't believe that any more than I do."

"If it was money they were after, they were sorely disappointed. At most, I had five dollars on me."

She reached up, stretching her fingers toward his swollen cheek. His skin tingled there, anticipating her cool touch. Heck, his entire body tingled just being near her. He was reacting, and she hadn't even touched him. He clamped his jaw together and kept his gaze straight ahead, remembering what he'd said back in his room about wanting more from her than friendship. He hadn't realized it was a full-blown thought until he'd growled it out, startling them both.

Just short of brushing his cheek, she closed her hand into a fist and then lowered it into her lap. "It wasn't random."

He let that pass, still dealing with the sensations pulsing through him, and the awareness of her next to him. Keeping an eye on her until Stuart arrived might just be the hardest thing he would ever do.

"Caleb, I can't have your injuries on my conscience."

"Then, don't put them there. I knew what I was doing when I agreed to help. I knew there might be more to the situation. Besides, better that I'm the one who is roughed up. Not you."

Her eyes flashed with anger—and something more. "I don't think of you like that. Like…like you are expendable."

"Well, you'd be the first of your kind not to."

"Of my kind," she repeated. "What do you mean?"

He blew out a long breath. "I've seen the newspaper articles. You're heiress to the Lansing fortune, the princess of Nob Hill." And he had to keep his distance.

Storm clouds gathered on her face. "Don't talk that way. Not you."

"How I talk doesn't change what is."

"Caleb, please understand. People depend on me. Besides my family there are hundreds of others that depend on Lansing Enterprises for their livelihood. Men with families to support like Stuart and Rachel. That's why this is important. That's why I won't give up—*can't* give up—until we find out the truth. For them."

He had considered the effect the lost ships would have, but it surprised him to hear her give voice to his thoughts. He'd assumed she was stubbornly charging ahead for Dorian and herself. Guess it was more than that. She understood more than he'd first realized. She had compassion for the far-flung implications. Realizing that made it even harder to think of her as he first had—as selfish. Now he could only admire the spirit that drove her. "Well, perhaps for once we agree," he murmured.

They rode in silence until the first wooden structures of La Playa came into view.

Hannah shifted on the leather seat as they passed a large warehouse that hadn't been there when she was young.

"Been some changes, as you can see," Caleb said.

Like me, she thought. *Like you.* Her memories of this place were special. Too special to muddy with who she was now—a Lansing. When she'd lived here she'd been Stuart's little girl—Hannah Taylor.

And she'd been happy. Stuart had seen to that. In keeping his promise to her mother to look out for her, he'd been the best father any girl could hope for. She'd felt loved and protected.

"Caleb? I…don't want to talk about Lansing

Enterprises or about the ships. Not now. Not while we are here."

His gaze held hers a moment, thoughtful. "If that's how you want things."

"I'm so tired of worrying about it all. Weary of trying to make the pieces fit into tidy answers."

"You don't need to explain," he said when she would have continued. "I figure today is for soaking up that warm ol' sun."

She nodded. "For both of us."

He met her gaze, his green eyes intent. "Something like that."

I want more.... The words he'd spoken that morning seared through her for the thousandth time. They had thrilled her and scared her all at the same time. Did it mean... Was it possible he would forgive her? Forgive her for the choice she'd made so long ago?

Would that ruin the promise she'd made to Grandfather? She'd already broken it by coming here, by seeing Caleb again. But surely Grandfather would understand. It didn't mean that she was forgetting who she was. She would still carry out Grandfather's wishes if necessary to save the business. She would still consider marrying Thomas.

The thought stopped her. Could she do it? Really? Oh, how she hoped it wouldn't be necessary. That was what hinged on finding the truth of the missing ships.

They drew up in front of the parsonage, and Caleb slowed the carriage. A fresh coat of white paint made the building look new. Climbing roses entwined along the white picket fence.

"Looks like there are new owners," Caleb said, drawing back on the reins.

As they looked over the yard, the door to the carriage house cracked open and a young girl in a bright yellow pinafore squeezed out, chasing after a squawking hen. The door swung wider, and behind the girl followed a tall, slim woman carrying a bucket filled with seed.

Hannah straightened in her seat. She recognized her! "Elizabeth!"

The woman stopped abruptly and set down her pail. Then she walked to the fence that separated them. With her hand over her brow, she shielded her eyes from the afternoon sunlight.

"It's Hannah…Taylor," Hannah said.

"Hannah?" Recognition lit Elizabeth's eyes. Her jaw dropped open. "You're talking!" she blurted out. "Rachel wrote to me that you could speak, but to hear you!"

Then, before Hannah could answer, Elizabeth's gaze lit on Caleb. "And Caleb! Oh, my! This is a surprise! How good to see you both."

She unlatched the gate and hurried through. "What brings you here? Can you stay awhile?" Suddenly she stopped short. "What happened to your face, Caleb? You're still working at that saloon, aren't you? Sam mentioned it the last time he came by."

Caleb didn't correct her false conclusion. A sly smile split his face. "Come see me sometime. I'll buy you a drink."

Elizabeth shook her head. "Not on your life, Caleb Houston. I have a reputation to uphold."

Hannah was moved by the unaffected warmth in Elizabeth's eyes. She'd always thought Elizabeth a nice person, but now she actually seemed lit up from inside—happy. "You bought the parsonage?"

Elizabeth dimpled, nodding. "My husband did, when I agreed to marry him. This is Molly, my daughter."

"Married?" Hannah studied the girl. The resemblance struck her then. Had Rachel ever told her? Had she been so caught up with her own life that she hadn't asked after Elizabeth? The thought bothered her.

"Oh, we really must catch up. I'll put on some tea."

Suddenly, Hannah wanted more than anything to do that. She glanced at Caleb. There was a slight hesitation before he answered, "I've got a few things to check at the mercantile. I'll collect you when I'm done." He offered his arm.

She held on and climbed from the buggy, aware how strong his bunched muscle felt beneath her hand. Her fingers tingled where she grasped him.

His green gaze held hers as she descended. It was as though he didn't want to let loose of her, didn't want her out of his sight.

She broke eye contact first, but the tingling sensation coursing through her did not diminish. It was just a cup of tea. Why, she'd be done in the blink of an eye. She turned toward Elizabeth and her daughter.

Forty minutes later Caleb stepped through the gate at the old parsonage and froze upon hearing a woman's full-bodied laugh. At first he thought it belonged to Elizabeth, but then he realized with sudden clarity that the sound came from an altogether different source.

He stood still, listening.

Hannah was laughing!

Emotions tightened his chest. A silent shy smile had been the only thing close that had crossed her face when she'd been a child. What would she look like? Her blue-gray eyes would probably be sparking, her cheeks a little flushed. He swallowed hard.

He refused to acknowledge the feelings that tried to climb out of the pit he'd buried them in. Didn't matter that'd he'd always wondered about that laugh. Here Elizabeth had coaxed it out of her within minutes of reacquainting herself. He set his jaw when he realized it was jealousy raising its ugly head inside.

"It's Caleb, isn't it?" A bear of a man approached, his hand outstretched. The flash of a pearl-handled gun peeked out under his plain black coat as he shook hands. "Tom Barrington. I just heard all about you from Miss Lansing," the man continued. "Guess this was once your house."

So this was Elizabeth's husband. Caleb relaxed and shook his hand. "My sister and I rented two rooms upstairs. That's all."

"According to Elizabeth, Reverend Crouse always spoke well of you and fondly of Hannah."

Caleb couldn't have been more surprised. "You have me confused with someone else. I gave him grief and then some, the couple years I lived here."

"No. If my wife said it, I'm sure it's fact. You nearly burned the town down at one point is what I heard." There was no condemnation in the man's look, only friendly interest. "You're welcome to come in. We've made some changes to the inside."

A trip down memory lane wasn't in his plans right now. "Maybe another time. Hannah and I are heading up to the lighthouse. As it is, it will take the rest of the day to get there and back before dark."

"Understood. I'll fetch Miss Lansing for you."

"Thank you. And give my best to your wife."

Hannah emerged through the front doorway,

pulling her blue shawl around her shoulders and then tucking a wayward strand of blond hair inside her bonnet. In the half hour that she'd been inside with Elizabeth, something had changed. She walked down the front path with a lighter spring to her feet and a sparkle in her eyes that he hadn't seen before.

He hadn't wanted to leave her there, hadn't wanted to miss a moment of being with her—especially with Stuart arriving tomorrow. But now he realized taking a moment with Elizabeth was something Hannah had needed.

Elizabeth waved from the doorway. "Now, Caleb—don't be a stranger! Come back and see us."

He tipped his hat to her. "Ma'am."

Hannah handed him a package wrapped in newspaper before climbing into the buggy. "Some sandwiches in case we get hungry."

"Elizabeth didn't need to do that," he said, frowning. He'd picked up apples at the mercantile, figuring that would hold them until they got back to town.

"I told her as much, but she wouldn't take no for an answer. Oh, Caleb, you should have come in. Elizabeth has decorated the place so pretty."

He walked around to his side of the buggy and climbed up, storing the package in a sack at his feet. "I always figured her for the town's old maid."

"I can't believe you said that!"

The truth was the truth. "Looks like marriage agrees with her," he allowed. He flicked the reins and the horse jerked into a slow trot. Then, his elbows on his thighs, he turned his attention to avoid the ruts in the road. Better that than on the woman sitting beside him—a woman he'd never gotten to laugh.

The wood-and-adobe buildings of La Playa disappeared behind them, and he turned the buggy toward the ridge road.

"Next to you, Rachel and Stuart, no one here remembers me—except Elizabeth."

"You didn't exactly get into town much when you were little."

"No. It's more than that. I...I don't know if I can explain it."

"We've got time."

She took a deep breath. "In San Francisco... the people I see are mostly Grandfather's business associates. The conversations revolve around negotiations and the state of the economy, even at the social gatherings."

He snorted. "Sounds like a great time."

"The men—and even their wives—have their own agendas. It is always something they want from Lansing Enterprises. Otherwise they wouldn't be there."

"Not exactly close friends, then."

"No," she said with a heartfelt sigh. "Not like tea with Elizabeth."

He glanced sideways at her. "You hardly know her."

"There is something comforting in knowing that someone else on this earth shares a piece of my life, shares my history. I suppose it would be that way if I had a brother or sister. You're lucky to have Rachel."

He mulled over her words as the buggy climbed up to the top of the peninsula's ridge. Rachel had been the one to keep him grounded and to hold him accountable after their father left. She'd been as much a mother to him as a sister. For a while he'd hated it and had given her all kinds of grief. It was Stuart who'd set him straight. Funny how all their lives had woven together from the moment they'd met.

The closer they got to the point and the farther from La Playa, the quieter Hannah became, but unlike before, this silence was easy, comfortable. A time or two, he caught her closing her eyes and raising her face to the afternoon sun. Caleb guided the buggy over the last rise in the dirt road, and the lighthouse came into view.

The limestone house, with the huge light springing from its roof, looked peaceful and serene against the cloud-studded sky. On the black iron catwalk surrounding the lamp, a flag of the stars and stripes flapped in the wind. A rush of memories enveloped Caleb. When his sister had first forced him here so that she could keep an eye on him while she'd tutored Hannah, he'd hated it. He'd thought life and excitement was the other way—toward San Diego—and not out here on this lonely stretch of land.

How wrong he'd been.

The memories he had were special. He'd changed here—become a man. He wondered how much Hannah remembered.

By the new cistern, a gray-haired woman hung clothes on a line near the shed. A wiry, white-haired man stepped from the house and walked over to touch her shoulder. They turned and watched as the buggy approached and came to a stop in front of them. Caleb climbed down, walked around to the boot and withdrew the sack of apples he'd purchased at the mercantile. He reserved two, one for Hannah and himself, and handed the sack to the light keeper, introducing himself at the same time.

"I worked here a few months before you took over and remember how I missed the taste of fresh fruit."

The man peered closer. "You must have been knee-high to a jackrabbit. What brings you out here today?"

"A picnic," Caleb answered. "We're taking the road to the beach. Just wanted to pay our respects."

"Well, it's a fine day for that. Fine day."

Caleb climbed back into the buggy. "You ready?" he asked, trying to gauge Hannah's mood.

She nodded silently.

He tipped his hat to the light keeper and guided the horse toward the beach road. The ribbon of dirt hugged the ocean side of the peninsula and ended just above the beach. He helped Hannah climb from the buggy, grabbed the sandwiches and started toward the water. At the three-foot drop-off to the beach, he stopped. Hannah would need help here. At a gasp and a scraping noise behind him he turned just in time to see her off balance and flying toward him. Dirt and pebbles sprayed out from beneath her slippers. It didn't look as if she had plans of stopping anytime soon. He caught her arm as she skidded by, steadying her until she regained her footing.

Her face flushed, and she brushed off her skirt as she said ruefully, "I suppose after that display, my dignity is irredeemable."

A smile tugged at the corner of his mouth. He jumped to the sand and turned to help her down.

But she wasn't looking at the drop. Her eyes were fixed on the waves crashing to shore fifty feet away. "How long before the tide comes in?"

"A while yet. Dusk." It took him a moment to realize she was thinking back to another time, a

time when the tide had trapped her in the cave.
"That was a long time ago."

"Sometimes...I have nightmares."

Her admission kicked him in the gut. Maybe
this trip had not been such a good idea after all.
He'd just wanted to get her away from town, away
from that room. "We'll be on our way before the
tide comes in. You can count on it."

He extended his hand, a subtle—or maybe not
so subtle—challenge.

She hesitated, meeting his gaze, holding it for
a moment. Then she grasped on to him, using
him for balance as she climbed down. She let
go immediately on reaching the sand. Stepping
forward, the pointed toe of her shoe caught on a
small tear in the hem of her skirt. "Drats," she
muttered as she examined it and then dropped
the fabric into place.

"Such salty language for a cultured lady," he
teased, enjoying the blush spreading on her face.
"Relax. No one here but me. The gulls sure don't
care how you talk."

"Still...I shouldn't..."

He shook his head. "Come on, Your Highness.
You can pick the spot."

She marched across the small expanse of white
sand and chose a knee-high flat boulder. Dropping the sack on the rock, he turned to survey
the narrow strip of rock-studded beach. A bank
of clouds rode low up and down the coast. Once

the sun headed farther west, the day would turn gray and cold. Blue-green water crashed against the large rock that jutted out into the surf—his once-upon-a-time fishing rock. He glanced sideways at Hannah, hoping her memories were not only of her time in the cave, but about the good times, too. "You were quiet back there with the light keeper."

"I wanted to see the house, see my old bedroom, but I knew everything would be different. I...I didn't want it to change. I wanted to keep it in my memory how it once was."

"They were good memories, then."

"The best."

"Then, let's relive them—if only for a few hours."

A smile began—first just the hint of it and then growing to fill her face. And he felt as if finally things were as they should be...as they should have been all along.

The rocks and crevices had changed little in fifteen years. In the pools, hermit crabs trundled sideways on their pointy feet, their shell homes swaying on their backs. Sea anemones and starfish perched colorfully on the water-smoothed rock walls. In one particularly large basin, a hand-size octopus darted gracefully away from them to hide in a crevice.

The sound of the waves and cry of the seagulls had always been a balm to him. It was one of the reasons he liked to fish. As they explored the pools, he was relieved to see the last ounce of tension drop from Hannah's shoulders and dissipate in the breeze. He stooped down and picked up something white, half-embedded in the sand. From his crouched position, sitting on one heel, he held it up to her. "For your treasure box."

She examined the sand dollar. "You remember that?"

He shrugged. He remembered a lot more than that.

"You told me once about the miniature doves inside."

"It takes breaking the outer shell to set them free."

She smoothed her hand over the sand dollar, her gaze pensive. "It's sad that something so precious can only come from destruction."

"I don't see it like that. It's more like letting go of the old to take hold of the new."

Her gaze clouded. "Are we still speaking of seashells?"

"You are."

She closed his fingers one at a time around the flat cream-colored shell. "Some things are too important to break. You keep it. My treasure box is full."

He set the creature back on the wet sand. "I doubt the bank will honor it."

When he stood, she was staring at him, the

thoughts reflected in her gray eyes as turbulent as the crashing waves behind her. He smoothed his knuckles over her cheek, surprised when she didn't jerk away. It gave him the courage to step closer and rub his thumb lightly over her lower lip. How would that softness feel pressed against his mouth? He wanted to find out. To kiss her there. All he needed was the slightest encouragement.

He was a fool to even consider it. She was leaving. Probably tomorrow.

She moved from his reach and headed back to the rock where they'd stored the sandwiches.

It was obvious she felt something for him. Desire surged between them like the constant pull of the tides. Yet it seemed the ocean that separated them was far wider than either of them could cross.

He strode back to the rock at a slower pace and plopped down on the sand, unwrapping one of Elizabeth's sandwiches and handing it to her.

She left it in her lap. "Caleb, we should talk."

He bit into his sandwich and concentrated on the wave that crashed to shore forty feet away. He had the feeling he wasn't going to like whatever it was she had to say.

"There is something I haven't told you. Something you should know."

He braced himself for her next words.

"When I return to San Francisco, I'm going to marry."

It was the last thing he'd expected her to say after all this time. "*What!* Who?"

"Thomas Rowlings. A business associate of Grandfather's. I've known him for years. He's honorable, well-read…"

Caleb had visions of a man Dorian's age. "How old?"

"Not ancient, if that is what you are implying. He's forty."

It was bound to happen eventually. Hannah was beautiful, cultured, rich… "You waited long enough to tell me. Was it because you were afraid if I knew I wouldn't help you?"

She frowned. "No."

"I don't believe you." A dark tone crept into his voice.

"This…place…this peninsula…has always been special to me. I didn't want my life in San Francisco tarnishing my time here. I wanted to keep them separate."

"So why tell me now?"

"I want you to understand, because…well… you've admitted you care for me. And I care for you—as a friend. It can't go any further. Thomas has a good head with business matters and knows the shipping industry inside and out. By joining his insurance company with Lansing Enterprises, they both will be protected."

He could barely listen to her, barely see past the anger growing inside. "So that's what this is? A business decision?"

"You talk as if it is a bad thing. People have been making such marriages all along."

Maybe he was the one who didn't live in the real world. Like a wave, he kept crashing against the rock that divided Hannah from him. Why couldn't he accept the inevitable? She would always be out of reach. Wasn't that what Dorian had said all those years ago? "What about that school you always wanted to start? Or have you given up on that?"

Her eyes clouded over. "I suppose that depends on what we find out about the ships."

"This Thomas… Will he help?"

"We haven't discussed it, but I'm sure he will once he understands how important it is to me."

That didn't sound convincing to him. More as though Thomas was placating her until he wed her. "What about children?"

Her mouth tightened into a straight line. "That isn't appropriate to discuss with you," she said firmly.

"Appropriate?" he said, rising to his feet. "Do you realize that you pull your big words and Nob Hill social rules around you like that cloak whenever I ask something that makes you uncomfortable? What has happened to you? What has Dorian molded you into?"

She jumped to her feet and faced him. "Things change. You said so yourself. We both grew up."

He brought his fist to his chest. "Underneath, where it counts, people stay the same. They don't change as much as you have."

Her chin trembled. "I can't be that girl anymore."

"Why not? What was so wrong with her? She was wild and stubborn and frustrating—but she was you."

Hannah curled her fingers into tight fists. "She was weak!"

Tears gathered in her eyes—tears she tried to hold back. He was getting closer to the truth. He lifted her chin with his fingers. "What happened after I left, Hannah? What did Dorian say to you?"

She swiped her eyes. "I don't know what you are talking about."

He untied the bandanna from his neck and handed it to her. "After we kissed."

"That was a long time ago, Caleb." She turned away, toward the ocean.

He took hold of her shoulder, swinging her around to face him. "Something happened, and I want to know what."

"Why? Why must you dig and prod so? Just let it go."

"It matters. And I think it has everything to do

with now, with us. It's why you suddenly showed up in town."

She jerked out from under his hand and walked a few steps away. "I made a bargain—a deal."

Her shoulders seemed smaller somehow. Frail. "What kind of a bargain?"

"A promise. My voice in exchange for you."

That stopped him.

"What… Nothing to say to that? You see, I can be as coldhearted and selfish as Grandfather. I'm even good at it." She spit out the indictment of herself.

He pulled back, staring at her. This callous, cold woman was a stranger to him. "What did Dorian demand?"

She blew out a long breath and raked her fingers through the loose hair at her temple. "If he allowed me to see the hypnotist, his requirement was that I never contact you again. Ever. And I agreed."

"Until now." His thoughts whirled with the implications of all she'd said. "What was he so afraid of?"

"You, Caleb. He was afraid of you." Her eyes held a hint of vulnerability. "He knew how I felt about you."

The breath rushed out of him. How she felt about him? "But you were only sixteen. We were friends. Just friends."

"He saw more. He saw what could happen.

Kathryn Albright 213

And...I felt it, too." She closed her eyes, spoke with them shut. "I still feel it."

His head might explode with all that she'd said—with the possibilities that Dorian had ripped from them both with his ultimatum. Yet she'd made the decision herself. The realization tasted of vinegar to him. "That clears up a few questions I've had."

Anger over that day had simmered inside him for five long years. The frustration he'd felt at not knowing why she'd suddenly turned her back on him had crystallized into a hate for anything Lansing. "I thought I'd done something..."

She shook her head. "Oh, no. Never. I never wanted you to feel that way! It was all my doing. Mine alone."

But it wasn't just *her* doing. Dorian had had more than a hand in it.

Hannah glanced away, fidgeting with her hands. It took her a long while before she spoke again, her eyes focused on the waves. "Knowing the truth now...can you... Do you think you can ever find it in yourself to forgive me?"

Could he be that big of a man? Because of that day, the course of his life had changed drastically. He'd thought to settle there near family. But Dorian's goons had escorted him to the wharf and onto one of his ships. Dorian hadn't trusted Hannah's promise. He'd taken the matter into his own hands.

Hannah waited for Caleb's answer. He could feel her waiting in the sudden stillness of her stance. "If you had it to do over, would you make the same choice again?"

His question took her by surprise, her eyes widening. "Yes," she said softly. "If I had to, I would."

He let that sink in. It made him angry—but not at her. Dorian was the madman here—the one who'd insisted it was either/or.

"I've never been without my voice. What right do I have to judge you?"

Slowly she turned to him.

"Yeah," he heard himself say. "I can forgive you." He met her gaze. "I do forgive you."

Her chin trembled.

He realized then that he hadn't been the only one hurt. What had the choice she'd made done to her over the years? "However, I'll never forgive Dorian."

"No, I can see that you wouldn't."

"He had no right to ask that of you."

"He was afraid…because of my mother."

"Your mother? How does she figure into this?"

Hannah pressed her fingers to her forehead. "When she ran off and married my father, it broke my grandparents' hearts. Then it turned out that Father wanted only one thing—to gain access to the Lansing estate. When Grandfather cut them out of his will, Father took out his frustration

on Mother. It was Stuart who stepped in, who
stopped him. I was too young to remember…but
I overheard Stuart arguing with Grandfather once
and questioned them. And certain images have
disturbed me ever since my voice has returned. I
think they may be memories."

It sickened him to think what Hannah had been
through—as a child and then again, reliving it as
her memory came back. "So Dorian didn't want
it to happen again," he said quietly. "He saw me
as that big of a threat?"

She nodded. "I'm like her. At least, that is what
he has always told me."

Caleb waited for her to explain herself.

"Mother…let her emotions rule her. I can't let
that happen to me."

Good Lord. That's what she was afraid of?
Dorian had pounded the idea into her head until
she was afraid to trust her feelings? "Hannah,
your mother made a mistake and she paid for it.
That doesn't mean you'll repeat it. You are not
your mother. This marriage you are contemplating benefits Lansing Enterprises and Dorian."

She nodded.

"But not you."

She glanced away. "With Thomas, I know what
to expect. He'll treat me well. And he has promised to build two more ships as a wedding present."

"Then, why bother coming here to find out

about the two that are missing? Why put yourself though all of this?" Couldn't she see the reason standing right in front of her?

Comprehension spread slowly over her face. "No, Caleb. My trip is to find out about the safety of the route and, if possible, the merchandise. The company can't afford to have more ships disappear."

Caleb wanted to shake her. "I'd like to believe you. It would make things neat and tidy for the both of us. But I don't. Not totally. There is another reason you're here. You just can't face up to it."

She shook her head, avoiding his gaze. "No, there's no other reason. You're wrong."

"Am I? You're selling yourself, Hannah."

"That's ridiculous! It's how things are done." She started across the sand toward the buggy.

He snorted. "Not in my world."

She turned away. "Now you're being ugly. Just…don't!"

He swung her around to face him. "Don't… what? Don't…care? I can't stand to think of you living the rest of your life with a man you don't love."

"I may grow to love him."

"You won't be happy."

"I'll be content. And that is important. I'll be keeping my promise. To want more, after all that Grandfather has done for me, is selfish. I don't expect you to understand about family loyalty. How could you? Your father left."

"I understand loyalty…and family. I have Rachel," he growled. "But she doesn't control my every decision."

"Grandfather is not like that."

"He's not? Listen to yourself! You said you were weak. Well, I don't see the choice you made as weak. You cared about me then. It was in everything you did that night, everything you said. It took strength to end what we could have had. It was a terrible thing Dorian did, making you choose, but you did it. And look—you're speaking now. But he's doing the same thing again—making you choose his way. How many more times will you let him control you? He's got you so scared to listen to your own feelings that you can't see the beach for the sand!"

She shook her head, near tears. "I know what you're saying. But I made a promise—a promise I can't go back on."

"You're an adult now. And you've already broken your promise. You're here. So renegotiate. It's time."

"Not with this promise."

He wanted to shake some sense into her. Instead he turned and paced the width of the beach. When he stood before her again he'd calmed somewhat, but not enough to heed the warning pounding in his head. "If you won't listen to your own heart, your own conscience, then listen to mine." He lowered his head, and before she could fathom his intent, he kissed her soundly on the lips.

Her hands flew to his chest. He thought she would push him away. It made him kiss her that much more fervently. This was his only chance to convince her of what she'd miss. But she didn't push against him; instead, she grasped the edges of his vest and held on tight as if he were a lifeline. He splayed his hand across her upper back, gently but firmly holding her against him, and poured his feelings into the kiss.

Her rigid frame softened in increments until she pulled him closer. His pulse kicked to a faster gait. He hadn't expected this. She was letting him kiss her, actually wanting him to kiss her! He stole his hand up to the nape of her neck where her skin was warm and satiny smooth, drawing her closer—close enough that he felt the beating of her heart. Slanting his mouth across hers, he deepened the kiss. A soft moan emerged from her.

The sound cautioned him. What was he doing? Forcing her to see things his way? If so, he was no better than Dorian.

Reluctantly, he pulled away and set her from him.

She stumbled back, her eyes big. One hand covered her swollen lips.

"You may be safe with Thomas," Caleb said,

frustration teeming inside him, "but understand this. He won't kiss you like that. Your heart won't pound inside your chest. You won't plaster yourself against him the way your body did to mine just now, wanting more. You'll feel nothing."

She stood there—shaken, her eyes still wide.

Didn't she understand what was happening? The woman could frustrate a saint—and he was no saint. "What you're contemplating…" He let the thought go unfinished. What right did he have to tell her anything?

"Caleb. Please." She closed her eyes. "We should go. We need…to go."

He bent down and snatched his hat from the sand. He turned it in his hands, giving his pulse a chance to slow to halfway normal.

She turned toward the buggy, took a few unsteady steps.

"Hannah."

She stopped and looked at him, her expression a mix of confusion and shock.

He shoved his hat on his head, kept his distance. "You might want to think on this. You don't love Thomas. The man you love—is me."

Chapter Twelve

It wasn't possible. She couldn't love Caleb. She
cared about him, yes, but love? He didn't fit—
not into her carefully thought-out plans, not into
her life. His words of that morning came back to
taunt her—*I want more. And there's the crux of
it. You can't see me like that.*

Yet that kiss… Heaven help her, she wanted
more…she *craved* more. Was that what it had
been like for her mother? The kiss had made her
entire body explode with awareness of Caleb. It
carried an unspoken promise of things to come,
and she wanted to know what those things were.
Thomas had never inspired those feelings with
the perfunctory touch of his lips to hers. Not
ever. She darted a quick look at Caleb as he handled the reins, maneuvering the buggy down the
main street of town. He hadn't said more than two
words on the ride back—simply stared straight
ahead.

It was dark now. Gas lamps burned steadily along the main street. Caleb turned the horse and buggy in at the livery and then walked her back to the Horton. With each step, she remembered what was waiting for her—the scattered clothes, the ink-stained carpet. Even if the maid had cleaned the room, it didn't change what had happened there. She didn't want to admit it, but she was frightened. And she dreaded the moment when Caleb would leave.

He walked with her all the way to her suite and opened the door with her key. He strode through the two rooms, checking to make sure nothing had changed since that morning and that no one lingered in the shadows.

Then he stood in the doorway between the two rooms, watching her, his expression closed. Even quiet, he simmered with controlled energy. He had to go to work now. If he was going to learn anything more about the ships, he must. She was only postponing the inevitable by keeping him here.

"Thank you—for everything," she said carefully.

He stepped toward her.

"No, let me finish. I…I didn't want to be alone today. Not after…this happened. The ride, the picnic…helped."

"Hannah…"

"I'll be fine now," she said quickly. "And I'll be careful. We can speak tomorrow."

"You're not staying here tonight."

"Of course I am. Where else would I stay?"

"I'm not letting you out of my sight. Not until I hand you safely over to Stuart."

"But you have work to do."

"And you're coming with me."

"To the saloon?" She could hear the sound of the piano coming through the open window. The music sounded cheery, inviting—directly opposite to her off-kilter mood. Yet it was one thing to enter the establishment in the morning before it was open, but now... "Caleb—it isn't proper."

"At this point I could be up to my neck in the mud with a herd of horses stampeding toward me and it wouldn't make me care what anybody thinks. None of that is important. I'm concerned about you. Only you. Whoever did this could come back."

"But he wouldn't! He knows now that I have nothing to steal."

The furrow between Caleb's brows deepened. "What if this man is not out to steal from you? What if he has something worse in mind?"

His implication registered, alarming her all the more.

"This isn't the time to choose some rule of being proper over common sense. And it's not open to discussion. I'm not taking that chance.

Not with you." He seized her silk reticule and shoved it toward her. "Grab what you need. You're coming with me."

The town was revving up for a lively Saturday night, Hannah realized. Five cowboys rode down the main street and dismounted in front of the saloon. They tied their horses at the hitching rail, and then laughing and elbowing each other in the ribs, they sauntered in through the swinging doors. The last one glanced from Caleb to Hannah before winking at her and following his friends.

"Any other time and I might take offense at that," Caleb mumbled. "That young whelp's got more sass than most."

"You know him?"

"Yeah. And it's lucky for him that I've got more important things on my mind tonight."

Hannah paused at the step to the boardwalk. How could she go in there with all those people?

Caleb tightened his arm on her waist. His eyes darkened with determination. "Nothing is going to happen. I'll look after you. Trust me."

"I do," she whispered. *I always have,* she wanted to add, but didn't. He'd always been there for her. She'd just never realized it before now. Grandfather had colored her memories and eroded the faith she'd once had in this man—and she had let him do it.

"We have to move forward if we are going to get answers."

He was right. One little thing and she was giving in to her fears, letting them control her. A thing she hated. She squared her shoulders. "I'm ready."

A tight grin appeared on his face. Together they entered through the swinging doors.

Noise, music and a smoky blue haze filled the room. Here and there, raucous laughter punctuated the low drone of conversation. Men surrounded several tables, playing cards and placing bets. The cowboys who'd entered before her had gathered in the corner around the billiard table and were choosing cues. A dark-haired barmaid swatted at one of the men, ducking out of his reach with a saucy smile. Over at the bar, Jim grabbed three mugs apiece in each hand, turned to the keg behind him and filled them up.

No one was paying any attention to her. Maybe a glance or two, but then they turned back to their own interests. They were all absorbed in their own fun. Realizing it helped her relax a bit.

"What happened to you, love?"

While Hannah had been surveying the room and patrons, the barmaid had approached. She reached for Caleb's bruised cheek. The concern in her eyes was real, but Hannah didn't like the fact the woman touched Caleb so familiarly—or the fact that he allowed it. She wore a red silk dress that emphasized her pale complexion. A black velvet choker circled her neck and onyx earrings dangled from tiny white ears. With her black hair swept high on her head, she looked almost regal.

Compared to her, Hannah felt windblown and tired. She checked her chignon, tucked in a few blond strands of wayward hair and reset a hairpin. At her side, Caleb moved away. The slight was nearly imperceptible, but Hannah felt as if a chasm had opened between them.

He grasped the barmaid's wrist and lowered her hand from his face. "Hannah, may I introduce Miss Fischer?"

The woman glanced over her shoulder and eyed Hannah with cool interest.

"Lola, this is Miss Hannah Lansing."

The barmaid's eyes narrowed. She looked Hannah over from heels to head. "Oh."

That one word said it all. Caleb had been talking about her—and not in a completely positive light. Hannah's throat tightened with hurt.

"Be nice, Lola," Caleb warned.

"I'm the essence of niceness," Lola said, finally turning toward Hannah. "You know that."

"I do, but Miss Lansing may not be in the mood for your particular humor. She's had a trying day."

"No doubt made worse because she's had to spend it with you."

Shocked at her words, Hannah pulled herself

up to her full height, ready to call her on it. "Mr. Houston has been most helpful today. He's seen to my every need."

Caleb pressed his lips together. Still she perceived a slight grin. She glared at him.

"Your *every* need, would you say?" Lola arched a brow.

Hannah's cheeks heated. Why was the woman baiting her?

"Lola…" The warning was back in Caleb's voice.

"You all right, miss? You look a mite flushed."

Hannah turned toward the unfamiliar voice. The young cowboy—the one who'd winked at her on the street—stood at her side. A sparse sprinkling of red facial hair accentuated his youthfulness.

"I…I'm fine. Thank you," she answered, noticing that, beside her, Caleb's jaw had tightened into stone.

"'Cause if you'd like to join me and my friends, I'd be happy to buy you a drink. Name's Josh."

Caleb drew closer. *Staking his claim?* Goodness. How was she to handle this? "Ah…how nice to meet you, Josh. Another time, perhaps?"

"Suit yerself. You let me know if I can do anything for you. Be happy to oblige."

"I will. Thank you."

Josh tipped his hat to Caleb, his gaze communicating something Hannah didn't quite understand.

As the cowboy sauntered away, a cocky swagger to his stride, Lola shook her head. "If that don't beat all. He sure was full of himself to barge in like that."

"He's green," Caleb said, shaking his head. "Hasn't got the rules down yet."

"Well, he'll get that handsome face of his mashed if he ain't careful. Maybe I better set him straight on a few things." Her blue eyes danced with merriment.

Caleb's eyes narrowed. "Don't spoil his fun, Lola. He should learn like the rest of us."

Hannah suppressed a smile. That boy had nothing on Caleb. She glanced up at the tall man at her side, content to be with him. Safe, just as he'd said. Caleb oozed strength and confidence just by breathing.

She realized suddenly that Lola watched her with a bemused expression, almost as if Hannah had passed some unwritten test. The barmaid seemed to come to a decision. "All right, then, Miss Lansing. Once I get those yahoos their drinks, what can I get for you from the bar?"

"Tea would be nice."

"Tea?" Lola glanced at Caleb. "You have got a blue blood here, sure as I'm twenty. Her daddy know she's with you?" She didn't wait for an answer, but headed toward the bar.

Hannah arched a brow. "Twenty?"

"Plus a few years," Caleb said.

"Nice friends." It didn't escape her attention that Lola had staged the entire interchange in order to make sure Caleb was all right. "She's worried about you...with me."

"She and Jim don't like me missing work. Makes their load heavier."

"It won't be much longer. Maybe as soon as tomorrow."

He pressed his lips together in a thin line.

"Can't we call a truce for tonight?"

"If that is how you want to play this." He indicated an empty table and guided her toward it.

He sat with his back against the wall, positioning himself so that he could watch all that happened in the large room. After a brief wait, Lola emerged from the room under the stairway with a steaming cup of tea, stopped at the bar to grab a full mug and then maneuvered her way among the tables to them. She set the mug before Caleb and the steaming cup in front of Hannah. "I hope it's how you like it."

"Thank you, Miss Fischer," Hannah replied, cupping her hands for warmth around the delicate rose-painted china. Caleb, she noticed, took the proffered mug without preamble and tossed half the contents down his throat.

While her tea cooled, Hannah considered all that had happened that day. From the moment she'd walked across the street to the saloon, it had been full of surprises. Over the rim of her cup, she studied Caleb's face—the straight blade of his nose, the high cheekbones. The swelling under his eye had receded a bit. She had the urge to touch his cheek there, the way Lola had, and in doing so, wipe away the other woman's touch. Of course, she didn't act on it. "Your bruises look better."

"I heal quick," he said, his tone clipped.

She caught herself gazing at his lips and re-focused on the swirling dark liquid in her cup. "I've realized something. Even if I find out what happened to the ships, it won't bring them back. The money is gone, no matter what. I didn't face that before."

"You might still recover something. And now that the sheriff and the port authority are aware of the situation, they'll alert other ships. It will make the passage safer."

She sighed and took a sip of tea. There was a different, foreign spice to it. She took another sip, trying to figure out where she'd tasted it before. Warmth seeped through to her bones. More re-laxed now, she settled into the chair.

"I need you to understand something, Caleb," she began. "Grandfather is only looking out for my best interests. He's pushed himself to excel his entire life. The shipping business he's built *is* his life. It's important to him that it doesn't turn to dust after he leaves this earth. He thinks Thomas will make sure of that."

Caleb leaned toward her, his voice low and earnest. "Look at what happened to Rose, Hannah. He controlled Rose with such a grip that she slowly suffocated. It was the same with your mother, and she tried to escape it. Now he's doing the same thing to you. Out of love—but it's a strange kind of love that leaves no room for your wishes or dreams."

Hannah circled a water spot on the table with her index finger, absorbing what Caleb said. "I thought we agreed to a truce."

He leaned back against the wall, balancing his chair on the two back legs. "You're the one who brought up Thomas." Then he tipped the chair down with a bang. "You're impulsive and stubborn all at the same time. Good grief, Hannah! You're the girl who dashed to the beach all by herself to find a lost puppy!"

"That was a long time ago, Caleb. And that nearly was the death of me." It only proved that she made poor decisions when she thought with her emotions. Even then.

"You did it because you cared about that little pup."

"And I'm doing this because I care about Grandfather."

He shook his head. "I don't buy that. The pup was helpless. Dorian is not. But I do see how you care about the other families that work for you. You're the one who should run the company. Not Thomas."

She had to keep to her own counsel here. Grandfather would give her the business—if she followed his rules. Thomas was part of those rules.

But marrying him… Could she honestly go through with it now after knowing Caleb's kiss? He'd made his point all too thoroughly. He might as well have branded her.

Over the years, she'd convinced herself that the kiss she'd shared with him when she was sixteen had become too special in her memory to be true. Today had crushed that imagining. Her skin had tingled. Her knees had gone weak. Desire and conflict had raged inside her. Had he continued his lesson in passion, she would have undoubtedly succumbed and ended up becoming a miserable replication of her mother. Providence had aided her in keeping his kiss short and succinct— or was it otherwise? Had it only made her yearn for more of the same? One thing she did know: Caleb was the one who made her feel full of possibilities—not Thomas.

Heated words between two men at the billiard table broke through her thoughts. "I called the pocket! Now hand over your bet. Fair is fair."

Three of the cowboys she'd noticed earlier had

bunched together and stood facing two other men. Lola stood in the middle of the fray.

"Cowboys," Caleb muttered, standing. "There's always trouble when they come in off the range looking to corral all their fun into one night."

"Who are the others?"

"They aren't regulars." He frowned. "By their clothes, they could be men from the docks."

He wound through the tables toward the men. Hannah held her breath. Of course he would be all right, she told herself. This was his job. He'd probably handled situations like this a hundred times before. Still, she couldn't shake the worry that mounted with each step he took. Caleb glanced across the room at Jim. A slight nod from the barkeep, a subtle shift in the man's stance, and Hannah regained a small amount of reassurance. At least Caleb didn't face the men completely on his own.

He slowed as he approached, his steps deliberate and steady. As one, the men's hostility shifted and focused on Caleb. Energy ricocheted off them like powder kegs ready to ignite. A wrong word, a wrong look, and the situation would explode.

"Move away, Lola."

She nodded at him and scooted out of harm's way. As she sidled by, he whispered in her ear, all the while keeping his gaze trained on the men. Lola made her way over to Hannah.

"If things go bad," she said in a low voice, her

dark eyes held a warning, "you're to follow me
and be quick about it."

Hannah's gaze snapped back to Caleb. Tension escalated around the room. The men at the
table next to hers had stopped playing poker and
watched the proceedings with interest.

She couldn't make out what Caleb said, but noticed the steady timbre of his voice. She'd heard
it before. He'd used it on her that morning when
she'd discovered her ransacked room. Along with
the ring of authority, he'd injected a calming note.

Suddenly the cowboy next to Josh pulled a
knife. With lightning speed, Caleb moved in,
gripped the boy's wrist and wrenched his arm,
sending the knife clattering to the floor. In a second move, he pulled his own gun from its holster,
pointing it at the men.

"Now the count is even," he said, continuing
his tight hold on the young cowboy. "But you'll
take this outside, or the man who makes the
first move to fight will find himself with a hole
through his gullet. Wyatt doesn't take kindly to
riffraff destroying his place."

He pointed his gun at each of the four, one at
a time. The fire diminished in their eyes, and
slowly each man shook his head and eased back.
The challenge wasn't worth anyone's life. They
grabbed their things and left.

Caleb waited until all but Josh had departed
before releasing the cowboy. With a reddened

face, the boy grabbed his knife off the floor and sheathed it at his waist, then strode out the door. Caleb said something to Josh. Josh glanced at her and then nodded at Caleb. He followed after the others through the door.

At the bar, Jim lowered his rifle and stashed it back under the counter. Hannah exhaled, her heart gradually slowing to a normal rhythm.

When Caleb returned to her table, she asked, "What did you say to Josh?"

"Just told him I saved his neck, and in payment, I'd appreciate it if he'd stop casting cow eyes at you." He pulled out his chair and sat, stretching his legs out under the table.

When he was settled, she arched a brow. "Cow eyes?"

He scowled. "He understood. I also mentioned that he's way too young for you, that you are the ripe old age of twenty-one and he's not a day older than seventeen. He didn't care much for that assessment—although he mentioned he thought older women were more appealing."

A smile escaped. She couldn't help it. "Anything else? It's quite an education learning how you coerce others around to see things your way."

He held back, apparently debating how much to say, and then plunged ahead. "I mentioned that you were so far out of reach that he'd likely see frogs rain down before he'd get a second look from you."

"A movement of biblical proportions? Don't you think that's a bit exaggerated?"

He met her gaze. "No."

She lowered her cup, troubled. Was that really how things stood between them? After all they'd been through, all they'd spoken of, even in disagreement she felt closer to him than anyone she'd ever known. "I honestly don't know how I would have managed today without you, Caleb. Thank you."

A tightening of his jaw was the only acknowledgment he gave.

She nodded toward the billiard table. "You handled that situation so well, and here I was worried for you."

"Maybe I've redeemed myself, then. Getting jumped last night was a blow to my ego."

"Would you have fired?"

A long minute went by. "If I had to."

"You have before." She hadn't meant for the words to come out as an accusation.

"Yes."

She swallowed hard, only then beginning to realize there were parts of Caleb she knew nothing about. He truly was a law unto himself.

"It's my job, Hannah. This isn't Nob Hill. Here, things aren't covered by a layer of etiquette. I don't have the option of 'pistols at dawn' or whatever gentlemen do in San Francisco. To stop a fight I do what I have to."

"You'd kill a man?"

"In self-defense."

"For any other reason?"

"To protect what's mine."

She quieted, absorbing that. With Caleb, things were either black or white. Shades of gray existed, but he didn't let them muddy the line between. Perhaps she'd known, deep down, that he would feel this way, and because of it, she'd known she'd be safer with him than anyone else—safe in a way that Grandfather, with all his money, had never made her feel.

The evening wore on, and she became aware of the deference paid to Caleb. Most of the men steered clear of him, tipping a hat or nodding to him from across the room. A few stopped by to ask his opinion on one thing or another. He politely introduced her and then steered the conversation to whatever the particular man had on his mind.

When heated words erupted between two men at the bar, Caleb nodded to Jim, and Jim quietly corked the bottle between the men.

"If you've got a problem with this, take it up with Mr. Houston over there," Jim said, indicating Caleb.

The men turned and looked at him and then settled down. It became clear to her that the calm competence he exuded touched every corner of the saloon.

When the piano player began repeating songs for the third time, her head started to nod. One melody blended into the next as blue smoke from the men's cigars and pipes drifted upward, thickening the haze that hung low from the ceiling. The individual sound of deep voices faded into background noise that no longer made any sense.

"Doesn't look like we are going to find out anything more tonight," Caleb murmured, his voice sounding far away. Opening her eyes, she looked around the large room and realized that the saloon had emptied of everyone except Jim and Lola.

"I'll lock up," Jim said, wiping down the bar one last time.

"Thanks," Caleb replied, taking her hands and pulling her to her feet.

She stumbled once between two tables, and he caught her arm. "I'm more tired than I realized," she murmured against his shoulder.

A low chuckle rumbled through his chest. He slipped his arm behind her knees and suddenly her feet were off the floor, and he carried her. "Sorry you had to stay up so late. I couldn't chance letting you out of my sight."

She must have been heavy for him. Really, she should insist he put her down. He was the one who'd suffered a beating last night. This wasn't necessary. She struggled against the pleasure of feeling utterly cared for and tried to wake up sufficiently to walk. The rocking motion of his gait told her they were on the stairs. She pushed weakly against his chest. "I can walk," she mumbled, lifting her head slightly. What must Jim and Lola think?

"Shh, Hannah. Be still."

Was that a kiss on her forehead? She sighed and burrowed into his shoulder, relaxing into his strong, warm arms. After all, it was the safest place on earth, and it was where she wanted to be.

Hannah's sigh fluttered Caleb's open collar and tickled his skin as he twisted the brass doorknob to his room. He'd never known her to be this unguarded, this at ease with him. After all the turmoil of the day, finally in her exhaustion, she could no longer hold on to the reins of control.

He made his way through the dark room and laid her on his bed. Moving to his dresser, he struck a match and lit the kerosene lamp, then turned and stared at her for a full minute. The light cast wavering shadows on the line of her neck and delicate jaw. Her dark lashes lay still against her skin—skin that had grown more golden over the past few days. When she'd first arrived, she had seemed so untouchable, so perfect—like an alabaster statue. Yet he'd held her today—kissed her—and she'd been soft and warm—*real*—in his arms. He blew out a long breath. What had he gotten himself into by bring-ing her here?

Those men from the docks had been in to-night to send him another message. They hadn't gone far when they stepped outside. Jim had seen them hanging around the land office down the street. Caleb studied the sleeping beauty in his bed. Maybe it was a good thing he'd been com-pletely out of it last night with that beating. At least he'd slept hard. With her here, and with the possibility of those men still outside, he'd best sleep with one eye open tonight.

He leaned over and pulled the pins from her hair, lingering a moment on the feel of the silk as he uncoiled the strands. Her skirt had twisted about her legs. He tugged on the fabric, releas-ing it from beneath her. Then he unbuttoned her high-topped shoes and slid them from her feet, letting each in turn drop on the floor. At the noise, she stirred and turned away from him toward the window.

Thin fingers of clouds stretched over the face of the moon. Blue light filtered in through the panes, slashing across her cheeks and leaving just enough light to see her. She was something to look at—a cool marble with that blue cast to her skin. In another life, she would have been one of those sirens that lured men to their doom. Heck—maybe even in this life…. At that image, he smiled. Probably not an apt description since she couldn't bear the open sea.

Half the men who had come up to talk to him this evening had done so to get a closer look at her. He'd known it. The men had known it. Only she seemed unaware of her inherent charms. To hear her talk, all the attention she received occurred because of her relationship to Dorian and his money. How much of that insecurity was because of Dorian's influence?

The thought sobered him. How could he let her return to San Francisco? When the time came to part, could he say goodbye? His chest ached at the thought of it.

Years ago when they'd separated, he'd had plenty of anger and frustration built up. Telling himself that Dorian had molded Hannah into someone cold and calculating had made it possible to bury her memory.

But now—now that she'd railroaded herself back into his life, he realized it was all a lie. How could she give herself to a man who only saw her as a business arrangement when Caleb wanted to give her the moon?

He loved her.

He sank into the one chair in his room and, his elbows on his knees, held his head in his hands. He loved her. Admitting it to himself was a relief, even though it didn't change a thing. They were still worlds apart. The fact that she was four feet from him in the same room didn't make any difference. It couldn't. As an heir of the Lansing fortune, she was destined to be rich. She'd been groomed and schooled for it. Someone like him didn't have any business wanting her for himself.

She'd gotten herself into one big mess by asking questions—smart, legitimate questions—about the business. When she left with Stuart, he would find the answers. He could do that much for her. But first he had to make sure she stayed safe. Turning her over to Stuart's care was the first step. He wished he could say it would be a relief, but he knew he'd never see her again once that happened, and that lay like a stone in his gut.

"Caleb?"

He raised his head at the sound of her sleep-filled voice.

"You won't get any sleep in that chair. Come lay down. I'll make room."

His heart pounded. "That's not a good idea."

"Morning will come soon enough. You need decent sleep."

"I'll get more here than there." But even as he spoke he tugged off his boots and set them aside. He stood and loosened his shirt from the waist of his pants. Then, taking the chair, he dragged it to the door, wedging the back under the doorknob. It wouldn't be strong enough to stop someone determined to break in, but it might slow them down enough for him to grab his gun. He turned the wick down on the lamp until the flame sputtered out, dousing the yellow glow in the small room until only the moonlight offered its pale blue view. Then, drawing his gun from its holster, he placed it within easy reach on the floor next to the bed.

He gazed down at her, hesitating, still not sure if he should go through with this. Taking one pillow with her, she scooted to the far side of the mattress against the wall. She might trust him, but by the absolute stillness that had come over her, she was nervous about sharing a bed. Could it be she didn't trust herself? The thought made him smile. What a pair they were.

He took up the wool blanket from the foot of the bed and spread it over her, tucking the edges in as if she was a child. Then he lay down on top of the blanket, laced his hands behind his head, and stared at the dark ceiling. His heart beat louder with each passing moment, and the blood rushed in his ears. Yep. This was gonna be a long night.

"Caleb?" she whispered. "I know I've been difficult at times. Just…thank you."

He didn't know how to answer that. He didn't want her thanks. He wanted her to see him as more than a good friend. He closed his eyes, breathing in her scent. He was in one heck of a fix.

"Caleb?"

"Hmm?"

The bedsprings squeaked as she turned toward him. In what felt like the most natural move in the world, he circled his arm around her, drawing her closer while she put her head on his shoulder and moved her hand up to rest on his chest. A contented sigh escaped through her lips.

"Hannah?"

Her breathing deepened, evened out. Whatever it was she'd planned to say evaporated into the night.

"Hannah?"

No answer.

He studied her face in the shadows. How easy it would be to raise her chin just enough to kiss her on the mouth. He ran the pad of his thumb lightly over her lower lip, debating the wisdom of such an action. Thinking like that would only frustrate him further. The night would be difficult enough, and the first rays of dawn over the eastern mountains were only a handful of hours away.

But he'd had plenty of regrets in his twenty-nine years. He didn't want to make this one more. He brushed a wisp of hair from her face, leaned over and kissed her on the lips. "Sweet dreams, darlin'."

Chapter Thirteen

The weight of something heavy across her waist woke Hannah. She opened her eyes to daylight streaming in through the dusty window and confronted the fact she'd slept in Caleb's arms all night. His eyes were closed, his breathing deep and even. This close, she could see the individual hairs that made up new beard on the straight line of his jaw.

The saloon was noticeably silent after the raucous noise of last night. The only sounds were those coming from early risers up and about on the street outside—the *clip-clop* of horses' hooves against the packed dirt, the squeak of wagon springs and the occasional greeting.

The room smelled of the sea air—cold and damp—yet heat poured off Caleb like a balmy day in July. She shifted slightly, fingering the button on his shirtfront.

Caleb had said she loved him yesterday. She'd

blocked it out. How could he know her mind when she didn't even know it herself? Yet sometime during the evening she'd given up fighting it. He was right. She did love him. A tremor coursed through her as she realized the import of her thoughts. What good did it do to say the words out loud when nothing would change? She had her duty to her grandfather, her duty to the company. She swiped at the wetness that gathered in the corner of her eyes.

"Mornin', Hannah."

She glanced up to find him watching her, his green gaze steady. His day-old beard scraped her temple. When she started to pull away, he tightened his hold on her. "Don't go. Not just yet."

So she quieted, resting her head back on his chest, feeling the rise and fall of his breathing, listening to the steady beat of his heart. "Yesterday I said there was no safe place. Remember?"

"Yeah," he said guardedly.

"I was wrong. There is. With you."

His breathing slowed for a moment and then started again. A minute later she felt him tug softly at a wisp of her hair at her temple. "Know what I've been thinking half the night?"

She raised her brows, unsure how to answer that.

He grinned. "Well, along with those thoughts… I was wishin' I could have been there that day you first spoke."

"Why? What could you have done?"

"Don't know," he said with a shrug. "Whoop it up a bit. Celebrate. Just would have liked to be there with you."

She closed her eyes, savoring the feeling of being cared for, protected. So much had changed between them in the past twenty-four hours. It was good, this cleansing of old wounds. She hadn't realized how freeing his forgiveness would be. She didn't want it to end. Not ever.

And that scared her.

"Last night something happened." She looked up into his eyes. "You kissed me."

"I kissed you yesterday, if you'll remember. Didn't think you'd forget so fast." His expression didn't change—still guarded, still quiet.

"I'm not talking about that. That was the heat of the moment." *And startling, unnerving, passionate,* she wanted to say. Yet so different from the one last night. She wanted to be sure it hadn't been a dream or wishful thinking on her part. The kiss on the stairs had been full of tenderness and something more. "It's last night I want to know about. Did you kiss me again?"

"Technically—yes. But seein' as how you were practically asleep standing up, I can't say that it counted."

"So you took advantage of me."

He frowned. "Now, I wouldn't go that far—"

Feeling a bit bolder, she walked her fingers up his chest. "And did I kiss you back?"

A slow grin spread across his face. "Sad to say—only in my dreams."

"Hmm. I don't think that counted, then. Technically."

He shifted slightly to see her better. "What are you up to, Hannah? Is this part of the truce? Or are we makin' new rules here?"

"Hmm. Yes."

His gaze sharpened. "I never took you for a tease."

She leaned toward him. "New rules completely. New territory. I'm not teasing."

She rose up on her elbow and pressed her lips to his softly, tentatively. He went as still as stone.

"Caleb?" she murmured. Was this his answer? Her face heated with embarrassment. She pushed away and sat up.

"Where do you think you're going? Thought Lansings always went after what they wanted." The challenge in his tone was unmistakable.

"We do. In business. This is different."

"Make up your mind, Hannah, but be sure about it when you do. There's no use denying that we both have feelings for each other. Strong ones, if you ask me. The thing is—either you want something to happen here or you don't."

"I thought I was showing you that."

At her words, he pulled her into his arms with

a sureness, a strength of purpose she'd come to know as his alone. His lips found hers, and immediately she could tell this was a different kind of kiss from the two she'd known yesterday. It urged her to give back measure for measure—this stirring of heart and desire.

Melting into him, she did just that. Her heart beat in time with his—perhaps it always had; she'd just never listened until now. His lips were firm but giving, surrounded as they were by the prickly new stubble of beard. Everywhere he touched, she thrummed with awareness—his mouth on her lips, his hand on her upper back, his fingers splayed and kneading her neck.

When he nipped her upper lip, she gasped and opened her mouth slightly. He swept his tongue inside, startling her further. She started to pull back, but he held her neck and wouldn't release her. His tongue stroked hers, slowly, *deliberately!* Like liquid gold, warmth raced through her veins and pooled deep inside. What was happening? "Caleb?"

"Shh. I know…" he said, his voice raw. He pressed slow kisses against her jaw, his breath tickling her cheek. She exhaled softly against his ear and a fine tremor raced through him. Knowing she'd caused it gave her a sense of power she hadn't known was possible. Yet changes were happening inside her, as well. Her breasts tingled—actually, ached—with wanting attention.

His kiss deepened, demanded more, and suddenly she was nervous and afraid of where this was going, of what he was asking without words. On the one hand she wanted it with a craving so intense it hurt, but on the other hand…how could she… "Caleb…stop, please."

He squeezed his eyes shut and seemed to have some sort of inner argument with himself. Then, breathing hard, he pulled back and swiped a hand through his dark hair. He swung his feet to the floor and put his back to her.

She reached for his shoulder but stopped just short of touching him. "Thank you."

He didn't turn to her. "I can wait…do things proper. Not all that excited about it, mind you, but you're too important to me to mess this up." He let out another slow breath, reached down and tugged on one boot. "You do realize this changes things."

At her silence, he looked up from his task.

"It can't change, Caleb. I can't—"

Thunderclouds gathered on his brow. "I must be the biggest fool west of the Continental Divide. Even now you are thinking of going through with marrying Rowlings?"

"Don't you understand? I can't think about just me!"

He stood and buckled on his gun belt, shoving his gun into its holster. "Don't explain it. I don't want to hear it again. Look. I don't fault you for being loyal to your family, but you need to figure out if that is more important than being loyal to yourself."

She squeezed her eyes shut. More and more her head told her one thing and her heart another. Grandfather was right. She *was* weak—just like her mother. The realization stung. She covered her face with her hands.

A moment later the chair scraped as Caleb moved it away from the door.

"Where are you going?"

"Not far. Just need some air."

"You mean distance. From me."

His eyes were hard as he slipped on his Stetson. "That, too. Stay put. You're safe enough here."

"Caleb…"

"You're not sixteen anymore, Hannah, and you can't have it both ways. If you leave this time, don't ever contact me again."

She stared at the closing door and listened to the sound of his footsteps fading away on the stairs. His parting words echoed over and over in her mind. She couldn't leave things like this. She had to make him understand.

Quickly, she straightened her blouse, buttoning the top button again. When had that come undone? She combed her fingers through her hair, twisted up the side strands and looked about for her pins. The task was futile. Giving up, she released her hair and opened the door.

No one stirred as she entered the hall, but she

heard Jim's slightly out-of-tune whistling coming from somewhere a floor below. She descended the stairs, passing Jim as he hoisted the last chair onto a table and grabbed his broom. Caleb was nowhere to be seen.

After a quick stop at the necessary, she checked the kitchen for Caleb. A teapot gurgled on the stove, and the scent of baking muffins filled the small room. She found her teacup—already cleaned from the night before—and, using a strainer, poured herself a cup of tea.

From behind her, someone pressed a cloth to her nose and mouth. A pungent odor filled her nostrils.

"Don't fight it, little lady. Won't do you no good."

She clawed at the large hand, broke his hold and spun away from her attacker. He was large and wide with a face riddled with scars and pockmarks. She sucked in a big breath, preparing to scream. No sound came out! Stumbling backward, she tripped over something bulky and soft on the floor.

"That's right. Ain't nobody to help you now." The man rushed her, once more forcing the rag against her face. His beefy hand had a red, puckered scar running the length of his index finger. She gripped his hands, trying to force them off. Her heart beat erratically, the blood pulsing strangely in her head. This couldn't be! Spots swam before her eyes, and the edges of her vision dimmed. She tried again to wrench free but couldn't.

Caleb! She needed Caleb!

Unable to keep from breathing, she inhaled again. The kitchen receded to a pinpoint of light as the man hauled her against his huge frame.

Then the light went out.

Caleb took the stairs to his room two at a time. He hadn't meant to leave Hannah alone so long—nearly half an hour—but he'd been waylaid by Alonzo Horton interrogating him in Wyatt's office about the damage to Hannah's hotel room. He was none too happy about the situation and made it a point to mention that Caleb wasn't welcome there ever again.

Caleb knocked on the door.

No answer.

"Hannah?" He opened the door. Empty. Irritation set in. She knew how dangerous it was for her to go anywhere on her own. He strode to the bedroom and saw her reticule in the corner. She wouldn't have gone far—perhaps just to get some breakfast or use the necessary. Still, the fact that she wasn't here set him on edge.

Sifting through their conversation, he realized with a jolt that she might have gone back to her hotel. Or she might have left *him*. He had given her that ultimatum. He should have kept his mouth shut. Cooled down a bit. He had meant what he said, but he knew as much about a woman's moods as a jackrabbit knew about swimmin', so a little caution might have been in order.

Descending the stairs once more, he called out to Jim, "Hannah around?"

Jim quit humming and leaned on his broom. "You two have another spat? I thought you were mendin' fences all right last night."

Caleb didn't have time to jaw. "Where'd she go?"

"Heard something in the kitchen. Check with Yin."

Caleb strode to the small kitchen area. A pot lay upside down on the floor, water seeping into the cracks of the wooden planks. The canister of coffee beans was on its side, with the dark beans scattered all over the hutch. And Yin—Yin was slumped in the corner with blood trickling down his face.

"That'll teach me not to whistle," Jim muttered from behind Caleb. "Didn't hear a thing."

Caleb scowled and slammed through the back kitchen door. He glanced up and down the narrow alleyway. Except for a dusty yellow cat that yowled and raced between two buildings, no one stirred.

He turned to Jim. "See to Yin and then get Wyatt. I'm going after the sheriff."

He started down the street before he realized

he might learn more at the Horton—might even find her. He charged into the hotel and strode straight through the lobby.

Mr. Bennett braced himself as Caleb approached. "You were instructed not to frequent here, Mr. Houston."

"Have you seen Miss Lansing this morning?"

"No, sir. And after what happened last evening, Jackson has increased his patrolling of the property."

Caleb's hand closed into a fist. "She's gone. Missing."

"Didn't she leave with you last night?"

Caleb didn't need this desk man to infer that he'd done a lousy job protecting Hannah; he already knew that. What he needed were answers. "I haven't seen her in the past hour. I thought she might have returned here."

"No, sir."

"I'll check her room."

Mr. Bennett pursed his lips. "If you don't mind my saying so, perhaps she needed a moment of privacy."

"I don't have time to argue. There's evidence of a struggle at the saloon. I think she's been taken against her will."

Mr. Bennett's attitude did a turnabout as he grasped the situation. Caleb didn't wait for him, racing up the stairs two at a time. He shoved open Hannah's room door and found the place much as he'd last seen it, with chairs overturned and cushions on the floor. He walked through the suite with Mr. Bennett dogging his heels.

"She's not here," Mr. Bennett said.

Caleb ignored him. There had to be a clue—something to tell him where to look next. He searched through the two rooms. Nothing surfaced.

She'd disappeared completely.

"I'm sorry, sir," Mr. Bennett said with a look of genuine concern on his face.

"Keep an eye out for her."

Without waiting for the man's acknowledgment, Caleb spun on his heel and left.

The sheriff's office was two blocks down the street. As Caleb approached, the door swung open and Sheriff Cramer pushed Josh out to the street. Must have gotten into more trouble after leaving the saloon last night. The kid looked at him through bleary eyes and then stumbled to his horse tied at the rail.

"Next time, keep your wits about you. I don't want to see you back here again," the sheriff called out, and then turned as Caleb approached.

"Miss Lansing is missing."

"When?"

"An hour ago."

"You sure she's not just powdering her nose somewhere?"

Caleb scowled but then detailed the situation in

the kitchen. He noticed Josh hadn't ridden off but sat on his horse, listening to their conversation.

The sheriff noticed, too. "You got something to say, Josh?"

"That purty blond gal? She the one you're talking about?"

Caleb nodded. "Have you seen her?"

Josh lifted his Stetson and scratched his forehead. "Not exactly."

The sheriff's eyes narrowed. "Just what did you see?"

"It was just a feeling I got. Could be nothing. Two men carried a barrel down the street this morning—one of them big ones. The way they were complaining, must have been heavy. They shoved it on a flatbed wagon and rode off."

"What's unusual about that?" Caleb asked.

"Well, they were the same men from the saloon last night—the ones so fired up to start a fight."

A sinking sensation hit Caleb. "Men from the docks."

"Not much to go on," the sheriff said. "They were probably just doing their job."

"Well, like I said—it was a feeling I got. Take it or leave it."

"Wait a minute, Josh. Which way did they go?" Caleb asked. At this point, he'd chase any lead he could find, anything that would bring him closer to getting Hannah back.

"South. Out of town, I guess. Heck, I was locked up here. How would I know for sure?"

"Thanks, kid. Keep your eyes open," the sheriff said.

Caleb reached up and shook hands with the boy. "Appreciate your help."

"Sure hope you find her. Seemed like a nice lady." He reined his horse away from the railing and rode down the street.

Caleb turned to the sheriff. "I'm going to the docks."

"I still think you're jumping the gun. She could be anywhere—a warehouse, a saloon, even a church, for that matter. There's no tellin'."

"I realize that. But wherever she is, she didn't go willingly. I have to find her—and fast." Hannah might be in the company of men who would hurt her—or worse—kill her if she didn't do what they wanted.

"You leavin' now?" the sheriff asked.

Caleb nodded.

"I'll go with you."

Before they headed to the docks, Caleb and the sheriff swung by the saloon again on the off chance Hannah had shown up. She hadn't, but Jim had staked out a place to keep a lookout for her.

He'd let her down.

Caleb's stomach roiled with the thought. She had depended on him, trusted him, and he'd messed up royally. He should have never left her alone—not for a minute. Regret was a hard thing to have to swallow.

When they turned the last corner to the harbor, Caleb heard the lone whistle from a steamer making ready to depart. He set off in a run.

On the pier, men carrying crates and barrels headed up the ramp to a steamer. A flatbed wagon, nearly empty of freight, parked halfway down the dock. Caleb raced to the wagon and jostled one of the barrels, then moved to the next one. It was a long shot, but if he heard a cry from inside, he'd tear into it.

"Here! Here!" a burly sailor ran up and shoved him aside. "What are you tryin' to do? These ain't your property."

"What do you have in these?" Caleb demanded.

"Leather hides."

"This your first load?"

The man frowned. Behind him, Sheriff Cramer quickly approached. "Who's askin'?"

"Just answer the question," Caleb said, tensing. He didn't have time for a game of Twenty Questions. "How long have you been here?"

A tall man took Caleb by the arm and spun him around. "I'm Captain Porter. I'll vouch for what's in the barrels."

"Open them."

The captain cocked his head. "Not exactly a polite request. Judging from that shiner, I'd say you've run into some trouble. Now, why don't you make this easy on the both of us and tell me what you're looking for before I get the sheriff?"

Sheriff Cramer smiled wanly. "That won't be necessary. I am the law here. We are looking for a woman of some consequence who disappeared two hours ago. Could be foul play. You'd do well to let us examine the barrels before loading them."

Captain Porter raised his brows. "Very well. I won't be part of anything shady. Go ahead." He nodded to his first mate.

There were twelve barrels in all. Two of them contained beer—evidenced by the sloshing noise inside. The other ten, when opened, contained leather hides.

"Sorry for detaining you," the sheriff said.

The captain waved off the comment. "Word to the wise," he said, directing his words to Caleb, "watch yourself. The kind of men who would take a woman aren't going to think twice about running you through if you get in their way. You can't go off half-cocked or you'll end up dead."

Caleb realized the man meant well, but he didn't need a lecture. He needed to find Hannah. Every minute spent jawin' was a minute less he could look for her. He turned back toward town.

When they arrived at the saloon, the sheriff

tipped his hat. "I'll let you know if anything turns up. I'd appreciate the same back."

Caleb nodded and watched him head back toward his office. At least the man was following up on his leads. Not fast enough for Caleb—but at least he was working it. The scent of lemon wax invaded his nostrils when he entered the saloon. Jim always cleaned when he was agitated about something. Claimed it helped him think.

Wyatt sat at his regular table, his back to the wall. "Sounds like you've been doing more than just escorting Miss Lansing to high tea. Want to talk about it?" He shoved out the chair next to him with his boot.

Caleb straddled the chair backward, his arms resting on the straight back in front of him. Maybe Wyatt, with his connections about town, could help.

Just then the door opened, and a small dark-haired boy stepped inside. He looked to be about ten years old with eyes too cunning for such a young face. Bruises on his knuckles and a scab on his lower lip spoke of his scrappy existence. Like many of the boys who lived by their wits, he was barefoot, his thin shirt and pants torn and muddy.

"I have message. Man say you pay."

"What man? Where?"

"First, *dinero.*"

Caleb laid two quarters on the table.

Faster than a snake striking, the boy grabbed the money.

Caleb slapped his hand down hard on top of the boy's.

The boy winced and twisted beneath his grip.

"The message, muchacho," Caleb said.

The street urchin glared, but then reached into his pocket with his free hand and pulled out a wadded piece of paper. He threw it on the table. Caleb relaxed his grip, and before he could blink, the boy dashed toward the door.

"Hold on there!" Wyatt jumped to his feet. He caught the boy and dragged him, kicking and resisting, back to the table.

"Let me go! *No entiendo!*"

"You'll wait," Wyatt said in a tone that brooked no argument. "What does it say?" he asked Caleb.

"It's a ransom note. She's been kidnapped." He met Wyatt's gaze. "Ten thousand dollars."

"Son of a gun."

It was more money than he had and, he suspected, Wyatt had, too. Caleb turned to the boy. "The man who gave you this note… What did he look like?"

The defiance in the boy's eyes was his only answer.

Caleb tried again. "Was there anyone else? A woman, perhaps?"

The boy stopped squirming. "No. No one."

"Where were you when he gave this to you?"

The boy clamped his mouth shut.

"He doesn't know anything," Wyatt said.

Caleb couldn't accept that. Hannah's life was in danger, and he needed answers. To encourage the boy to remember, he grabbed his ankles and turned him upside down. The boy flailed about, his small fists beating anything that came close— the table, Wyatt's leg, Caleb's stomach. "Where did you get this message? Tell me!"

"*Sí! Sí!* Put me down!"

Caleb turned him back over and set him on his feet, keeping tight hold of his arm.

The boy gave Caleb a dark glare. "Market Street. I do not know the man."

"We should take him to the sheriff," Wyatt said.

At the word *sheriff,* a frightened look came over the boy's dirty face. "I know nothing!"

"I believe him," Caleb said. He gave the boy a stern shake and then released him. "Whoever did this is dangerous, muchacho. Stay away from him."

At being set free, the urchin dashed toward the door. Caleb glanced again at the careless handwriting in the note.

If you ever want to see Miss Lansing, bring ten thousand dollars to the main dock at midnight tonight. Alone.

Hannah must have been scared out of her wits. Despair knifed through him. How had he let this happen? He handed the wrinkled note to Wyatt.

Wyatt read it over. "I can help some, but not much. My cash is tied up. Maybe you should wire Lansing. He'll send the money."

"He doesn't have it. Hannah said something about an investment that went sour. He was counting on those two shiploads to stay solvent."

Wyatt rocked back on two legs of his chair. "The papers would have a time with that piece of news."

"Hannah discovered it. He kept it secret—even from her."

"Understandable. A man in his position would. Doesn't help now. I'm sure those who are holding Miss Lansing believe he can cough it up easily enough."

Caleb let out a long breath. He'd rather do just about anything other than telling Dorian that Hannah had been kidnapped.

"You've got to tell him."

Caleb stuffed his hat on his head. "Yeah. I know. I'll wire him. And Rowlings, too. Maybe he can come through with the cash."

Wyatt got to his feet. "What about the sheriff?"

"The note said 'alone.' Cramer will get in the way. I haven't sorted it all out, but I'll have something by tonight. I have to."

* * *

Forty-five minutes later, after sending the wire, Caleb stepped out of the telegraph office with Wyatt. His entire body throbbed with tightly controlled frustration. No one was moving fast enough to suit him. Every minute lost meant Hannah could be farther away—farther out of reach. He couldn't think beyond getting her back from whoever had taken her. That was his priority. "So we wait for Dorian to wire the money."

Wyatt nodded. "He'll go to Rowlings."

"I can't stand waiting," Caleb muttered, feeling jumpy inside. Hannah's life hung on what happened next. The situation demanded action, not sitting back and waiting for other players to come to the table. He looked down the street. The sun hovered straight overhead. "Ten hours. Not much time," he murmured.

"I've seen that look before," Wyatt said, falling into step with him. "Whatever you're planning—try running it by me."

"What's it to you?"

"I don't want to train another manager."

"Then, you better keep up," Caleb said without slowing down.

Wyatt's stride matched his until he turned in under a large brass sign—Wells Fargo Bank. "Just what do you have in mind?"

"I have a little saved up."

Wyatt stopped. "Your land."

"Never said for sure I'd use it on the land. This seems as good a reason as any."

"Is there enough?"

Caleb shook his head. "'Bout half. Enough to tease them, or stall for more time."

Wyatt's gaze narrowed on him.

"Say it," Caleb said. "You think I'm crazy."

"You're taking a big risk. You're good at reading people—you'd have to be with your job—but this isn't some squabble over a card game. This is a woman's life we're talking about."

"Think I don't know that?"

"Houston—they will expect full payment. Understand your options here. You may end up paying the balance in blood."

"And Hannah's in the thick of it." He didn't want to hear any more reasons to move cautiously. He stormed up to the teller's window and gave the small mustached man standing there his name. "Withdraw all of it."

The teller hurried over to the vault.

"Are you sure about this, Caleb?" Wyatt asked.

"I'm not waiting to find out if Dorian or Rowlings comes through. There's no time for that."

Wyatt studied him. "Whoever wrote that note could slit your throat as soon as you hand over your money."

"I know. It's a risk. But my entire life has been a risk of one sort or another. This one is worth it to me."

"It is if you love her."

Caleb went still. He wasn't ready to admit anything, especially not to Wyatt. The man was his boss, not his buddy. "Look, I let her down. I'm the one she came to for help, and I gave her my word. This is my responsibility."

"Is that all she is to you?" Wyatt probed.

Caleb frowned. "That's all she can be. She's marrying Rowlings."

"And you're willing to die for another man's woman?"

The teller thrust a note across the counter. Caleb scrawled his signature, grabbed the small sack of money and headed for the door.

Outside in the bright sunlight, he turned on Wyatt. "Sure, I have feelings for her. Strong ones. Plain enough? It doesn't change a thing." He spun on his heel and strode back to the saloon, not caring if Wyatt followed or not. He'd said enough. They'd both said enough. And he wanted answers, not needling.

Once inside the saloon, Caleb slammed the money bag into the safe behind the bar. He spun the combination lock thrice, and then gave it one more turn with a vengeance. He hated feeling helpless. He needed to snap out of it. Needed to think clearly.

"I could use a drink," he said, rising from his crouched position at the safe. He rounded the end of the bar and drew two beers on tap, shoving one to Wyatt.

Wyatt took a swig. "I figured it was something like that."

Caleb matched him, taking a long draw on his drink. He plunked the mug on the bar, watching the amber liquid slosh to the rim.

He'd meet with her captors tonight—and hopefully live to tell about it. What they might be doing to Hannah—the horror she could be facing even now—scared the juices right out of him. He had to get her back, had to tell her he was sorry and he had to tell her he loved her. If it took the rest of his life, he'd make this up to her.

He glanced at the safe. It was money he'd been saving—for land, or a business venture or...*something*. Four thousand dollars and some change. Opportunities had come up every now and then, but for some reason he couldn't part with the money. Something had always felt wrong. He didn't have that ominous feeling now. Maybe this was what he'd been saving it for all along. For Hannah. "There's enough to bluff with and that's all," he said, thinking out loud.

"Might buy you some time," Wyatt murmured. "You'll have to negotiate. Unfortunately, patience never has been one of your finer skills."

Caleb scowled. "There's always a first time."

Chapter Fourteen

A cool breeze raised goose bumps on Hannah's damp skin. The vague odor of ammonia mixed with sweat and the tickle of Caleb's whiskers confused her dream. Something was wrong. She needed to open her eyes. Instead she licked her lips and tasted salt on the cracked, dry skin. Nearby, the low rumble of voices came to her, along with the keening cry of a gull.

"She awake?" a man asked.

"Yes, sir," a boy's voice answered, higher pitched than the other. "I done just like you told me."

Someone grunted.

"So I go with you next time." Again—the boy's voice.

"You know that's up to the cap'n."

Another voice spoke. "Bad luck bringing her here. Mark my words. Cap'n shoulda known better."

Captain?

She opened her eyes. Pink light filtered over her knuckles and onto the rocky ground. A stone's throw away, the outlines of two men and the boy emerged. They sat on small boulders that surrounded a fire pit. One poked a long stick at the charred remains of a cook fire. Above his head, the rock ceiling was blackened with smoke.

Hannah's pulse quickened. She pushed up on her elbow. Not a cave!

The boy rose from his seat. His sun-bleached hair hung in oily snakes to his shoulders. His pants and shirt, streaked with dirt and sweat, would make better rags than clothes.

She had to get out! She scrambled to her feet and, for the first time, realized she was barefoot. It didn't matter! Memories of another time, another cave overwhelmed her. She must get out!

She raced toward the opening. Behind her, the men emitted surprised guffaws.

Following a narrow worn path between two hillsides, she picked her way along. Sharp rocks and nettles scraped and cut her skin. The path ended abruptly—with the sea. She tried to block out the panic threatening inside.

To each side of her, a steep, shrub-covered hill rose high above the sea's surface. Everywhere else, indeed to the horizon where the sun hovered, was the ocean. A peninsula? A sliver of hope pumped through her. Perhaps near the lighthouse? But then, why did nothing look familiar?

She listened, straining to hear the sound of pursuers, only to hear nothing but the wind and birds. Where were those who had taken her? Why go to that trouble only to let her leave? She crouched and removed a thorn in the arch of her foot. Blood smeared across her skin.

"You were better off asleep."

She froze.

The boy squatted on the hillside but twenty feet away. "You don't look like you're worth ten thousand."

A ransom? That's what this was about?

"Me name's Jamie. A word to the wise considerin' that there foot. Blood draws sharks like honey draws bees. I wouldn't consider swimmin' if I was you." He jumped down from his perch and stuffed a short dagger into his pants waist.

The breeze chilled her damp skin. She shivered and then hugged herself while he walked away. Why would she swim? And why was he leaving? Wasn't he worried she'd try to escape? She glanced up the hill. Unless…

Stealing herself against the punishment her feet would take, she grasped a clump of weeds and started to climb. One hundred feet from the path, she came to the top of the small ridge. The sun shone on the hill and beyond, sparkling over a wide expanse of ocean all the way to a long white strip of mainland—so far away.

Hot tears burned in her eyes. No wonder the men hadn't worried that she'd escape. She plopped down. What now? What was she to do now?

Did Caleb even know she'd been kidnapped? If only she could hope for that. But after the words they'd spoken, he probably thought she'd left of her own accord. More than likely he'd washed his hands of her. She wouldn't blame him if he did. Once again, she'd chosen family—Dorian—over him.

The sun sank below the horizon and immediately the air cooled further. Staying outside wasn't an option any longer. Rising to her feet, she made her way back to the cave. As she entered, the men finished their argument, the shorter one squinting his eyes at her.

"Well, looky here. 'Bout time you came back. Got a good look about, did you?" His harsh laugh ended as he doubled over in a violent coughing spasm. The sound sent shivers through her. When he straightened, he spat a wad of brown juice on the rock at her feet.

He stepped over to a large barrel near the wall and grabbed a cup from inside it. A steady drip, drip, drip pinged into the barrel from the roof of the cave. He dipped out a cupful of water. Disgust rippled through her.

The man leered at her. "Why don't you ask for it?"

She wouldn't give him the satisfaction. She was thirsty, but the thought of drinking from the same barrel—with the same cup—made her nauseous. She opened her mouth to speak, but no sound came out.

"Go ahead. Beg me for a drink."

She'd dry up and blow away before she'd do that. Stubbornly she closed her mouth. Yet a slow panic began to build inside. Why couldn't she talk?

She was scared. That was all. When she calmed down, the words would come.

An interested gleam came into his eyes. "Don't think I've ever known a woman to be quiet before. Not in a situation like this. Usually they scream—or whimper like pups. But then, they don't have your history."

There had been others? And what fate had they met? Then the full import of his words hit her. He knew her past! He knew about her, yet she didn't remember him.

"Leave her be, Teddy."

"Quit actin' like you're boss. I don't answer to no one but the cap'n."

The larger man shrugged and tossed a small log into the fire pit. "Get this going, Jamie."

"Yes, sir, Barker." The boy took up a metal box from a ledge and began striking it with flint over and over, trying to coax a spark from it. Before long, a steady thread of smoke drifted toward the ceiling, and then a flame caught hold and burned.

As the fire grew, she looked around her and began to make out large shapes toward the back of the cave. Boxes and crates. A small boat's anchor and chain. Large white sails. A wooden crate with the words *Lansing Enterprises* stamped on the side.

Anger rippled through her. Her grandfather's wares! What of the sailors and the captain? Were they all dead? Or was the reason this man knew so much about her because he sailed on the ships?

"Figured it out, missy?" The thief called Teddy jabbed a dirty finger at her shoulder. "Took you long enough. I figured you for smarter."

The man's touch felt like evil crawling on her skin. She jerked away, stumbling on the uneven ground. A yellow, toothy grin stretched over his face. "Guess you noticed the ships didn't go down in a storm."

Hannah's heartbeat quickened. They weren't even trying to keep it from her. They didn't care if she saw everything! Which meant they never planned to let her go—ransom or not.

Teddy took a menacing step toward her.

"Stand back," Barker said, speaking in a commanding voice from the shadows. "And shut yer trap."

"Just havin' fun. That grandfather dotes on her.

You said so yourself. He'll pay no matter how she is returned." He snickered. "If she is returned."

"The captain will decide. Not you."

Teddy scowled but moved back to the tiny fire and cuffed Jamie. "Hurry up."

Her legs suddenly weak, Hannah sank back against the damp rock. They didn't mean to honor their ransom pact. She'd never get away. Never see her grandfather again. Drawing her knees up, she wrapped her arms around them.

It wasn't her grandfather she wanted to see, she realized. It was Caleb. Caleb would know how to handle these men. She'd never felt so safe as when she was with him.

Where was he in all this?

Fifteen minutes early. Caleb jerked the collar of his leather coat up against the chill of the damp night air and scanned the deserted dock. Wind whipped the iron triangle at the pier, its striking bar dangling from a weathered rope. It was strangely silent. No sound, no clanging interrupted the darkness except for the creaking and groaning of an old fishing trawler tied along the wharf.

Caleb paced the width of the dock, on edge, alert for the slightest movement. When ten minutes had come and gone, an old man shuffled from the shadows. A rim of straggly hair hung from his head to his thin shoulders. After eyeing

Caleb and noting the sack he held, the man raised a gnarled hand. "Yer to follow me."

"Is Miss Lansing all right?"

"Don't know and wouldn't say if I did. I don't ask questions, just follow orders, and you'd be wise to do the same."

Caleb tightened his grip on the burlap and looked once more for any more men lurking in the shadows. This fellow wasn't big enough to kidnap a child, let alone Hannah if she put up a fight.

"I will take that gun."

His hand went to his piece. "I prefer to keep it."

"Then, we aren't goin' anywhere."

Caleb had expected to lose his firearm at some point—just not to a man half his size. He had the feeling this guy didn't have any idea where Hannah was being held and was just a go-between—like the boy who'd brought the ransom note. Threatening him wouldn't answer any of the questions he had. Caleb drew his Colt from its holster and handed it over. The man stuffed it under his arm and started walking.

Caleb followed him along the waterfront a piece, and then through several back streets until they entered the Stingaree district. His guide stopped in front of an old two-story shingled house with round Chinese lanterns hanging from the porch.

When Caleb followed him inside, ducking through the door, he felt as if he'd entered a different world. A few widely spaced candelabras lent flickering golden light to the shadowed parlor. Deep red swaths of fabric covered the windows, blocking out any moonlight and interested views from the street. The overwhelming scent of opium hung low in the air. A woman in a shimmery, formfitting black dress stood behind the brocade settee and massaged a cowboy's shoulders. The bored expression on her painted face disappeared when she noticed Caleb, sizing him up with interest, and then she returned to her task, trailing her long bloodred nails along the man's neck.

Caleb's guide nudged him through the house to the kitchen and indicated a table and chairs. "Wait here."

Caleb settled onto a chair. A burly man stood by the back door, his arms crossed over his chest. Caleb recognized the stance of a seasoned guard. He'd stood just that way hundreds of nights at Wyatt's establishments contemplating what he'd do with the money he had saved up while keeping his eyes open for the start of arguments. That was the only way he could have stayed sane into the witching hours of the night.

Tonight any dreams for that money would take a walk out that door. Well, so be it. Hadn't his life been like a deck of cards? One minute all aces and kings and the next minute reshuffled and holdin' deuces.

Being straight with himself, he didn't want Dorian to put up the cash, whether the man was able to or not. Course, all the man had to do was sell his last ship—or his mansion—and he'd be solvent. But that took time—something Hannah didn't have. And it was his own fault Hannah had been taken. So it was his problem. He was the one who had to find the solution.

He still couldn't get over the fact that for a moment that morning, before the world had crowded in, Hannah had wanted him. *Him!* She'd ignored her overactive conscience and for once let herself feel.

What had Dorian done to her and for how long to make her believe her emotions, her gut instincts, were so wrong? Was he trying to mold her into a female version of himself?

He frowned. Rachel *had* tried to tell him things weren't good for Hannah at home, but he'd been so angry at the way Hannah had treated him that he'd shut everything else out. Guess it didn't matter much now. Nothing mattered anymore but finding her. Fast.

He tapped his heel on the plank floor. This sitting and waiting had him itching for action. Wyatt's words about being impatient came back to haunt him, and he tried to stop the telltale sign.

He wouldn't give Hannah up without a fight. Not to these clowns and not to Rowlings either.

Could you give her up if it is what she wants?

The thought stymied him. That was asking too much. If he got her back he'd never let her go. Somehow, he'd find a way to make her stay.

You'd make her live above the saloon? You think she'd be happy? She was accustomed to a soft brass bed and tea parties and dresses for every day of the week. Why would she choose to stay with him? He didn't have a thing he could give her that Rowlings couldn't give tenfold over him. She'd never choose him—not in a million years. He was foolin' himself to think otherwise.

The iron knob on the back door jiggled. Caleb pushed all errant thoughts aside and readied himself. He couldn't be swayed by anything other than getting to Hannah. Time enough later to figure out where she stood in his life.

The guard stepped aside, and a man entered—heavyset, with a bulldog face and short, scraggly black beard that didn't match his body. He carried a knife with a wide blade slung low on his hips, and with a quick glance took note of Caleb's weapon on the hutch. Caleb reached forward and turned up the wick on the oil lamp. When the light illuminated his features, Caleb recognized him. "Corcoran."

A condescending smirk curled the edges of the man's thick lips.

"Been a long time," Caleb said.

"Probably not long enough by your yardstick.

I owe you for that decking you gave me," Corcoran growled.

"If I remember right, you had it coming. You still thick with Trask?"

Corcoran's gaze narrowed. "I see you brought the money."

Caleb raised his bag and lowered it, tucking it into his gut protectively. With his boot, he shoved out the chair across the table from him. "I want answers first." He figured his only chance—Hannah's only chance—was if he took control of the situation from the outset.

Corcoran ignored the chair. "In case you haven't noticed, you ain't in a position to bargain."

"So how do I know you really have her?"

The man spit a wad of tobacco juice on the floor. "Might just have to take my word on it."

"Now, there's an encouraging thought—believing the word of a thief."

"I wouldn't start name-callin' if I was in your position. From what I hear, she was sittin' mighty close to you last night. Lansing know about that? Not that I blame you. She's a pretty little thing. Hardly struggled at all when I nabbed her. Soft, too."

The man was trying to get him riled. Unfortunately, it was working. That this ape had even touched Hannah made Caleb want to smash him into the floorboards. "Like I said—how do I know you really have her?"

A wicked smile spilled over his opponent's meaty face. "I figured you'd want some kind of proof. Thought about cutting off her finger—"

Caleb's stomach turned over.

"Oh. She needs those fingers, don't she? Can't talk without them, poor thing. Least not now."

How much did this man know of Hannah's past? And hadn't she screamed or tried to bargain her way out of his grasp when he'd nabbed her?

Corcoran slapped his hand on the table, keeping something covered, and watched Caleb closely. It could be a finger or it could be nothing under his palm. This was a game to him—a stinking game! But until Caleb knew where he held Hannah, he had to play along no matter how his stomach roiled at the thought.

With another smirk, the wharf rat slowly raised his hand. The abalone-and-silver pendant gleamed back at Caleb. His gut clenched even as he reached for the necklace and curled his fingers around the shell, which was, ironically, their good-luck piece.

"I'll take that money now."

Caleb dropped the burlap bag on the table.

Corcoran grabbed hold of the sack and tossed it to the guard. "Count it."

Caleb wrestled with whether to tell him right off that it wasn't the complete amount or whether to let him add it up and hopefully discover Hannah's whereabouts during the counting.

"You've got your money," he said. "When do I get Miss Lansing…and where?"

Corcoran held up his hand. "Time enough for answers."

Caleb had waited long enough. He nodded at the guard. "You won't find all of it there."

Corcoran drew his dark brows together. "Part's not what I asked for. Lansing can afford my asking price."

"Yes, but he's not here. And wiring that much takes time. A man in your position should know that."

Corcoran picked up the pistol and waved it about carelessly. "You're uppity for someone who's on the wrong end of this."

Caleb shrugged, although a deep-burning anger was taking hold of him. "You don't want to do that. Kidnapping is one thing. Murder is another thing altogether. You'll hang for murder."

Corcoran ignored him and turned to the guard. "How much?"

"Four thousand."

"Tsk. Tsk." He shook his head in an exaggerated move. "Not even half."

Caleb stared down the barrel of a rusty S&W revolver. His pulse jumped up a notch. "I brought all that was here in the bank. The rest is being wired from San Francisco. You need to give me more time."

Now the wavering metal pointed at his gut instead of his chest. He resisted the urge to wrestle it from the man's hand. He figured he could overpower the wharf rat, but the guard was another matter entirely—and it didn't mean either would give up the information he wanted.

"Miss Lansing don't have time. She's a good-lookin' wench, if you know what I mean."

Caleb thought he might vomit. He knew exactly what the man meant. "I expect her to be returned undamaged. That's what Lansing is paying for."

The man's brows drew up. "Undamaged. Now, there's a laugh. It's no secret she was with you all night. Ironic, ain't it? She was stolen right out from under you. What did Old Ironhead have to say about that?"

Caleb wanted to climb over the table and ram a fist through the man's face. Instead his mind caught on the fact that the man had called Lansing by his unofficial nickname.

"Sounds like you know Lansing."

Corcoran grunted. "We have a history. Goes back a few years."

Nothing connected this man with the downed ships—only with Hannah's kidnapping. Corcoran could just be after the Lansing money because of Hannah's name. Then again, two people might be all it would take to kidnap a woman and demand ransom, but it would take far more than that to sink a ship of seaworthy sailors. He needed to find out who else was in on this.

"The money won't go far, split between the rest," Caleb said, hoping to get more information. "And the leader will take the larger share."

"Enough talkin', Houston. We're leaving," Corcoran said to the guard. "Tie him."

The guard whipped out a thin hemp rope from the hutch and grabbed Caleb's arms.

This wasn't in Caleb's plans. How could he follow them if he was tied? He felt the jerk as the guard tightened the knot and yanked on the rope. "Wait just a minute! I kept your demands. No one followed me."

"Not my problem. Why should I care how you come out of this—or if you come out at all?"

"You surprise me, Corcoran. You know I'll tell the authorities the minute I get free."

Corcoran paused. Turned.

"Lansing's not stupid. And he'll never stop trying to find you. You'll be looking over your shoulder the rest of your life—even if Miss Lansing is returned without a scratch."

"Well, then…we ain't leavin' you behind. You're insurance—at least until I see the rest of the money. After that?" Corcoran shrugged, then stuffed his gun in the waistband of his canvas pants and nodded to the guard. "Bring him."

The guard hoisted Caleb to his feet.

"Sure you're not after her for yourself?" Corcoran sniggered and held up the bag. "I thank ye for unloading this little bit of pleasure. It'll keep the crew satisfied for a day or two."

So there was Caleb's answer. Corcoran had to be involved with the disappearance of Dorian's ships, and since he and Hannah were suspicious of that, they were a liability—a liability that would have to be dealt with. If Caleb didn't escape, he was as good as dead—and Hannah, too.

Chapter Fifteen

Hannah wanted to gag. The spicy scent of food could not disguise the odor of unwashed bodies sitting across from her. A few feet away, the two men shoved their supper of refried beans, cheese and tortillas down their throats, oblivious to her discomfort.

A bell clanged twice in the distance. At the sound, the thieves ate faster, as though fearful the food would be snatched away. The boy, Jamie, walked over with a small plate of food. When she didn't take it from him, he set it on the rocky ground in front of her. "Suit yerself. But there's no more vittles till tomorrow unless Cap'n brings some."

No sooner had the words been uttered than a band of rough-looking men filed into the cave. Hannah counted eight as they settled on the floor or any available flat rock. Scruffy and smelly, they ranged from thin and wiry to hulking.

One man with a gray beard carried in a sack and tossed it at Teddy. "Be quick about it."

"Yes, sir, Mr. Trask." Teddy moved to the back of the cave and opened the bag. Immediately movement in the bag turned into the distressed squawking of birds. He reached in and pulled out one disoriented chicken. With a twist of his hands, he snapped the bird's neck and tossed it to Jamie. The boy plopped down on a rock and began plucking out feathers. Teddy did likewise with the next chicken and worked on his bird while keeping a foot on the opening of the flailing sack.

A dark-haired, heavyset man strode into the cave. By his air of authority and the deference the others gave him, Hannah realized he must be the captain. He wore a cream-colored linen shirt with sweat stains under the arms. On the sleeves, gold nuggets took the place of cuff links. His black pants, frayed at the hem and nearly worn through in the seat, were a size too big.

Trask leaned in and said something to him in a low voice.

"Well and good," the captain answered him, although he kept his gaze on her. He walked toward Hannah. "Hope yer enjoyin' your stay, Miss Lansing. Don't usually entertain a lady here."

The evil smile that crawled onto his face made the back of her neck tingle. "From what I hear tell, Dorian Lansing is in a bit of a money bind.

O'course, our activities might have had something to do with that." He chuckled—a cold, mirthless bark of a sound as he circled her, looking her over from her toes up. "I had a brace o' words with your bodyguard. Took guts to face me without all of the ransom money. I'll give him that. Guts—or he's a bigger fool than I remember."

Bodyguard? Caleb? A hundred questions formed on the tip of her tongue. Where was he now? Was he safe? And how did this man know him?

The captain's eyes glittered black and cold, and she had the feeling he knew exactly what was going through her head. An involuntary shiver coursed through her. This was not someone to bargain with—and Caleb had tried.

He motioned to the back of the cave. A scuffle ensued until a man hidden in the shadows was forcibly yanked into the light of the fire. Hannah recognized him even though a cloth covered his eyes. His stance, his clothes, were familiar. Caleb.

She started toward him.

"Hold!" A hand shot out and blocked her path. The captain yanked her by the arm. "Where do you think you're going?"

She stumbled and then regained her footing. Cruel laughter echoed off the walls of the cave.

"You'll face me when I'm talkin' to you, missy." He backhanded her.

Too shocked to cry out, she palmed her stinging cheek. Hot tears pooled in her eyes.

"Now we understand each other. Nothin' like a bit of discipline to smooth the way. You'd best get used to the rules here. I make 'em and no one is comin' for you. No one knows you're here except Houston. And he's in no position to help. He doesn't even know where we are."

He nodded to Caleb's guard, who removed the cloth. "Well, you've seen for yourself that Captain Corcoran is a man of his word. Nary a hair touched on her rich little head."

Caleb's initial relief at finding Hannah alive quickly gave way to anger. A reddened blotch stained her right cheek. Her hair hung unkempt and tangled down her back. Bruises formed on her arms. The blouse she wore was wrinkled and stained with dirt, and was that a bare toe that peeked out from beneath her skirt? A bloody bare toe.

Yet, it was her face—those large gray eyes surrounded by dark lashes—that haunted him. Frightened. Scared. A wounded animal.

Any illusions she might have had about decent treatment because of her background had been shattered. And the cave—it would have to be a cave of all places—did it remind her of the other time? The other cave she'd been trapped in? No wonder she wasn't talking.

"You and I have differing opinions on that," Caleb said, answering Corcoran's claims of decent treatment.

Corcoran scowled. "That weren't rough. She'll know it when I'm rough."

"You've got the money now—and more is being wired. Let her go. I'll take her back to her grandfather—and disappear."

"I took you for a smarter man." Corcoran released his grip on Hannah and motioned to Trask. "Keep an eye on them." Then he strode over to the fire. The other men gathered around him, and Caleb could feel anticipation in the air. They were planning something. Although Corcoran spoke in a voice too low to decipher the words, the subject held their interest.

"Don't get no ideas, Houston," Trask said. "You were quick enough with your fists at one time, and I ain't no fool." He turned and headed back to the rest of the men.

Left alone, or nearly so, Caleb strode over to Hannah and searched her face.

She gripped his leather jacket, clinging to him as if he was a buoy and the sharks were circling. She buried her face in his jacket.

He didn't move. He was someone familiar— that was all. This was nothing more than her relief at seeing someone she knew among such men. It couldn't mean she might finally be realizing there was a heck of a lot more between them. If he thought that, he might go soft. And going soft wouldn't help them escape.

But she wasn't talking, and that got to him. He raised his arms, still tied at the wrists, and circled them around her. "Don't fade on me now, Hannah," he murmured close to her ear. "We have to figure a way out."

She shivered, and in response, he pulled her closer. Her skin was cold. He hoped, holding her, that some of his warmth would penetrate.

"Aw, looky here," Trask said, loudly enough for the men to hear and turn to look. "A hoity-toity gettin' all wet-eyed over a bar bruiser." He sauntered over to them and took hold of Hannah's chin, forcing her to look at him. "Maybe you'd enjoy a little attention from me. I got skills you ain't never experienced."

Hannah stiffened within Caleb's arms and pressed even closer to him. Her eyes flashed with anger, which she quickly banked. Good. She would need that fire inside to escape.

He curled his hands into fists, ready to fight. Didn't matter that he was tied. But he couldn't protect her properly bound like this. Reluctantly, he moved his arms from around her and stepped back slightly. He had to be ready in case something happened.

She took hold of his hands, turning them over, staring at the raw and bloodied skin of his wrists, then began tugging and working at the ropes binding him.

"Here, now! None of that!" Trask said, shoving the butt of his rifle against Caleb's back, separating him from Hannah. Then he pushed him to the far side of the cave.

Those who had stopped to watch turned back to their discussion. Caleb waited until he was sure Trask was going to leave her alone, and then he sat down on a nearby rock. It was just as well. He couldn't think with her in his arms. And he needed to think. Needed to figure out an escape.

Where were they? Once he'd been blindfolded, Corcoran had forced him onto his ship. The trip to this cave had taken a few hours. Was he along the coast? North or south?

The men cooked hunks of chicken meat on sticks at the fire. The odor of cooking meat filled the cave. Firelight flickered along the walls, illuminating crevices he hadn't noticed before and distorting the men's faces into grotesque monsters.

Jamie approached Hannah and extended a small cooked portion of meat. "Captain said you're to have some."

At first she didn't take the food. Jamie stepped closer. "Be quick about it. He'll see if you don't, and then there'll be blood to pay. Both o' ours."

Caleb was relieved to see she tore off a bite-size portion of meat and popped it into her mouth. She'd need that to sustain her.

"Barker and Teddy will stay behind," the captain said, loud enough for Caleb to hear. "Sorry you'll miss the fun, men."

He didn't look sorry at all.

"Barker, hail me when you spot the ship."

Ship? Caleb tensed. What was happening?

Corcoran walked up to Hannah. "Guess you don't remember me. You were a little princess when I worked for your grandfather—no more than a yardstick. It were only a brief spell. Old Ironhead thought I was stealin' from him. A little here. A little there. He had no proof, but he let me go. And me with a wife and baby to look after."

Corcoran's voice dropped low as he spoke, but Caleb heard the banked anger, not wholly under control.

"Where is your family now?" he asked.

Corcoran's eye narrowed, but he turned away from Hannah. "Gone. Disappeared. All because of a Lansing. So you see, I have me own score to settle."

He expelled a grunt and then raised his voice to address his men. "This'll be our last sting for a while, men. Things are getting too hot. After this, we lie low."

A sharp whistle pierced the air. The sailors stood and headed for the cave entrance. Jamie jumped up to join them. With his thick arm against the boy's gut, the captain blocked his way.

"You said I could go!" Jamie said indignantly.

"Changed me mind."

"Well, I ain't stayin'! I always have to stay."

"Last time I checked, I was the captain. You'll do as I say."

"I'm sick o' bein' left behind like a girl!" He doubled his hands into fists ready to fight.

The captain smirked. "Try it, Jamie. I'm waitin'."

The boy glared at Corcoran, a man twice his size. Although his chin quivered, his eyes held mutiny.

"Your duty is to guard the woman—along with Barker and Teddy. Do your job well and you'll get a portion of the take. Otherwise…nothing." He released Jamie. "Get a move on, men. Don't want to be late to our own party!"

Jamie turned away, his gaze colliding with Caleb's. He set his jaw. "What're you lookin' at?" He stomped to the fire pit and scowled into it.

The cave finally emptied except for those who were to stay behind and the captain. Corcoran spoke in low tones to Trask, giving last-minute instructions. Hannah glanced over at Caleb, sitting with his back against the far wall, his knees drawn up. She couldn't quite make out his face, half-hidden in shadow, but a movement between his knees caught her attention. She focused on his hands.

Ship. Stuart, he signed.

Her heart quickened. Corcoran planned to attack Stuart's ship?

Caleb's subtle nod convinced her. But how did they know he was coming? How— Then she realized…Mr. Webberly—or someone else in the port authority office—had learned of it. Perhaps Stuart had telegraphed ahead to say to expect him. Perhaps Grandfather's telegram to her had been intercepted. It could be any number of ways that Corcoran knew.

This was personal. And Corcoran would not stop his rampage until every last one of Grandfather's ships met its end at the bottom of the sea.

What can we do? she signed back to Caleb.

The thieves had already scuttled two Lansing ships and crew. They had the process perfected. Lethal mercenaries with no conscience—they would have the element of surprise on their side and strike under the cover of darkness. How could Stuart and his crew stand against them?

A shadow fell between them. Trask stopped in front of Caleb. "Get up. Yer coming."

Caleb didn't budge. "I'm not going anywhere without Miss Lansing."

"Not your decision." Trask hauled him to his feet and stood nose to nose with him. "Captain's orders."

This couldn't be happening. What would happen to Caleb? He knew so much now—too much.

"You created your problems when you kidnapped Miss Lansing. I'm not moving from here without her."

Trask snorted. "You're talkin' like you have a choice. You don't." Trask leaned close to Caleb's ear, but he made no effort to lower his voice. He intended Hannah to hear. "We're cleanin' house tonight, if you know what I mean. Would you have her witness your end? Won't be pretty."

Caleb met her gaze. Frustration, longing—it was all written in that look. Whatever he had done, whatever would happen next, was all because he loved her. She didn't need sign language to understand.

And she'd taken that precious emotion and stomped on it—once years ago and a second time just this morning. She hated herself for that.

Why had he come after her? Why? After all she'd done to hurt him, she didn't deserve it. She'd never deserved him.

She trembled, barely able to draw a breath. She had to tell him, had to let him know that she believed in him.

That she loved him.

"Move it!" With a hand to his upper back, Trask shoved Caleb forward. Caleb tightened his jaw, his face firming with resolve. With one last look at her, he headed outside.

She watched until his silhouette faded into the darkness. What would become of him? Could she do anything, anything at all to help him? To help Stuart? Sinking back to the damp floor of the cave, her thoughts raced. How had she come to be here? There had to be a second ship—or boat. Could she find it and use it to escape? At the thought, bile rose in her throat. She'd have to. No matter her fear of the water. Somehow, she'd have to overcome it.

But where would she go? To the mainland? How would that help Caleb? Or Stuart?

Stuart was heading straight into an ambush. He had no idea these men were lying in wait and would attack. They would scuttle his ship—just as they'd sunk the *Margarita* and the *Rose*. And they would kill him and his crew without a second thought. Even using the small boat, she wouldn't be able to beat the thieves' ship to the *Tourmaline*. It was foolish to consider it. Her eyes burned with frustration. There had to be a way—if only she could figure it out.

Barker threw a cursory glance her way before joining Teddy at the fire. They spoke in voices so low she couldn't make out what they said, but it sounded as though they were hatching plans. Every once in a while, one of them would chuckle. Even that sounded sinister.

She drew her knees up, rested her chin on them and stared at the fire. The warmth of the flames did not reach her, and she welcomed the cold. She deserved the cold. At least she *could* feel. But what she felt was small, and miserable, and... and hopeless.

This was where her impulsiveness had led her—running from a marriage she didn't want, thinking herself smart enough to untangle the mystery of the lost ships. In the process she'd risked the lives of those she truly treasured— Stuart and Caleb.

The flames danced, causing the shadows on the walls of the cave to leap and dive. She rubbed her sore cheek, all the while keeping a wary eye on the two men and Jamie. She didn't want any more of their hospitality. Whatever she figured out, if they caught her, she wouldn't get off so easily again.

Maybe that was the problem. She was only thinking of herself.

Her mind fixed on the thought. She was only thinking of herself. Just like when she'd been so determined to get her voice back. She'd thought only of herself then, and look what it had cost her in the end. Caleb. Others were risking their lives for her, and here she was thinking again of herself. Hadn't she learned anything? Thinking about what would happen to her would only hinder her. At this point, if she saw morning alive, it would be a miracle.

She said a quick prayer for Stuart and for

Caleb—lingering a bit on Caleb's image in her mind. Twenty-four hours ago she'd been in his arms—safe and protected. It seemed like a lifetime ago. What she wouldn't give for one more chance to be there again.

A sharp hiss drew her attention to the fire. Both men hovered around Jamie. "That's the last piece o' bird, and it's mine!" Barker said, a warning in his voice.

"I pulled out the feathers. I'm the one should get more."

"You're not big enough to have more."

Jamie ran to the other side of the fire and then inched toward the cave's opening.

"Where you going, boy? You know there ain't no escape."

Like an ambushed rabbit, Jamie froze against the cave wall.

Watching the scenario play out in front of her, Hannah was truly worried for the boy. Barker approached him, twice his size, with a menacing look to his dark eyes. "You shouldn't o' caused such a snit. Captain don't like to be questioned—especially in front of his crew. You know the penalty. Now, be a man and take your due."

Hannah rose to her feet. Dread spiraled inside.

Teddy took hold of her arm. "Don't get any ideas about leaving." A leer replaced Teddy's usual grumpy countenance. "Don't worry. Barker will take care o' things just fine."

Jamie tried to duck and run, but Barker caught him and circled his fingers around the boy's neck. Reckless power shone in Barker's beady eyes as he raised the boy up. Jamie grasped Barker's forearms, his face turning red and then pale. His hands dropped to his sides.

"Stop!" she rasped out. "You're hurting him!" She twisted her arm, trying desperately to wrench free.

Teddy studied her. "I see you got your voice back. Just funnin' us before?"

She snarled and scratched his face with her nails.

Surprised, he let go.

Scrambling to the fire, she picked up the end of a glowing log and raced toward Barker and Jamie. "Stop!" she cried out, her voice still hoarse. "Stop!"

Barker ignored her, too engrossed in his domination of Jamie. With all her might, she dashed the heavy log down on the larger man. He stumbled, then lost his footing and crashed to the ground.

"Eh! What are you doing?" Teddy yanked the log from her hands. "Looks like ye got a champion, Jamie. A lassie!" he chortled. "Won't help you none, though."

Jamie's color went from blue to pale. Hannah breathed a sigh of relief.

"Barker! Get up, you worthless sea cod." Teddy

jostled his fallen comrade with his boot. The larger man groaned, turning slightly, but didn't open his eyes. Something dark and wet smeared along the ground under his head.

Teddy turned on her. "He'll have a headache for sure, missy. And you'll pay. Ain't no one to help you now."

Jamie leaped onto Teddy's back and held his knife to the man's neck. Teddy grabbed Jamie's hand, but his grip on the log compromised his balance.

Quickly, Hannah dashed the log from his hands, turned it around and tilted the burning end into Teddy's chest. The old cotton shirt caught fire. Teddy stumbled backward, and as Jamie jumped from his back, Teddy fell backward onto the cave floor. "Yer done now! Both of ye!" Teddy roared. He batted at the flames racing up the cloth on his arm and chest.

Jamie tugged on Hannah's arm, pulling her along. "We gotta get out of here!"

He would help her? It took a moment for the realization to sink in. He would help her! But leaving wouldn't help Stuart or Caleb.

"What are you doin'?" Jamie cried, already at the cave's entrance. "I ain't waiting! If they catch us, they'll kill us for sure." He took off running.

She stared at Teddy, writhing on the ground with flames and smoke billowing from his clothing and choking up the cave. A fire! A warning fire! That was it!

She raced back, skirting around Teddy, and grabbed a handful of small sticks and kindling from a pile near the fire pit. Making a sling of her skirt, she tossed twigs and kindling into the gathers, then picked up another large burning stick from the fire. With a prayer on her lips, she raced outside.

There was enough of a moon to see—although darkly. Jamie had jumped in a boat and was untying the lines that held it moored. "Get in!"

She watched for a split second. It was so tempting to do just that—jump in and get as far away as possible. But if she did that, she wouldn't be able to live with herself. And she'd had enough of regrets. Stuart must be warned, and she was the only one to do it. "Get out of here, Jamie. Save yourself. I…I can't go with you."

She turned toward the hill behind her.

"Teddy'll be upon us!" Jamie called, frantically hoisting the two sails.

"There's something I have to do. Just go."

She clambered up the side of the hill, gritting her teeth against the sting of cutting thorns and jagged rocks. She had to get above the line of sea spray. As it was, the constant dampness in the air would make it hard enough to start a fire and keep it burning.

At a point halfway up the hillside, she dropped

the smaller sticks from her skirt, pushing them under a pile of brush. She stuffed the burning stick into the mix. *Please, catch on! Don't go out! Stuart must see the fire.* A small stream of white smoke trailed upward in the moonlight.

"You stupid dame! You'll pay for what you've done."

At the harsh voice, Hannah spun around. A dark figure climbed toward her.

"Where do you think you have to run?" Teddy said with a sarcastic snarl. He ripped the burning stick from her hand and threw it far down the hill. Then grasped her arm and pulled her back to the patch of brush she'd ignited. The flames sputtered, unable to catch on completely. Teddy stomped on the glowing embers.

"No!" she exclaimed.

"You're not going anywhere. You or the boy—"

Jamie! Hannah peered down the hillside, able to make out the boat's sail bobbing in the night. "What have you done to him? Jamie!" she yelled. "Run! Get out of here!" It was his only chance.

Teddy backhanded her and sent her flying. "That'll teach you."

Her vision darkened.

Just then a wild yell pierced the air and Jamie appeared out of the dark, flinging himself against the larger man. The two grappled—the outcome inevitable. Hannah screamed and rushed to help Jamie, but slipped on some loose gravel and skidded to the ground. Sitting down hard, she grabbed a handful of pebbles and pitched them into Teddy's face.

He howled and rubbed his eyes. At the same time, Jamie rammed into him like a young bull.

On the steep hillside the larger man stumbled, flailing his arms for balance. His foot slipped out from under him. He reached for Jamie, gripping his shirt.

"No!" Hannah scrambled to her feet and beat on the man's arm. "Let go!"

Crying out, the brute did just that. Momentum suspended him in midair. He reached again for Jamie. With a cry, Hannah pulled Jamie to her. Teddy tumbled down the steep hillside. A moment later she heard a grunt and then a large splash.

They peered into the darkness.

"I don't see nothin'," Jamie whispered. He dragged in a big gulp of air and turned on her. "What was that all about? You could have got us both killed! That fire will bring the others back if they see it. An' we don't stand a chance against them."

"I told you to go. You didn't have to help."

He scowled. "I owed you for helpin' with Barker. But we gotta get out of here afore the others come back or we're dead meat."

Hannah looked once more at the hillside, dark except for the shadows created by the moonlight. She shook her head. "I can't, Jamie."

He stared at her. "Corcoran will be back. He won't like this."

"I have to warn the *Tourmaline*'s crew. I have to."

"Well, I ain't a-waiting."

"I told you to go. When you get to town, tell the sheriff what happened here."

"Are you crazy, lady? I ain't goin' to no sheriff."

She pressed her lips together. She didn't have time to discuss this. "Thank you for your help, Jamie. I won't forget it."

She turned away from him, knowing her actions confused him. She knew what she was doing. And there was little time to lose.

Racing back into the cave, she stopped short at the sight of Barker, sprawled on the ground near the fire. He was breathing but looked to be unconscious. She grabbed two sticks from the fire and slipped away.

She made her way up the hill again. Her calves ached as she laboriously crawled upward to the same area of brush. At least it was semidry now. The first attempt at fire had burned off the coating of mist from the sea air. She gathered more twigs and needles into a canopy on top of the brush and thrust both burning sticks into the center. For more dry fuel, she ripped off the bottom eyelet band of her petticoat and added that to the pile. Slowly the dry needles and twigs ignited, and then gradually grew into a slow, steady flame.

Choking back a sob of relief, she plopped down on the ground and looked out to sea. *Please, Stuart,* she urged silently. *Take heed!* She stared over the water into the inky night. Somewhere out there two ships sailed—each carrying a man dear to her heart.

Chapter Sixteen

He was as good as dead if he didn't escape. Caleb sat on the slimy floor of the cook's galley with his hands tied behind his back. He'd strained against the rope over and over until his muscles screamed and his wrists bled. By its feel, the rope was old—sun rotted in parts and frayed on the ends. With luck, he might be able to break it at its weakest point. Unfortunately, his fingers had gone numb over an hour ago when Trask had returned and given the knot one more sharp tug before leaving him there. He hadn't returned. Guess the rat figured he'd never get free.

He hadn't expected the captain to drag him along—not to the island. At least now he knew where Hannah was. Guess she'd gotten her answers—in spades. He'd noticed the crates lining the cave wall—many with *Lansing Enterprises* written all over them. She had to have seen them, too.

Fat chance those two guarding her would leave her alone for long. A few of the others had mentioned her beauty and just what they'd like to do with her. It had made his blood run cold to hear them. When Corcoran had hit her, Caleb had nearly come apart. He'd wanted to break the man in two. He kicked the iron leg of the stove with his boot and felt the impact jar him to his hip. At least part of him could feel, even if his hands couldn't. He slumped back against the wall.

Outside, the talking of the sailors quieted. Had they already drawn that close to the *Tourmaline?* Caleb struggled anew to loosen his bindings. Somehow he had to break free and warn his brother-in-law of the trap. He couldn't give in. He eased off the rope and felt it loosen. Of all the sailor's knots he knew, only one knot did that.

Footsteps sounded just outside the galley door. "Too much moon tonight," Captain Corcoran mumbled. "We won't use the twenty-four pounder, just the swivel guns."

"Aye, aye," Trask said.

"Captain, take a look!" a new voice cried out.

Trask swore under his breath. "Should have finished that dame while I had the chance. She'll get hers, she will."

There was no doubt he was talking about Hannah. What had happened? What had set him off?

"Target sighted off the port bow!" another man called.

He'd run out of time! Caleb pressed his back against the wall, inching upward until he stood. Squeezing his shoulders together with the help of the wall, he felt the ropes give again. At the same time he pushed the frayed end toward the center of the knot.

Again it loosened.

His heart beat so loudly he figured Corcoran and Trask had to hear it. He glanced through the galley doorway. They stood shoulder to shoulder looking out over the ocean. Whatever had their attention, Caleb was grateful for it. It kept their minds off him.

Working the ropes a little more, a little more… and suddenly he was free! He looped the rope together. For the moment it was his only weapon. Keeping to the shadows, he stepped close to the door.

Then he saw what had Trask's ire up. Back on the island, a river of fire raced up the hillside.

Cursing a blue streak, Corcoran headed aft, leaving Trask blocking the doorway. Whatever hope Caleb might have of escaping, *now* was the time.

The *Tourmaline* sluiced toward them, cutting silently through the moonlit water not more than three hundred feet away. No doubt Corcoran's ship had been spotted, a silhouette against the backdrop of the flaming island. Then Caleb heard the bark of Stuart's voice. The *Tourmaline* veered right at the last minute and dropped its sails to keep from ramming straight into their vessel. Along the railing, their rifles aimed and ready, stood Stuart's men.

"Damn!" Trask said, crashing into the galley. "Hope she was worth it to you, Houston. There won't be nothing left—" He stopped short when he realized Caleb wasn't where he'd left him.

From behind, Caleb looped the rope around Trask's neck. "You first—"

They struggled, Caleb tugging at the rope ends, Trask pulling to loosen it and struggling for air. He reached for his gun.

Sharp, stinging pain tore through Caleb's thigh. He faltered and then yanked tight on the rope ends. Before Caleb could set his stance again, Trask used the momentary easing of the rope to gain leverage.

Together they crashed to the deck, Trask's pistol flying and then clattering across the wooden planks. Caleb dived, grabbed it and turned, firing a shot in one fluid motion. Trask toppled onto Caleb and expelled his last breath.

Stunned momentarily, Caleb lay there. Gunshots volleyed over the small divide of ocean. A grappling line hurtled onto deck. Caleb shoved against Trask's weight, sliding his carcass off. He had to stop Corcoran or Hannah would never be safe.

Scrambling to his feet, his fingers closed again on the gun.

"Won't do no good," a familiar voice said behind him. "That pistol only has two chambers and I can see well enough that Trask shot you once." Caleb glanced down at the weapon in his hand. Corcoran was right. And he knew without looking that the man would have something else trained on him.

"Trask always did have a sentimental attachment to that ol' relic. Me, now, I always have preferred knives. Timeless, quiet—they do the job just fine. Turn around, Mr. Houston."

Caleb turned. Slowly.

Corcoran drew back to throw the pearl-handled knife like a dart.

A stunned expression crossed Corcoran's face before his gaze narrowed on Caleb. In one determined effort, he pitched the weapon. His knife whistled by Caleb's ear and drove hard into the galley wall. Then Corcoran toppled forward onto the deck, a pool of blood growing on his shirt. Someone had shot him in the back.

Too close. That had been too close. Caleb expelled a shaky breath. A young crewman pointed a shaking gun at Caleb. "Don't try anything, sailor."

A large hand clasped the crewman's shoulder, and then Stuart stepped into view. "I'll handle this, Mr. Perkins. You help contain the crew in the ship's hold."

He raised a chin to Caleb. "Should have known you'd be in the thick of this."

"Good timing."

"Where's Hannah?"

"The island." *If she's alive...* But he didn't add the last. He couldn't voice his greatest fear.

Stuart's eyes hardened as if he, too, could read Caleb's thoughts. His gaze stopped on Caleb's leg. "You need a surgeon."

Caleb looked down. Blood spread insidiously over his inner thigh. White-hot pain radiated from its core. "Not yet." He yanked off his bandanna and tied it over the bleeding. The extra pressure increased the pain, but he couldn't be bothered with it. Not when Hannah's life hung in the balance.

Stuart's lips drew together. "Your sister will have my hide if anything happens to you."

Caleb met Stuart's gaze head-on. "Nothing is going to happen to me. Make way for the island."

Stuart nodded. He ordered another man to help, and together, supporting Caleb on each side, they half carried him across the railing and onto the *Tourmaline.*

Nothing could make Hannah enter that cave again. Nothing. She hunkered down in the small alcove, protected from the ashes and glowing embers that fell all around her. It wasn't because Barker might harm her. No. It had everything to do with what had happened to her as a child. She might be shivering, but even if she died of exposure on the hillside, she wouldn't return to the cave.

Their hideout was a death trap. Not because the fire she'd started was a danger to them physically—they were safe enough in the cave. It was because the smoke was visible from the mainland. People would wonder—and they'd come. She held no illusions of what would be her fate if the thieves found her. They'd want retribution. Her only hope was Caleb. He had to come for her first.

Caleb could be dead. By all counts he knew too much—just like her.

The thought had taken hold in the early hours of the morning and she couldn't shake it. He could be dead, and it was all her fault. Impulsively, selfishly, she'd dragged him into this. And she'd led him to his death.

If only she'd stayed back in San Francisco, none of this would have happened. Caleb would have no idea that anything was amiss with her and her grandfather. Stuart wouldn't have come anywhere near San Diego after his stop in Los Angeles and would be heading home to Rachel by now. She'd ruined so many lives with her impulsiveness. The thought made her angry. What was impulsiveness but another form of thinking with one's emotions?

If she got out of this alive, she'd go home to San Francisco. She wouldn't marry Thomas. Not now. Not ever. She loved Caleb. She knew that with a sureness unlike anything she'd known before. It had been Caleb all along, and if, in the end, he gave his life for her, she would honor that, honor his wishes for her. And if he lived, she'd get out of his life once and for all so that she would never cause him pain again.

Overhead, the gray light of dawn accentuated the dark column of smoke billowing skyward. The west wind blew it toward the coast, away from her side of the island. The flutter and snap of cloth caught her attention. She jumped from her hiding place onto the trail—and then froze. It could be the thieves.

Someone shouted. Friend or foe? Stuart's man—or one of Corcoran's? Oh, Lord—what should she do? She strained, listening hard.

"Hannah!"

This voice was much closer. Caleb! "I'm here! I'm here!" She tumbled out of her hiding spot. He stood at the entrance to the cave. His eyes lit up when he saw her. Streaked with sweat and dirt and blood, he was the most precious sight she'd ever seen. She raced down the hillside, barely feeling the sting of the stones and thorns on her bare feet, and threw herself into his arms.

"Thank God, you are safe," he said against her hair, hugging her hard.

"I didn't think I'd ever see you again. I thought…I thought…" Her voice broke, and she was unable to speak her greatest fear—that he would be gone from her life forever.

"Shh. It's over. You're safe now."

She clung to him, near to sobbing her relief. "You came."

A troubled looked passed over his face before he tightened his hold on her. "How could you doubt it?"

Burrowing into his shoulder, she drew in a deep breath of his scent mixed with the salty sea air.

"Don't ever scare me like that again, Hannah," he whispered near her ear.

She pulled back and drank in everything about him—the fading bruises on his cheek, the drawn, worried look in his eyes. She wanted to smooth every line with a kiss. She stood on tiptoe to do just that when she sensed they were no longer alone.

Behind Caleb, men gathered. "They're with Stuart," he said. She released him and stepped back. As she did, she saw his thigh and the make-shift bandage. "You're injured!"

"A scratch," he said softly.

It was far more than that by the look of it. He'd risked so much for her. So much.

Seeming to need the same reassurance, he searched the length of her down to her bare, scratched and bloody soot-darkened feet. He stopped there, frowning slightly. Before she could allay his fears, he scooped her into his arms.

"Put me down!" she gasped.

He breathed into her hair. "Never."

"I can walk."

"I'm sure you can. But it will be when I get you back on board the *Tourmaline,* safe and sound, and not before."

Caleb hadn't expected to see Hannah alive—not this side of heaven. He'd wanted to touch her—hold her—mostly to reassure himself that she was real. He leaned close, sucked in a whiff of her scent—which was tinged heavily with smoke—and finally, finally the pressure in his chest started to ease.

With each step back to the ship, his thigh throbbed a little more. He had to stop and catch his breath before carrying her up the wooden plank and onto the deck.

Stuart met them. "Good to see you in one piece. Take her to my cabin for now."

"I need a bucket of fresh water," Caleb said as he strode past.

He deposited her on Stuart's bunk, and she sat, her back against the side of the ship, just as one of Stuart's men entered with a bucket and a long-handled dipper. Caleb scooped out a measure of clean water and held it to Hannah's mouth. She grasped the utensil with both hands and drank greedily. The water dribbled down her chin in her haste, making darker spots on her cream-colored blouse. She took a second dipperful, this time slowing her gulps.

Watching her, he realized what had caused her desperation, and the acid churned in his gut. Corcoran had never offered her something so basic as a drink of water. He sank onto the rope bed and took the dipper from her. "That's enough. Too much, too fast, and you'll toss it."

She pushed her hair away from her face, and her fingers caught in the tangles. Two bright spots of pink colored her cheeks. "I look a sight."

Even disheveled she was lovely, but he wouldn't let her sidetrack him. "You started the fire."

"Yes."

"Instead of getting away. What possessed you? You could have been killed!"

"I could say the same to you."

He scowled.

"Caleb. Please. I don't want to argue. We're both safe now. It's over."

He leaned in to wipe away the drips on her chin. A vibration hummed between them that had nothing to do with the rocking of the great ship. Why had he been so critical? He didn't want to argue either. It would be so easy to slip his hand around her neck, pull her closer…

Instead he grabbed a rag from Stuart's bedside stand, doused it in the water and wrung it out. Momentary dizziness washed over him. He checked the cloth at his thigh. No new drainage. He shook off the feeling and began to clean the dried blood, dirt and scratches crisscrossing Hannah's feet.

"I can do that," Hannah said.

"I know." But he didn't stop—he couldn't. He'd nearly lost her. *He* needed this, needed to touch her so that her presence felt real to him. The tightness in his chest eased with each stroke of the cloth. She was safe. She was here. He swallowed hard. Every scrape, every cut had happened because he'd stormed out of his room and left her alone.

"Caleb…" She leaned forward.

"I never should have left you, Hannah. If I'd done my job, protected you, none of this would have happened." He turned back to his task, angry with himself.

"It wasn't your fault. I should never have involved you in the first place."

"It was my choice to help. Don't blame yourself."

"But I do. Caleb—"

He felt a staying hand on his shoulder and looked up from his task.

"—stop…please."

Her eyes held a look he hadn't seen before. A look that begged to be kissed. And with it, he gave up trying to hold back. If this was only fleeting, only because she was so relieved to be safe again, well, he'd take it as that and be happy about it. Dropping the cloth, he slipped his hand behind her neck and pulled her to him, meeting her lips with his, slanting across them, sweeping her tongue with his. Then the blood rushed in his ears, and he wanted more, wanted to know with this kiss that she was truly his, for this moment.

The cabin door swung open. "I brought my—"

Hannah pushed away from him.

"—surgeon," Stuart said, stopping abruptly.

Her withdrawal felt like a slap in the face, even as Caleb understood her embarrassment. He turned to look Stuart in the eye. "She doesn't need one."

"Not for her. For you. You're as white as my sail."

Caleb checked his thigh. Bright red blood seeped through his pants and down the length of the material. The bandage underneath had to be saturated.

Hannah gasped.

"Guess I need stitches after all." The sight of the blood made him queasy. It didn't make sense, considering all his hunting and fishing.

"And food, I suspect," Stuart said.

Caleb tried to think back to the last time he'd eaten anything. Yesterday? Or the day before? The room tilted.

"I expect an explanation." Stuart's voice came from a distance.

The edges of Caleb's vision darkened. His thoughts grew fuzzy, distorted, but he knew what Stuart meant—Hannah. "Fair enough. When this is over."

Hannah sat in the galley eyeing her empty plate, unable to believe she'd eaten the entire serving of eggs and potatoes with the way her stomach had been clenched into a nervous ball. The surgeon and Stuart had been with Caleb for a full twenty minutes—long enough to set a few stitches. She had to see Caleb and know that he was all right. Rising from the long table, she walked outside to the deck railing. She had as much right to be in that room as Stuart. Frustratingly, it was Caleb who had demanded she leave.

What was he worried about? That she would think less of him if he cried out? Proud man. Proud and foolish to think so.

With that thought, she marched to the cabin, took a firm grasp of the handle and opened the door. "You'll not get me to leave, Caleb Houst—"

Stuart and the physician glanced up from their work and then quickly returned to it. She took in the bloody bandages lying near the basin of water and an involuntary shiver coursed through her. Taking a steadying breath, she stepped inside and shut the door.

"Almost done," the surgeon murmured. Over his left shoulder, a man held a kerosene lamp high to illuminate the work area. The assistant's arm shook with the weight of it—or perhaps the view he had.

Caleb lay across Stuart's large desk, the papers and charts having been pushed aside into a pile over a nearby trunk. Caleb's cotton shirt had been loosened from his waistband, and one leg of his pants had been ripped open at the seam to allow access to the wound. He followed the surgeon's every move, his jaw set, his lips thinned into a line of resolve. "You shouldn't be here, Hannah."

Moving to his opposite side, she pulled up a wooden chair and sat.

His face didn't change, but she felt his hand close against hers briefly before clasping the edge of the table. She'd make this up to him. If it took her the rest of her life, somehow she'd make amends.

A moment later the surgeon cut the catgut and announced he was done. He stanched the trickle of blood at the wound with a clean cloth. "If you would find something to secure this, Miss Lansing…"

She scanned the room. Nothing but charts and papers.

"Try there," Stuart said, indicating a squat wooden chest under the porthole.

Opening it, she found folded clothing and a soft, woven belt. She brought the belt to the surgeon, who then wrapped it around Caleb's thigh. "That will do," the surgeon said, stepping back to critically assess his work. He gathered his instruments. "Make sure you keep the weight off it for a few days. I'll see to the others now."

When the surgeon had departed with his assistant, Stuart helped Caleb sit up. "You'll do better in my bunk." He shoved a shoulder under Caleb's arm, assisted him up and helped him move to the bed.

Once Caleb was settled, Hannah drew the covers up. "What can I do? Would you like water? Something stronger?"

"Nothing."

She felt it as a rebuff and started to step back.

"You can stay."

She met his gaze.

Stay, he mouthed, but his eyes closed as though he were fighting to stay lucid.

"He's had some laudanum," Stuart explained, watching her closely. "And lost a lot of blood." He dragged his desk chair over and set it by the bed, by his actions giving her his permission to stay.

She settled against the hard, straight back. "Thank you."

"How they take you?" The question came from Caleb, his words slightly slurred.

Stuart remained in the room, listening. Should she declare in front of him that she'd spent the night in Caleb's room? That didn't seem wise. However, if he spoke to anyone in town, it could be common knowledge.

"Yesterday morning," he prompted.

She took a deep breath and plunged ahead. "I wanted hot water for tea. Mr. Avery was sweeping." She glanced at Stuart. He would not condone her presence in the saloon. It couldn't be helped, and actually, worse things than that had happened now.

"Someone put a rag over my face. It had something on it—the odor burned my nose. I couldn't get it away. Whoever held it was much stronger. That's the last thing I remember until I woke up and found myself on the island."

"You're lucky it was no worse than that."

"I know," she said softly, taking his hand, so glad he was alive, so glad they both were. "I was never so thankful in my life as when you appeared. I didn't expect to ever see you again."

"Who started the fire?" Stuart asked, drawing her attention back to him. His gaze darted from her hand in Caleb's.

"It's the only thing I could think of," Hannah answered. "You were sailing into a trap. If those men had caught you by surprise… Well, I just couldn't let anything happen to you. Jamie helped." She quickly explained about the boy.

Stuart frowned. "So you could have gotten away, yet you stayed to warn me? Hannah...you shouldn't—"

"Don't you dare tell me I shouldn't have done it—that I should have looked out for myself. There's been too much of that over the past few years," she said.

"It was brave of you," Stuart said.

Hannah gave a short laugh. "I'm not sure how brave it was, considering I was more afraid of that tiny boat on the water than staying put."

Caleb pressed his lips together and squeezed her hand. He understood. The knowledge comforted her. *He* comforted her.

"But if I hadn't run into Caleb..." Stuart's brows drew together.

She met his gaze. "I know. You would have never known I was there."

"You could have been stranded, Hannah."

She swallowed. The consequences of her split-second decision hadn't been lost on her. "I wasn't naive. You had to be warned. That was the beginning and the end of it."

Suddenly it dawned on her that Stuart didn't know about the cache of stolen merchandise on the island. "I don't think they'd thought my kidnapping all the way through. I'd seen the crates, the ones taken from other ships they'd sunk—

along with Grandfather's. The wares are all stored in the cave. The thieves couldn't let me go—whether or not the ransom was paid. I would have gone straight to the sheriff."

A look crossed between the two men.

"Go ahead," Caleb said, letting his head fall back on the pillow. "The sheriff will need proof. Not just our word."

Stuart stood. "We'll move what we can onto this ship. The rest can go aboard the other vessel." He looked from Hannah to Caleb, his gaze falling again on their clasped hands. "I'm not done asking questions."

"I'm not going anywhere," Caleb said, by his voice resigned to facing an interrogation.

Hannah wasn't so willing. Her feelings were raw, her emotions on edge. Caleb needed rest, and not the 'swinging from a rope bed on a ship' sort—the kind you got from your own room, your own bed. "Shouldn't the authorities handle it from here on out?" she asked.

"We're in Mexican waters," Stuart said. "If we leave and the Mexican authorities get wind of the cache, they won't let us within a mile of the island. They'll confiscate everything. Now is our best chance to get back what belongs to your company."

He left then, closing the door behind him. Reluctantly, Hannah pulled her hand from Caleb's grip. "You need rest."

A weak smile split his lips. "Rest? Not possible. Not around you."

She took in the bandage on his leg, the old, yellowing bruise on his cheekbone. Yes. *Bad* things happened. Knowing her was akin to knowing a nightmare.

Caleb closed his eyes, finally giving in to the effects of the laudanum.

She studied the planes of his face, committing them to her memory, and then knelt beside the bed and softly brushed her lips over his. "Thank you," she whispered.

He opened his eyes and watched her for a length of a Western sunset, his gaze trailing from her eyes to her lips and then back to her face until she felt she had to fill the silence with words—any words—or kiss him again unreservedly. His injury precluded that. Yet, by his expression, he didn't seem to be thinking about his wound. Rising on his elbow, he reached his other hand behind her neck, drew her to him. He kissed her slowly, deeply, deliberately. And she felt herself sinking into it. In that moment nothing existed but Caleb—his warmth, the softness of his lips, his scent—and she wanted the kiss to go on forever. He made her feel protected, cherished—loved.

Yes. Loved. For herself. Not her money. Not her position.

He'd risked his life for her. Why did she continue to fight against her own heart?

He lowered his head back onto his pillow. A long sigh escaped. His eyelids drooped and then finally closed as his breathing evened out.

She pulled back, searching every curve of his face. How could she bear to leave him after all they'd been through? Up to now she'd put her duty, to Grandfather and to the family business, ahead of all else. She'd risked her life and the lives of those she loved to get her answers. Well, she had them now. With the pirates out of the way, the shipping business could again grow and flourish.

But what about her? She'd never felt so alive, so necessary, as when she was with Caleb. He challenged her, encouraged her…and accepted her shortcomings.

She stood and pulled the covers to his chin. Surely, when she'd had some sleep, the answers she needed would come.

Hannah woke to the cry of the gulls. Early-morning sunlight streamed through the two portholes, the dust motes floating in the circular slash of light. She blinked, taking a moment to adjust to her surroundings. A room of richly polished wood, small and cozy…the floor shifting, rocking, beneath her.

Oh, yes—Stuart's cabin.

She was surprised she'd slept at all, curled up as she was on the chair. In that position, exhaustion had soon claimed her. She'd likely pay for it now with a stiff neck and shoulders.

She'd fallen asleep despite her attempt to remain awake for Caleb—in case he should need something. Her dreams had been restless. Thoughts of him had chased her, and she'd run from them like a dolphin ahead of a storm. Images during the past few days of him angry and frustrated, and then thoughtful and caring, played over in her mind.

Caleb slept, his arm flung out to his side, his hand dangling off the edge of the mattress. His other arm covered his face, leaving only his whiskered chin and mouth exposed.

In the corner of the room, curled on top of a blanket, slept a familiar-looking boy—Jamie.

Hannah straightened. How had he gotten here? Before she could give more thought to his presence, footsteps sounded near the door and Stuart stepped into the cabin.

Caleb woke and swung his feet to the floor. He winced and then rubbed his hand over his face. "How long have I slept?"

"Most of the day," Stuart said. "We've loaded everything and are starting back to port."

"No setbacks?"

"None. The two men left weren't in any shape to threaten us. I've put them in the hold with the others. And I found this one." Stuart nodded at the boy. "Seemed to know you both."

"Jamie." Hannah supplied the name.

"Looks all done in," Caleb said. "And your men?"

"A few injuries. They'll be all right."

Caleb tried to stand, favoring his injured leg.

Hannah started to rise from her chair to help him, but he gave her a quelling look. She hesitated, and then sat.

He tried again to stand. On the second attempt, he straightened to his full length.

"What are you doing?" she said, alarmed that the bleeding could start up again. "The surgeon said you're to keep your weight off that leg."

"I'm feeling better. And it's time you had your privacy. I'll bunk with the crew."

"But that's not necessary. You... You're family."

He slowed in grabbing up his Stetson, dropping it on his head. When he turned back to her, his eyes had hardened. He indicated Stuart with a tilt of his chin. "His. Not yours." Then he limped to the door. Stuart stepped aside for him as he made his way through.

"But..."

"Leave it, Hannah," Stuart said, moving to block her path when she would follow after him. "He knows what he has to do."

Chapter Seventeen

Caleb hobbled to the aft part of the ship, descended the steep ladder and flopped down on a seaman's bunk. It wasn't as nice as Stuart's cabin, but it would do. Caleb wasn't used to fancy anyway.

It didn't take long for Stuart to find him and start asking questions.

"You've explained about the ships and the tie-in with Dorian," Stuart said after hearing Caleb out. "Guess he made some enemies over the years. No surprises there. You've talked about the discrepancies Hannah found between the two records—which means someone was lying. Based on the fact Corcoran knew the time and the route I'd be taking, I'd say it was the port authority—or someone in that office. What you haven't said is why she came south in the first place."

"I already told you. For answers. She wanted to find out what happened to the ships."

"Dorian had an investigator on it, along with me. There wasn't a need for her to come...unless there's more to the story. You said Dorian was ill. It doesn't make sense that she would leave Frisco right when Dorian needed her most. Her trip here doesn't sound anything like her."

But it does sound like the Hannah I used to know, Caleb thought. "I thought it strange, too. Especially when she should be planning her wedding."

Stuart sank down on the opposite bunk. "Wedding?"

So he hadn't heard. "It's been a while since you were home. Maybe Rachel knows about it."

"Maybe." But Stuart looked doubtful. "Who does she plan to marry?"

"Thomas Rowlings."

The hard set of his brother-in-law's jaw told Caleb all he needed to know. "I take it you don't approve."

"The man owns half of San Francisco."

"That's not telling me anything new."

Stuart took his time removing his cap and then hooked it on a wall peg. "Dorian and Thomas are built from the same marrow. They don't comprehend the words *no* or *stop*. It's all about acquiring more—more land, more ships, more power. Dorian has had his sights on Thomas's holdings for years. This would be one way to make it happen."

Caleb didn't like what he was hearing. "That's not how Hannah described things. With what you're saying, sounds like Rowlings might be after Hannah to gain control of Dorian's shipping business."

Stuart nodded.

"So they're both using her." The new information lay like cold lead in his stomach.

"Hannah has always had to walk a tightrope between what she needed and what Dorian wanted. She's learned to do it so well that she doesn't even realize when his wishes bleed over and contaminate hers. It sounds like Dorian is using the fact that he's ill to pressure her into this union—a union that will benefit him."

"She understands all that."

A furrow formed between Stuart's brows. "And she still agrees with the marriage?"

"She's going into it with her eyes wide-open." Caleb hated that, especially now, knowing that she had feelings for him—feelings she was afraid to trust due to Dorian's influence. It was a bitter pill to swallow.

"Sounds more to me like she was running from it. The opening of the Hotel Del, the lost ships—could be they were an excuse or the impetus she needed. She wouldn't have done this—come this far on her own…" Stuart studied him, and too late, Caleb remembered that intense look of his that saw more than most men. "You're not telling me everything. What happened between you two?"

Caleb felt the weight of the question. What happened between him and Hannah, the private stuff, was just that—private. But he'd thought all along that he'd figured into her journey here. Stuart was only trying to make sense of it, same as him. "Are you askin' as Hannah's father or as Dorian's gofer?"

Stuart tensed his jaw. Quick as lightning he breached the space between them and grabbed Caleb's collar. "The answer better be all the same. What happened?"

Caleb forced Stuart's grip apart. "You can let go. Nothing happened. I know how things are."

Stuart relaxed his grip, but nothing else about him moved. Caleb didn't blame the man for his actions. In his place, he would have been just as direct. "Hannah contacted me to escort her around town—to the Hotel Del for its opening, to the port authority, to the newspaper office. She knew it wasn't smart to go it alone. Somehow, someone figured out what she was after—someone who didn't care for her snooping."

Stuart sat back down. "Anything else you want to tell me?"

"Let's just say we both care about Hannah and leave it at that. Clear enough?"

Stuart's gaze narrowed on Caleb.

The brief hesitation, the close assessment,

nearly made Caleb squirm like when he'd been younger and Stuart had caught him trying to hide something.

"Look," his brother-in-law said. "Dorian asked me to come, but that's not why I'm here. He's not my employer—hasn't been for years. I'm here because I care about Hannah and want her safe. I'd also like to see her happy."

"Why? Who is she to you?"

The blunt question made Stuart pull back. "She's not blood, if that's what you're thinking. I made a promise to her mother that I'd look after Hannah, and that's what I'll do. Linnea was… special to me."

A look of infinite sadness passed over Stuart's face and then was gone in the next instant. "Looks like Hannah squirmed her way into the middle of something dangerous, and by the old bruises on your face, she pulled you right along with her. Or is that her work because you were getting a bit too personal?"

Caleb had had enough of his probing. "I told you. Nothing happened between Hannah and me."

Stuart looked him in the eye, absorbing what Caleb said. "But you wanted it to."

Caleb pressed his lips together.

"All right. I think I understand things now."

Hannah stayed in Stuart's cabin and tried desperately not to think about the rocking of the ship.

It had been easier to ignore when her mind was occupied with worry over Caleb. Now, lying there on the bunk, she felt every shift and correction of the vessel, every tilt of the deck.

The orange sunset glowed through her porthole. Evening was fast approaching. It would be worse at night. She'd lost her mother at night. *What would you say at seeing your daughter in such a fix?* She squeezed her eyes shut and hot tears escaped, slipping across her temple and into her hair.

Angry at herself, at her weakness, she rose and paced the length of the small cabin, the brush of her bare feet against the worn wood floor sounding every bit as loud to her ears as the other noises of the ship. She wrenched open the cabin door and took the narrow stairway to the deck.

Caleb stood at the railing. Immediately he straightened, his jaw tightening. He glanced down at her hands. "It's the ship, isn't it?"

How could he know? She followed his gaze and realized she had wadded up a wrinkled, damp handkerchief. She joined him at the railing. "What are you doing up? What about your leg?"

"Don't worry about it."

His answer felt like a rebuff. What was wrong? Why was he suddenly distancing himself from her?

"I've been wondering where the money came from for the ransom. Grandfather couldn't wire it. He didn't have it. Was it Rowlings?" If so, he would be aware of her circumstances.

"I wired Dorian." Caleb turned to look at her. "I didn't get an answer. There wasn't time."

"Then, how—" Where did the money come from for the ransom? Her gaze flew to Caleb. "How—"

"I had a little saved up."

"Then, the thieves have it?" At his nod, she continued, "You'll get it back. I'll make sure of it."

She had so many obligations waiting for her back in San Francisco. The weight of them had been lifted for a time, but now she felt them settling back on her shoulders like a heavy cloak. Although Caleb had helped carry the load, it wasn't his burden to bear. It was hers alone. Still, she hated to think about the moment when they would have to say goodbye.

"Caleb, why not come north? You have family there."

He blew out a breath and studied her for an interminable length of time. His lips thinned into a straight line. "You know why, Hannah."

She closed her eyes. Yes. She supposed she did know why. He didn't want to be anywhere near her.

"I can see your mind spinnin'. Already you're figuring out next week's celebration when you arrive at the dock. What you should wear, who you should invite to your homecoming shindig…"

She bristled. "Caleb—don't."

"Figured out yet what you will say to Rowlings when he learns you are back? He'll expect an explanation."

She wasn't sure how Thomas would react. When she'd made the decision to head south, his feelings were the least of her concerns. "I'll think of something. I have a few days to figure it out," she mumbled.

His knuckles on the railing turned white. "You care about me, Hannah. Admit it. Heck, you trust me. Otherwise you wouldn't have come so far on your own. But you don't trust yourself—at least not where I'm concerned."

She watched the sun slip below the horizon and disappear. He was right. He knew her so well.

"I want you to stay. With me."

Blood pounded in her ears. "I…I…" She gripped the railing. "Caleb, don't do this." She turned away from his penetrating gaze.

"What happened back there in my room, Hannah? Was it nothing?" An edge of frustration crept into his voice.

"No. Of course not. But I can't…"

"You came here looking for my help, but also looking for me. You were running, Hannah. Running from the mold Dorian is trying to force you into. Running from a loveless marriage and an equally loveless life."

His words cut her. They hurt. He didn't understand her dilemma, didn't truly understand how it was for her living in that manor with her grandfather.

"You can run from your feelings, Hannah, but it won't change anything. Change takes courage—something I know you have in spades. But as things stand now, I won't have a coward for my wife."

His words shocked her—and made her angry. "That's the poorest proposal I've ever heard!"

"And you've heard how many?"

She glared at him. Yet beneath his words she heard the pain—and she'd vowed never to cause him pain again, so she kept her retort to herself.

The look he gave her was filled with disgust. He turned away and looked out to the mainland, completely shutting her out.

Caleb stood at the railing after Hannah had gone back to her cabin. He'd made a mess of things, but he'd meant what he said. At least she knew how he felt.

The ship maneuvered the deep channel into San Diego's harbor with the last vestiges of daylight. The beam from the lighthouse streamed across the sky. They'd make harbor by nightfall if the wind held.

Footsteps sounded behind him—the boy, Jamie, coming from the galley. Spying Caleb, he hesitated.

"So what's your story?" Caleb considered the boy. He was skinny and in rags, and Caleb wondered when he'd last eaten anything but fish. "How long were you there?"

"Too long."

"Why'd you circle back?"

Telltale color crept up his neck. "Miss Hannah—I'd have been done for if she hadn't helped me. I couldn't just leave her."

Caleb let out a long sigh under his breath. "Guess I can understand, then." Whoever the boy was, he understood loyalty. If he'd been more selfish, he would have been long gone by now. "Thank you for your help with Miss Lansing."

"We helped each other," he said with a suspicious scowl. "We're even now."

Caleb stifled a smile. Obviously the boy was not used to being thanked. "How did you come to be on the island?"

Jamie didn't answer.

"I'm not going to turn you in, if that's what you're thinking. That's not how I repay a debt. I take it that being a pirate wasn't all you'd hoped for?"

Jamie shook his head again.

"The law will be involved when we get back to port."

A frightened look came into the boy's eyes—
a look he tried valiantly to hide.

"You got any plans for when we dock?"

Jamie shook his head.

"A relative in town?"

"Maybe."

When the boy offered nothing more, Caleb
continued, "The sheriff will want to ask you a
few questions."

"Sure he will. Just before he locks me up."

"No one is going to believe that Miss Lansing
bested the pirates all on her own. Your name will
come up. It's inevitable."

Jamie studied the wide floorboards as though
his life depended on it.

"I'll leave town, sir. I promise."

"Can't let you do that, Jamie. You did a good
turn for Miss Lansing. That counts for something.
And the way I see it, you didn't have much of a
choice with Captain Corcoran. It was either become a pirate or die. The sheriff will take that
into account."

"The lady said the same thing," Jamie grumbled.

The ghost of a grin lifted the corners of Caleb's
mouth. *The lady*—she certainly was that. One
beautiful, brave, determined, *aggravating* lady.

Hannah hadn't emerged from Stuart's cabin
since they'd spoken. Short of kidnapping her
again, Caleb didn't have a plan. He couldn't force

her to stay. That would make him no better than Dorian.

Well, at least his conscience was clear. He wanted her to stay. Wanted a life with her. Of course, sayin' it hadn't changed anything. She was determined to go back to Frisco and take her place in the business. If that was what she wanted, the best thing he could do was stay out of her way.

Their time together was over. The quicker he faced that fact, the better. He didn't belong in her world, and she definitely didn't belong in his.

Chapter Eighteen

That morning, the *Tourmaline*'s crew unloaded the wares originally slated for the Hotel Del Coronado. The manager, Mr. Barstow, after learning of the pirate situation, was most accommodating. He apologized for his previous rudeness with Hannah. Diplomatically, Hannah said she had attributed it to his frustration at not being completely ready for the opening events.

Once docked in San Diego's harbor, Caleb left to get the sheriff. An hour later, Sheriff Cramer arrived by himself. Hannah waited, anxious to ask where Caleb might be, while Stuart accompanied the sheriff to check on the men tied in the ship's hold.

"I'll have them transported to the jail," Cramer said, once he was back on deck. "But first, I will stop by and question Mr. Webberly one more time. Seems he may know more than he has let on."

Stuart thought about that a moment. "I'll go with you. I'm interested in seeing those incident reports myself." He turned to Hannah. "We'll leave on tomorrow's tide. Is there anything you need in town before we go?"

She had expected he wouldn't want to stay long, yet although she wanted to get home to Grandfather, she didn't feel ready to leave. "I need to gather my things from the hotel. Have you seen Caleb? Perhaps he can escort me."

Stuart shook his head. "He's already left the ship. Said he had to get back to work. Took Jamie with him."

Disappointment barreled through her like a heavy cold mist. She'd wanted to spend more time with him—talk to him once more.

"Very well," she said, forcing a cheerfulness she didn't feel into her voice. "Is there someone else who might accompany me?"

"Mr. Gordon will help you. I'll call for him whenever you are ready."

Hannah swallowed hard.

Stuart cocked his head to the side. "Anything wrong with Gordon?"

"No. Of course not. It's just—"

He walked to her and drew her into a gentle hug, much like the ones he'd given her as a child. "Things will look clearer to you once you are home, back with your grandfather and surrounded by your friends."

She nodded against his shoulder, not caring that she was mussing her hair. Not caring about much of anything. "Thank you, Father."

An awkward silence followed.

"Been a while since you called me that."

"I never should have stopped." Grandfather had said it wasn't proper. That Stuart wasn't her real father, and it confused people. And like many of the things in her life with Grandfather, she'd accepted that he was right. Too easily.

"Why the sudden change?" he said gruffly.

She pushed away from him and looked him in the eye. "It is who you are...and you came for me." He'd always been there for her. In the strongest sense of the word he *was* her father—and family. Not by lineage and blood, but through love.

"As your father, then, I have a request. Look hard at what you're leaving behind. Absence didn't make you forget Caleb before, nor he you. Do you think it will be any different this time?"

She made several stops in town—the bank to redeposit the money Caleb had used for her ransom and then to pay her bill at the Horton Hotel. Then a few more places before heading to the saloon. Caleb was nowhere in sight. Lola escorted her up the stairs and stood in the doorway while she gathered her things.

"You're going, then...." There was mild condemnation in the woman's voice.

It wasn't any of Lola's business, but Hannah realized the woman only asked out of concern for Caleb. "I should get home to my grandfather. And I've had quite enough excitement."

"A man from the newspaper was here earlier."

Wonderful. How would her part of the past two days be painted in the morning paper? Quite sensationalized, she imagined.

"I didn't tell him nothing."

Relieved by the woman's loyalty, Hannah met her eyes. "Thank you. That was exceedingly kind."

Lola shrugged. "Figured it's your story to tell, not mine."

Only a few things in the room spoke of Caleb's presence. His leather coat hung over the back of the straight-back chair, his shaving cream, brush and comb on the tall dresser. She touched each item before turning to Lola. "I guess that's it. I'm sorry I missed Mr. Houston. I...I had hoped to say goodbye."

Jim peered over Lola's shoulder. "You're not leavin', are you? Surely your intended can take care of things in Frisco. I heard tell your grandfather's doing okay. Can't you stay a while longer?"

"How do you know such things, Jim?"

"Oh, I just keep my ears open. Lots going on around here."

"Then, you might as well know that I won't be marrying Thomas when I get back. I'm not going to marry at all."

There. She'd said it. Yet with the words, the tight hold she'd had on her emotions began to slip. All of this felt wrong, but there was nothing to do but go through with it. She ignored the quick sting of tears and held up her burgundy traveling suit, wrinkled from being tossed quickly into the carpetbag in her hurry to leave the Horton. She barely cared anymore.

The worried glance that passed between the two at the door did little to comfort her. "I'm leaving first thing tomorrow. Tonight I'll be staying on board the *Tourmaline* in case…"

Lola waited for her to continue.

She didn't. There was no point in hoping Caleb would want to see her again. She'd completely disrupted his life, whirling in and then whirling out of it again.

That evening, Stuart brought a few of his men with him to the saloon. Wyatt bought them all a round of drinks. They'd be shoving off at dawn. Stuart took Caleb aside just before departing.

"Your money is back in the bank," he said. "Just thought you'd like to know. Got any plans for it?"

"Wyatt has some land he's itching for me to buy."

"Land?" Stuart shook his head. "Doesn't sound like you."

"Guess that's why I've been putting him off. I always figured I'd spend it on a fishing boat some day."

"Well, don't be a stranger. Rachel, Lawrence— we'd all like you to come north. Like I've said before, you've got a position with my company. All you have to do is let me know."

Working with his brother-in-law would be a good life, but it was the other thing that stopped him from jumping at the offer.

"Don't know that I could be that close and see her married to someone else." They both knew who *her* was.

Stuart pressed his lips together. Finally he reached out to shake Caleb's hand. "Understood. Well, thank you for looking out for Hannah. I won't forget it."

Caleb returned the handshake. "Give Rachel my love."

"I'll do that, but she'd rather hear it from you." Stuart started for the door with his men. He turned back one more time. "Good fishing up north."

In the early hours of the morning, after the saloon had closed, Caleb walked to the docks and stood hidden in the shadows. He stared at the ship, half hoping to see Hannah once more. But it was late. Too late by the hour and too late to change the course of events taking her away. He'd given it his best try.

He did wish her well—to a certain point. He wanted her to be happy. He just wished that happiness could be found by staying with him.

That morning, even after hearing the first daily noises of the town waking up, Caleb remained in bed. The *Tourmaline* would be casting off. He couldn't bring himself to go down to the dock, couldn't bring himself to watch her leave one last time. She'd made her choice, he kept telling himself, and it wasn't him. It wasn't him.

Finally, unable to put it off any longer, he rose and padded to the window. Pale sunlight touched the street below his window. Lifting his gaze to the horizon beyond the town, where the ocean and the sky met, he made out the tall sails of Stuart's ship near the entrance to the harbor, heading out to open sea.

Hannah was gone.

He let out a breath. From the moment she'd stepped back into his life, he'd felt as if he'd been harpooned and dragged under by the tether. Now, with her absence, all he felt was numb. He turned from the window and dressed in his jeans and cotton shirt, his actions slow and methodical. Once he had on his boots and Stetson, he headed downstairs.

The saloon was quiet—that early-morning quiet that he'd always enjoyed before. Now the silence pressed in on him. He needed to keep busy. He wasn't up to questions or being surrounded by people. Not today. Fishing sounded like a good idea. He walked outside and headed toward the livery.

Mr. Johnson hailed him from the doorway of the land office. "Mr. Houston! I expected you would come in today."

Before Caleb could remark on the strangeness of the man's comment, Mr. Johnson turned and reentered the building. Caleb followed him inside.

"Pull up a seat. This will only take a moment," Mr. Johnson said over his shoulder. He rummaged through one of his desk drawers.

Caleb sank into a hard-backed chair just as Mr. Johnson plopped a packet of papers on the desk between them. "They're all in order. All I need is your signature."

"What is this?" Caleb noticed a reference to the tract of land he'd been talking to Wyatt about. "Has Mr. Earp said something to you?"

"No, not Mr. Earp."

"Look, I don't know what's going on, but I haven't made up my mind about that piece of property. It's a lot of money."

"But you don't owe anything on it!"

"What do you mean?"

"Why the woman you were seeing—Miss Lansing—she stopped by."

"She was here?"

"Yesterday. For nearly an hour." He pushed the papers on his desk toward Caleb. "See if you agree with the contract."

Caleb picked up the papers and began reading. Lansing Enterprises had paid for the fifty acres he'd had his eye on. The words *paid in full* were stamped across the last page of the packet.

Caleb swallowed. "There must be some mistake. I never decided about that land."

Mr. Johnson pointed to a clause at the top, a clause Caleb had skimmed over too fast. "It's all in your name. You own the land free and clear. All you have to do is sign for it." Mr. Johnson handed him a pen. "Miss Lansing said you'd saved her company, and it was the least she could do."

He started to put pen to paper and then hesitated. Rather than feeling a rush of anticipation, he felt like a noose was tightening around his neck.

The land agent leaned forward, lowering his voice. "She said you might have trouble accepting it. Said to tell you that you earned it, if that would help."

"Guess I did, at that," he mumbled. But accepting it meant he'd be staying, putting down roots. And he'd always figured when the time came he'd put those roots down near family.

"She mentioned that she would be eternally grateful for all your help."

Caleb scowled. He didn't want Hannah's gratitude. He wanted her. Abruptly, he stood, his chair scraping across the hardwood floor with a loud noise that made the other two clerks in the office look up. "Sorry, Mr. Johnson." He picked up the paper waiting for his signature and tore it down the middle. "Sell the land to someone else. I won't be settlin' here."

"But what about the money?"

"Send it back." He tossed the words over his shoulder as he stormed out the door. He would ask her properly, on his knee if need be. And if she still had it in her mind to marry that Rowlings fellow, as foolish as that was, well, then, he'd make it mighty hard for her. He'd be there, everywhere she turned, so that she'd know she'd made the wrong choice. She'd know what she'd given up, and it would wear on her. Because, in the end, she belonged with him, and he belonged with her. Their love should be well served, not set aside.

According to Stuart, the *Tourmaline* would pull into port in Los Angeles. If he hurried, Caleb could meet her there.

He stopped at the saloon before leaving town. Lola and Jim sat at their regular table, having a morning cup of coffee.

"Tell Wyatt I won't be in tonight."

"Now, hold on," Jim said, standing. "You've

had an entire week off, and you think he'll let you have more time? You're stretching the boss's hospitality."

Jim would poke at a caged cougar just to irritate him, and Caleb didn't have that kind of time. He had to get movin'. "Matter of fact, you can tell Wyatt to find another manager. I'm leaving town."

He took the stairs two at a time and headed to his room. Jim would probably follow just to needle him. The man had a soft spot for Hannah. Caleb took his saddlebag off his bedpost and cleaned out the first drawer of his bureau, stuffing the things he'd need inside the pouch.

Jim appeared and leaned against the doorpost. Lola stood at his side.

"This wouldn't have anything to do with Miss Lansing, now, would it?" Jim asked.

"What's it to you?"

A meaningful look passed between Jim and Lola.

"All right. What's going on?" Caleb asked, wondering if he'd regret finding out. He tossed the shirt he was holding onto his bed and then straightened, giving them his full attention.

"She came by here yesterday to get her things," Jim said.

"Figured she might. So?"

"She wanted to say goodbye. I noticed you made yourself scarce. Where were you anyway?"

"Out." At the time he'd wanted to avoid her. His feelings had still been raw, still hurt that she wasn't seeing things his way. But he hadn't been able to go far. His leg hurt like hell with the stitches pulling. In the end, he'd holed up in the cantina in Old Town and nursed his wounded pride more than anything.

"I congratulated her on her upcoming wedding." Amusement laced Lola's voice.

Caleb scowled. He could do without their teasing. He stuffed a change of shirt into his satchel and then hooked his gun belt around his hips. "Anything else?"

"As a matter of fact, yes," Jim said. "She mentioned she ain't getting married after all. Apparently, she's changed her mind."

Caleb paused.

Lola winked at Jim before adding, "And that she was leaving at nine o'clock today."

Caleb finished buckling his belt with a quick jerk. "At nine? Impossible. The *Tourmaline* headed out at sunup."

"Hmm," Lola said with another knowing look at Jim.

Irritated, Caleb looked from one to the other. Suspicion mushroomed inside. "All right. I've had about all I can stomach from you two—" Suddenly he realized what Jim had said, what Lola had said. Hannah hated the water. "She didn't take the ship. She's on the train!"

Jim smirked. "You are thickheaded at times—but smart. And something tells me you *still* won't be workin' tonight." He shook his head. "I should have known. Wyatt may as well start lookin' for a replacement."

Lola stretched up on tiptoe and gave Caleb a peck on the cheek. "Let us know how things turn out."

Caleb took a moment to meet both their gazes. He owed them for this…big-time. He didn't need to head to Los Angeles. All he had to do was catch that train before it left the station. Without another look at the two grinning idiots, he slung his saddlebag over his shoulder and strode out the door.

Chapter Nineteen

"That's us," Mr. Gordon said.

Deep in thought, Hannah hadn't heard the conductor call for passengers to board the train. Beside her, Mr. Gordon grabbed the handle on her carpetbag, hefting the case with ease. He'd seen to her trunk earlier. She knew he'd rather be on the ship with the other men, and counted it as a testament to Stuart's judgment of character that the man was so solicitous. He followed her to the platform and boarded the train behind her.

Sliding onto a leather seat, she indicated to Mr. Gordon that he could sit on the one facing her. She'd half hoped Caleb would show up to say goodbye. It would have been difficult for them both, but she wanted one more look at him, one more memory to tuck away.

The whistle blew, signaling their departure. The wheels groaned and then jerked the car forward before easing into a steady rhythm on the tracks. The buildings sped by on one side, the harbor and fishing boats on the other. She barely noticed the sun sparkling off the water or the azure blue of the sky.

Suddenly, she realized Mr. Gordon had spoken, and she hadn't heard a word of what he'd said. "I'm grateful for your company, Mr. Gordon. Regrettably, I'm just not up to conversation at the moment." No, one thing occupied her thoughts—leaving Caleb and the ache growing deep inside.

Trying to turn away such morose thoughts, she pulled out her ledger, opened to a blank page and began to list the things that would need her attention upon returning home. Number one: Grandfather's health. She must see the doctor regarding that. Number two: unloading and cataloging the merchandise from Stuart's ship. Number three: contacting those who'd ordered the items and marking them for reshipment. Number four: speak with Mr. Rowlings.

She frowned and laid her pen down on the ledger, staring at the list. Mr. Rowlings—number four. That in itself should tell her something about her priorities. She didn't look forward to facing him. He wouldn't take kindly to being refused, more likely due to a bruised ego than any deep affection for her.

How could she have ever considered marriage as a business arrangement? Something so personal as living with a man, learning his habits, his likes and dislikes, sharing his meals...sharing his bed? When she thought of such things, it wasn't Thomas's face she imagined at the breakfast table—but Caleb's.

The list in front of her blurred. Had Grandfather cast his spell so completely that such an existence sounded normal? She'd been a fool. A naive fool.

A telltale drop of moisture splattered on the paper. As much as she tried to concentrate on her to-do list, the only thing she wanted to think about was Caleb. With each surge of the iron wheels, bits of her heart tore out and stayed behind with him. She curled her fingers into a tight fist in her lap.

Actions spoke louder than words. And Caleb... Caleb had come after her with no thought for his own safety. Knowing that he did not have enough money for her ransom, he'd still tried to bargain for her life. He could have been killed on the spot. He'd charged in and risked everything.

But what had she risked? Was she truly the coward he accused her of being? It would take courage to tell Grandfather she would not marry Mr. Rowlings. He'd be disappointed at first but, in the end, wouldn't dwell on it long. There were too many other decisions to make about the business that would soon occupy his mind. Yet she had a feeling that that wasn't exactly what Caleb had meant when he'd called her a coward. No, he'd meant she was afraid to stand up to Grand-father—about *him*.

Across the seat from her, Mr. Gordon dozed, his sailor's cap low on his forehead, his chin on his chest.

"Lookin' for a little company?" a familiar voice said.

She looked up, up, up to the tall man standing in the aisle. *Caleb.* "What are you doing here?"

"Not letting you go." His deep green eyes bored into hers, intense and serious.

"But I'm on my way back to San Francisco. I've already gone." The inane comment slipped out before she could stop it. Foolish.

"Yep. I see that."

"So…you're too late."

He reached out and caught one of her tears on his fingertip, then rubbed it between his finger and thumb before looking back at her. "Maybe… but maybe not," he said thoughtfully. "You going to make room for me on that seat of yours, or do I have to stand the entire trip to San Francisco?"

She scooted over, and he slid in beside her. Her heart scudded in her chest as he rested his arm possessively over her shoulder. "Please. Mr. Gordon could wake up. You are taking liberties."

"And your pulse is jumping like a Mexican bean on a hot plate. Why do you think that is, Hannah?"

"You know why. And you're not playing fair."

He leaned in and whispered in her ear, sending shivers all the way to her toes, "I'm not playing at all. I'm dead serious." He reached into his vest pocket and pulled out the abalone-and-silver necklace. "You forgot this."

"I thought you should keep it. It brought me luck."

"I'm not in the market for luck. I want a sure thing."

She could barely think with the way he was rubbing the outline of her ear with his fingertip. The onslaught of sensations he produced in her, right here in front of Mr. Gordon and the entire company on the train, was so unfair of him.

"Lola mentioned that you changed your mind about marrying Rowlings. That true?"

She opened her mouth, ready to sidestep the direct question, when she remembered her thoughts about risk and all he'd done for her. He deserved the truth. "What you said started to make sense. It wouldn't be fair to Thomas or to me to marry under the circumstances."

"Glad to hear it. Anything else I said that impressed you?"

"As a matter of fact…yes."

He raised his brows, waiting. Thankfully he stopped rubbing her ear for the moment.

"You said you wouldn't have a coward for a wife."

He waited for her to go on.

"A mother…" She stopped. Began again. "*My* mother…was not a coward when she let go of me in the water. She must have been frightened, but she did it because she loved me—and loved Father. She saved us by acting with her heart… with her feelings."

Caleb nodded, listening intently.

"On the island, instead of escaping, I started the fire to warn Father. I thought—and acted— with my heart."

She paused, realizing with sudden clarity another truth. "Coming here—I said it was all about the lost ships, but I was lying to myself. Grandfather was insistent that I marry Thomas. I felt trapped—just like on the island—and I reacted with my heart." She met his gaze. "I ran to someone I trusted. You."

"'Bout time you came to your senses."

"On the beach, when you said I loved you, you were right. I do."

He didn't move, didn't respond.

"I'm not a coward, Caleb. I like a good challenge once in a while."

A slow smile curved his lips. "You calling me a challenge?"

His voice flowed over her like honey—so suggestive, so intoxicating that, too late, she realized the trap he was laying. Funny thing, though, she didn't mind one bit. "Yes," she managed to whisper.

"Good. If things come too easy, they're not appreciated." He pulled away and settled back against the seat, angling his Stetson over his face to block out the daylight.

"What are you doing?"

"Think I'll take a little siesta."

"But…what about your job? Don't you have to work?"

"I gave my notice. Wyatt can find another manager."

"But…what about the land?"

"Don't own any land." He removed his hat and slid up in the seat, meeting her gaze. "I appreciate the gesture, Hannah, but I'm not one to be tied down by land. I think you know that."

She had known that. Deep down. But at the time she couldn't think how else to show her appreciation for his rescue. "Then, you didn't sign for it?"

He shook his head. "I've got other plans."

"Such as?"

"I've got a bit saved up—the money I used for your ransom. It's enough to buy a fishing boat and hire some help."

Of course. He'd always liked the sea. "That still doesn't explain why you are sitting beside me. And, might I add, being downright obtuse!" She wanted him to say he missed her. She wanted him to take her in his arms and kiss her the way he had in his bedroom above the saloon.

"There you go using that fancy talk again."

The wicked smile growing on his handsome face frustrated her all the more. The cad was playing her! Just like a fish! Reeling her in, then letting out a little line to make her think she had some control, then...

"Caleb—"

"I'm goin' to Frisco. Clear it up any?"

"Frisco?"

"Been a while. Thought I'd visit my family—Rachel and my nephew."

"You just thought you'd visit your sister?" she repeated, not believing him for a minute. "After all this time?"

He shrugged.

"Well, I'm sure Rachel will be happy to see you."

"What about you?"

Studiously, she smoothed out the wadded handkerchief in her lap. "I'm not family. You made that very clear on the ship."

"You can be." He stopped her motions with his warm hand. Then, turning up her palm, he placed the necklace in the center. "I want you to be." With two fingers under her chin, he raised her face until she couldn't help but meet his gaze or hide the tears brimming there that she refused to let fall. "You don't belong with anyone else, Hannah. I've known it since that first kiss. I'm doing the askin' now. Marry me, Hannah. You won't ever regret it."

She wanted so badly to say yes. So badly. But she had to know one thing. She was a Lansing after all. "What about Lansing Enterprises?"

"Keep it. I'll help you if that's what you want, or stay out of it. Whatever you decide. It's you I want. Not your business, not your money, just you."

She believed him. His actions, over and over, had proved his words. If he'd cared about the business or the money, he'd never have risked so much to save her or refused the reward she'd left him.

"You'll ask Grandfather for my hand?"

He grinned, and she realized she'd given him his answer.

"I'll *tell* him."

"Telling is not the same as asking."

"I'm not leaving our future to chance."

Our future. A future he'd risked his all for. How could she do any less? "Then, I will tell him. The minute I see him."

He raised his brows.

"I'm a Lansing, aren't I?"

He took her in his arms, his lips a whisper away. "Not for long, Miss Hannah. Not for long." He lowered his mouth to hers and kissed her thoroughly, right there in front of Mr. Gordon and everybody on the train. And she didn't mind one bit.

A moment later she pulled back to where she

could see him, although his face was slightly blurred. Her lips felt swollen—well kissed. Nothing had ever felt more right in her life.

"Hannah Houston…hmm. I believe I could get used to it."

* * * * *

MILLS & BOON®

Need more New Year reading?

We've got just the thing for you!
We're giving you 10% off your next eBook or
paperback book purchase on the Mills & Boon
website. So hurry, visit the website today and type
SAVE10 in at the checkout for your exclusive

10% DISCOUNT

www.millsandboon.co.uk/save10

MILLS & BOON®

HISTORICAL

AWAKEN THE ROMANCE OF THE PAST